PAYBACK

A SPORTS ROMANCE NOVEL

AMY DAWS

Published by: Amy Daws, LLC
ISBN 13: ISBN-13: 978-1-944565-26-8
ISBN 10: 1-944565-26-4
Editing: Stephanie Rose

Formatting: Champagne Book Design
Cover Design: Amy Daws

PAYBACK

CHAPTER 1

Allie

"**H**EY, VI. I JUST LANDED," I STATE EXCITEDLY INTO THE phone as I hurry through the bustling Heathrow Airport trying my hardest not to skip because I'm so happy to be off the damn plane. It's an eight-hour flight from Chicago to London, but the arrival is even more appreciated when you've spent an entire day in the airport with a never-ending delay.

"Hiya, Allie! So glad you finally made it." My cousin Vi's voice is warm and motherly like I remembered.

Ever since my cousins' mother passed away about twenty years ago, Vi took on the maternal role in their family. I was here for the funeral, and the death of my aunt, Vilma Harris. It changed the dynamic of our family, specifically the relationship between our dads—once brothers who were extremely close, now separated by so much more than an ocean.

"I'm glad I made it, too." I blow a piece of hair out of my face. "And I'm leaving no room for jet lag."

Vi huffs, "After the shit couple of weeks you've had, you didn't deserve to have flight issues."

"A shit half a decade is more like it," I mumble as I swerve to miss an airport employee who's pushing a woman in a wheelchair at superhuman speed.

1

"Have you heard from…Oh, what is the hilarious nickname you have for your ex?"

"Ghost Penis," I answer with zero humour in my tone and attempt to blink away the aching thump in my temples. I refuse to voice his full name ever again. "And yes, I've heard from him. But I'm ignoring his calls. I've wasted enough of my life on him."

Parker Frost and I met freshman year in college, and I thought he was going to propose after graduation. When he didn't, I remained patient. I told myself that we were still young and just starting our careers. We had plenty of time to plan our future.

Then, two weeks ago, I walked into the apartment I shared with my stepsister, Rosalie, and caught her on my bed. On top of my purple paisley comforter. Fucking my boyfriend like it was her last day on Earth. She didn't even have the decency to pull back my bedspread. *Fucking animal.*

Since then, my life has been a drunken blur of moving out, burning that horrible comforter, cursing the colour purple, and swearing to my coworkers that I wasn't Googling "how to get away with murder." I wasn't sure which of the offenders I wanted to kill more…My stepsister or my boyfriend of five years.

Vi's calming voice snaps me back to reality when she says, "Well, I'm glad you're not giving Ghost Penis the time of day. He doesn't deserve it. Neither does that joke of a sister you have."

"Rosalie is soon to be an ex-stepsister, so thank goodness for small favours."

"That's right," Vi replies. "This will be your father's third divorce, right?"

"Yep. And the timing couldn't be better," I grumble, shaking my head at how messed up my father is when it comes to his relationships.

When I was eight years old, my father, Charles Harris, divorced my mother, Karen, because he received a big job offer in the States and she refused to move. Weeks later, she met her current husband, Jon, in some travel-lovers club. They all but ran away together, leaving me to move overseas with my father—the stable-looking one in the marriage.

My father's second wife was some young thing whom I barely remember because their marriage only lasted for a year and they lived apart half the time. His third wife, Hilary, actually stuck around for over a decade but is now suffering the same fate as the others.

My voice is resigned when I add, "It will be nice not to be attached to my stepsister anymore, but I still haven't told Dad about what happened. I'm terrified that he won't be sympathetic, and I can't handle that iciness right now."

My dad and I have a bit of a strained relationship. Charles Harris has never been a warm and loving father like the ones I've seen in so many TV shows. I always assumed it was because he was British and they were built differently. But when he married Hilary, I realized he was capable of showing actual human emotion. At least he did when it came to her daughter.

Comparing Rosalie and me side by side, you'd probably think we were biological sisters. We were the same age and both had golden blonde hair and blue eyes. We were mistaken as twins a lot, which I actually loved. It was like I instantly got the sibling I'd yearned for all my life as an only child. Rosalie and I got along well, too, even moving in to an apartment together after college.

As time passed, I began to notice how much my father gave in to Rosalie's every need. I tried not to be jealous because her own father abandoned her when she was ten years old and I knew how hard that was on her. Apparently he'd gotten another woman pregnant with the son he'd always wanted, and he discarded Rose and her mother in favour of his other life. My parents may be selfish assholes but at least they haven't completely left me for another child.

"Have you spoken to your mum about everything that's happened?" Vi asks, her voice tight.

I exhale heavily. "No. She and Jon are backpacking through Poland this week. I didn't even tell her I was coming to London. I'm not going to be here long, and I don't need her drama on top of my own."

Vi tsks knowingly because most people are aware that my mother is a flake. Sweet and caring, but consumed by her own life.

"Well, it's good you're here," Vi states with renewed vigour, her tone taking on that matriarchal sound again. "My family may be loud, obnoxious, and completely dysfunctional, but we love bigger than life. I think you could use a healthy dose of real family right now."

Her last comment causes a knot to form in my throat that I forcefully swallow down to the dark part of my soul that's been holding in all of my emotions the past two weeks. *Not today, Satan. Not today.*

"And just you wait until you lay eyes on the date I found you for Aunt Fiona's wedding!" she peals into the line. "You won't give Ghost Penis another thought."

A smile tugs on the corner of my mouth. Hearing Vi say "Ghost Penis" out loud is seriously awesome, but that's not what pleases me. What pleases me is hearing that she's set me up with someone hot. My date is the exact reason I came to London. Frankly, it's the only thing I've been excited about since my entire life was turned upside down. The reason being, I have a payback plan all worked out for how I'm going to show Parker and Rosalie they haven't broken me.

Thankfully, Vi is well-connected and a willing co-conspirator. Her four brothers—my wild, unruly cousins—play professional soccer in England. Two of them play for their dad, Vaughn Harris' team, Bethnal Green F.C. That means that Vi is often surrounded by hot, sweaty athletes—the lucky bitch. Never mind that she's six months pregnant and engaged, she was still able to hook me up with exactly what I need.

Epic. Fucking. Rebound. Sex.

One night, no strings, and a payback to rival what those two assholes put me through. Then I'm back on a plane to Chicago to rebuild what's left of my semblance of a life.

"Tanner and Booker are picking you up outside," Vi explains, cutting into my Dr. Evil scheming. "They'll be in a big, ghastly truck, so you shouldn't miss them."

I smile as faint memories of my cousins seep into my mind. It doesn't surprise me that the Harris Brothers drive a big truck. They were never known to be discreet, which is what made them so much fun. As an only child, Vi and her brothers were always the most exciting part of family gatherings for me. They were like a live circus act existing solely for my entertainment.

I lost touch with the Harris clan after the move, outside of regular emails with Vi. I do, however, try to keep up with the boys' soccer careers because they're actually really impressive.

The oldest Harris Brother, Gareth, is a defender for Manchester United. Camden just signed with Arsenal a month ago, leaving his twin, Tanner, and their youngest brother, Booker, the last two still playing for the local London club, Bethnal Green F.C.

"Do Tanner and Booker know you set me up with their teammate?" I ask as I make my way to the passenger pickup area.

"Um, not exactly. Tanner's been a bit of a mess lately since Camden left the team, so I didn't want to stir things up quite yet."

"Won't he figure it out at the wedding?" I ask, my face scrunching up with anxiety over how badly that could go down.

Vi scoffs. "If I'm there to run interference, they'll be quiet as church mice. Being pregnant has made them treat me with kid gloves, so my large circumference should work to our advantage. It's basically my super power."

This makes me smile. "Lucky for me, pregnancy doesn't seem to affect your badass wing-woman skills."

"Not one bit," she laughs. "I can't wait to see you!"

We finish our chat just as I burst through the airport doors and into the damp summer air of the outskirts of London. Before I even have a chance to take in the scenery, my eyes zero in on something horrendous.

A big black pickup is parked by the curb, smack dab in front of the door. Standing up on the tailgate is a well over six-foot blonde, bearded animal with a man bun, inked arms, and a shit-eating grin to rival Jack Nicholson. As if his location in the bed of the truck alone isn't conspicuous enough, he's holding up a large sign that reads: WELCOME HOME FROM PRISON, COUSIN ALICE.

I stop midstride with my carry-on clutched firmly in my grasp and, to my horror, his eyes land on me.

"Alice?" The Big Foot-looking man shouts my name loudly over the traffic, and the people walking by turn to gawk at me.

I do a quick glance down the curb to see if I can lose him and hail a cab, but I know it's no use when he adds, "Booker, it's her! It's Allie!"

My eyes cut to the cab of the truck as Booker hops out of the driver's seat and makes his way toward me. His dark hazel eyes are squinting sympathetically as he pushes back his short brown hair. "I'm so sorry about Tanner. He's a special kind of wanker." He reaches for my bag and shakes his head like this is a normal occurrence and he's powerless against him.

Tanner puts a foot on the edge of the truck bed and drops lithely to the concrete. He still has that smile as he approaches, hovering over me like a giant. "Bring it in, cuz." His big arms wrap around me nearly twice as he lifts me up in a bear hug. "I told Booker I'd be able to spot you." He ruffles my long, golden hair, extracting wisps from their proper place and creating a curtain over my eyes. "I remember that one time I shampooed this mop with mud because I told you it would help your boobies come in."

I now appreciate the protective shield of hair as my face bursts into flames. "Thankfully, my boobs came in all on their own, no thanks to your cosmetology skills." I push my hair out of my face and glance down at the sign. "Prison, Tanner? Really?"

He holds it up again and shrugs. "Well, your flight from Chicago was delayed a whole day, so I had extra time on my hands."

Booker clears his throat and adds, "Speaking of time, we need to get moving. The reception for those of us not important enough to be invited to the ceremony is in a couple of hours, and I'm sure you want to get cleaned up."

I make a half-hearted attempt to fix my hair and catch sight of Booker's dimples as he tries to conceal a chuckle at the state of me. I follow them to the truck and mumble under my breath, "God, it's good to be back."

Sandwiched between Booker and Tanner for the forty-minute drive to the hotel, it's fun to listen to their British accents as they ramble on and on. Mine is nearly nonexistent after being in the States for so long, but it slips out every now and again from being around my father all the time.

More than their accents, it's even more fun being caught up on all the Harris family happenings. Booker is still living in their dad's mansion in Chigwell, though he may be moving into a place of his own next year. Vi is living with her fiancé, Hayden, but they are holding off on a wedding until the baby comes. Tanner's twin, Camden, is apparently all but married off after falling deeply in love with his knee surgeon only a few weeks ago. And Tanner admits he's in the middle of taking a naked tour of East London…Whatever the hell that means.

When they ask me about my relationship status, I have a sudden case of word vomit and end up sharing far more than I intended.

"The boyfriend is nonexistent on the account that I found him fucking my stepsister, slash former roommate, slash former best friend in *my* bed of all places. As if our very adequate two-bedroom apartment didn't have enough square footage for him to slip his micropenis in, they decided infesting my space with their sex drippings would be a blast. It's comical really, because he's been a jealous freak our entire relationship, barely wanting me to look at other men, let alone talk to them. He'd probably be jealous of you two even after being told we share a bloodline."

I stop talking and the cab of the truck grows eerily silent for a long, awkward length of time. Jeez…Did I say too much? Heck, Tanner was nattering about his sexual escapades, so I thought my drama would be par for the course. It felt good letting it all out with Vi, but I apparently should have kept my mouth shut with her brothers.

Just when I'm about to say something to lighten the mood, Booker interrupts me with his stone-cold voice. "Name. We need a name."

I frown at him and Tanner barks next. "An address would suffice. I have a former teammate who plays for Chicago Fire. He owes me a favour."

"Yes. Mitchem would do the job properly," Booker adds through clenched teeth. "Give us your bloke's work address. This prat deserves public humiliation. Something to make him lose his job. What a worthless fucking sod of a man…"

"Good thinking, Book," Tanner chirps, sounding oddly cheery, like they're in the middle of some kind of brainstorming session. "Where does he work?"

Tanner presses his phone to his ear, and I realise he's actually calling his Chicago friend right now. I grapple with him for a moment before freeing it from his grasp and quickly press END.

"I'm handling it," I snap, mostly angry at myself for revealing such personal information to two of the most caring freaks in the world.

"How?" Booker demands. "Details, Allie. We need to know how you're handling this because, as far as I can tell, this tosser needs to be castrated. And I think we need to hand your stepsister off to Vi." He shudders at that thought because Vi truly has her four brothers terrified of her.

Of course they don't know that Vi is already in the know. She has bent over backwards to help make this trip a diverting one. Something to get me out of my funk.

But hearing Booker and Tanner volley back and forth over how they are going to exact their own revenge is so moving, I'm not even surprised when tears well in my eyes. Blind loyalty…Is that what family is truly about? Rosalie and I were close during the ten years our parents were married, but I can't say I ever felt such a strong sense of protection from her. Is this a brother thing? Or a Harris thing?

Maybe both.

I stare open-mouthed at Booker and Tanner, feeling stunned because I haven't shed a single tear since the horrid Tuesday afternoon I found my stepsister and boyfriend in bed together. Not one tear. I just drank, moved out of my apartment and into a spare bedroom at my coworker's, and formulated my revenge. But here I am now, packed in between two overly-muscled nut-jobs being all noble, and I'm nearing emotional volcanic eruption.

My voice is shaky when I croak, "Thanks for all of this, guys, but it really isn't your problem." I clear my throat, praying they didn't notice the crack in my voice. "I'm not eight years old and needing you to attack the schoolyard bully. I'm twenty-four. And I appreciate the suggestion to have him stretched and quartered, but I think I have it covered."

I feel Tanner's eyes pinning me to my seat, but I refuse to look at him. I refuse to let these two do-gooders manhandle their way into my business or, worse, ruin my big plan for tonight. I'm actually excited about this plan! It feels good to be taking action against them after two weeks of avoidance.

After a long, uncomfortable moment, Tanner huffs loudly and states, "Did you really say 'sex drippings' a minute ago?" Booker cracks up laughing and I bite my lip to remain composed. "Fuck me, you're a bloody Harris if I ever saw one."

CHAPTER

Roan

"**D**eWalt! What are you still doing here?" a deep, familiar voice echoes off the changing room shower walls. I squint through the soap running down my face to see the team manager, Vaughn Harris, standing on the other side of the tiled wall. He's watching me with a scowl on his face.

"Sorry, sir. I'm almost finished."

"I don't mean in the showers. I mean here…Why are you still at the training grounds at this hour?"

I continue rinsing the soap off and reply, "I was watching films with Stephens."

"What films?" he asks, eyeing me seriously.

I turn my back to him, not wanting to see his reaction when I answer, "We were watching films of Camden."

"My son Camden?" he asks in confusion.

I nod. "Stephens thinks if I can pick up some of Camden's style, Tanner and I might get on better on the pitch."

The sound of the water running is the only noise for several long seconds before Vaughn exhales heavily. "Look, I know Tanner can be a bit of a pain in the arse. And I know it was a lot for you to leave South Africa so you could come here to play alongside someone who's only ever played alongside his twin brother. But

I think this can work, Roan. More than work. I think it can be brilliant."

I nod, still looking away from him because, *ag man*, do I miss home. Leaving my mom and two sisters behind for this team was the biggest step I've taken in my soccer career. And playing alongside Tanner Harris has been the biggest challenge I've faced in this crazy game. He and his twin, Camden, were killer strikers who worked in tandem with each other for years. Now the entire team and coaching staff expects me to step in and take Camden's place. It often feels like an unattainable goal, but I'm no fucking quitter. And my place on the team is more important to me than anything.

I school my features to look confident and turn to face my coach. "I understand what you're saying, sir. That's why I'm working so hard."

Vaughn looks at me firmly for a moment and then nods. "All right then. We'll see you at training tomorrow. Go home and get some rest."

I finish showering and head into the changing room where my suit is hanging inside a garment bag. I'm just unzipping it when my phone illuminates with a call.

I see Tanner's sister's name, Vi Harris, on the caller ID and quickly answer. "Erm, hello?"

"Hiya, Roan! It's Vi."

"I know," I reply with a laugh. "I saved your number after the last time you called."

"Oh, right," Vi giggles nervously, sounding a lot more tense than she did when she called to ask me to be their cousin's date at some wedding tonight. "Look, Roan, I'm calling to let you know Allie is at the hotel now, getting ready. I'm not exactly sure what she has planned for tonight, but I'm just warning you to be gentle…Okay?"

"Gentle?"

"She's…fragile, I think. She says she has some plan, but I don't know what it is exactly. I'm just worried about her. So, do you think you can be on your best behaviour?"

I frown at her request. "Did you expect I wouldn't be?"

"No, no, no. But, honestly, I'm the sister of four footballers. I know how you guys spend your nights. Bacon Sandwich Rule and all that."

"Bacon Sandwich Rule?" I ask, my face twisting up in confusion.

"When you lick something to mark it's yours and no one else can touch it…Oh, never mind. Just do whatever you think is best for Allie tonight, okay? Trust your instincts. I want this night to be exactly what she needs, because she's had a rough go of it. The problem is, I'm not sure what she needs. I just want whatever you do to her—"

"Do to her?" I interrupt, my voice rising in disbelief. "What exactly would I do to her?"

My blood pressure rises because I fear that Vi has my motives for agreeing to this crazy setup a bit out of whack. My hope is that doing this favour for the Harris family might earn me some points with Tanner. They are a close-knit group, and it's been impossible for me to infiltrate them in any meaningful way that might translate to better chemistry on the pitch. And Vaughn has told me time and time again that once I'm "in" with Tanner, I'm all in and I won't be able to shake him. So if Vi is worried about me doing something that crosses a line with their cousin, she's dead wrong.

"I don't mean you'd do anything. Sorry, that's not what I meant. I'm six months pregnant and this baby is sucking my communication skills out of me one hormone at a time. I'm just beginning to panic that this was a bad, bad idea!"

Vi's voice reaches a shrill level that rattles my ear, so I do what I do with my mom and sisters. Pulling out my most soothing voice, I defuse the situation. "Look, Vi. Despite what you might think, I'm a good person and I will take care of your cousin. I may be a professional athlete, but I was raised by a single mom and have two younger sisters. I'll be whatever Allie needs me to be tonight, even if it's just a shoulder to cry on. All right?"

PAYBACK

exhales a huge breath of relief. "Yes...Oh my goodness. Than you, Roan. I'm sorry I'm such a mess. I really do appreciate this."

" 's no problem." I inhale a deep breath and add, "And you're sure your dad won't mind me taking his niece out? I'm really trying hard to earn his respect on the team."

" m sure," Vi insists. "My dad isn't even going to the wedding and I l explain everything to my brothers. You're doing us a huge favou ."

N y shoulders relax. Vaughn Harris has taken me under his wing ince recruiting me, so the last thing I want to do is negatively affect my relationship with him because I let his daughter talk me into t king out his niece for the night.

" reat. I'm happy to help," I reply with a forced smile.

" ou're the best! Hopefully this is the last call you'll get from the cr zy pregnant lady!" She laughs maniacally, and I can't help but laugh back.

" Io worries. See you later."

" ye!"

I ang up and shake my head. Something tells me I'm going to regre agreeing to this night.

CHAPTER 3

Allie

By the time I get to my hotel room, I can't get in the shower fast enough. I need to wash off the flight, that car ride, and the memories of Ghost Penis railing my stepsister that fluttered to the front of my mind after retelling it all to Tanner and Booker. I need the flicker of tears I felt earlier to go the hell away. Crying over what's happened is not what this trip is about. This trip isn't even about attending my aunt Fiona's second wedding. She's the much younger sister of my father and uncle Vaughn, but she lived in Japan until recently, so I don't even know her that well.

This trip is about revenge sex. Something to completely obliterate any memory I have of Rosalie and Ghost Penis forever.

An hour and twenty minutes later, I've consumed two vodka Red Bulls and dressed myself in my sexiest little black dress with scandalous lingerie underneath. My blonde curls are loose down my back, and I slick on a matte red lipstick to go along with my dramatic makeup. I'm ready to meet my date for the evening, but I have one more thing to do. Before leaving my hotel room, I purposely leave my phone propped by the television behind a plant. Then I make my way downstairs to the hotel bar where Vi planned for us to meet.

It takes all my strength not to skip into the bar because I feel like a million-dollar whore in my platform heels and I'm ready to get th s show on the road. But skipping in this outfit wouldn't quite fit.

S ipping is an issue for me. Not an issue as in I can't do it. I'm an ex eptional skipper. It's an issue in the sense that sometimes I don't now when I'm doing it, and I don't just do it when I'm happy. Some imes I skip when I'm anxious or stressed. It's a nervous tic that I've h d my entire life, but it's a lot less adorable on a twenty-four-year- d than it is on a child.

I ake a deep breath to calm my nerves like a normal, non-skipping dult. Dressing up like this and meeting strange men in bars isn't l w I've spent much of my time the past few years. Don't get me w ong, I'm a girlie-girl and I like wearing heels and glamming up. B t it's an unnerving feeling to trust that my cousin can pick some ne whom I'll find sexually attractive. Then again, tonight isn't abou ne. It's about a fantasy. A plan. An escape from the shitty real-ity th t is my life. So I make the decision to embrace this feeling and let it el my inner skipping self.

V said my date will know who I am, which freaks me out be-cause hat means he's most likely seen a photo of me. But Vi insisted I be s rprised, so this is me trusting my cousin.

U on entering the bar, my eyes collide with a tall, handsome man ho is standing next to a stool in a custom suit that hugs his musc s a bit too tightly. His skin is bronze and his hair is nearly black He looks like a melting pot of different cultures that I can't quite ecipher, but everything about him makes my mouth water. Even he way he stands with his shoulders relaxed and his hands restir inside of his pockets like it's perfectly normal for him to ca-sually ark himself in a bar like some GQ fitness model.

J st when I begin inwardly cursing Vi for not setting me up with omeone as sexy and confident as him, he turns and begins walki g toward me. I glance over my shoulder to ensure that I'm not i the middle of one of those mortifying moments when you think omeone's waving to you so you wave back, only to discover they were waving to the person behind you. Good-god, that's embarrassing.

When the coast is clear, I turn back to find the man is now only two feet away from me. His light brown eyes are shockingly dazzling. They look like those filters you can apply to brighten eyes on a photo, but he is clearly without a filter right in front of me. His full lips look so soft and pliable that I want to reach out and squeeze them to see if they would melt like caramel.

"Are you Alice?" he asks in a warm, husky voice that makes my throat close up.

I swallow hard and nod. "I go by Allie."

He half smiles and his eyes drift down my body briefly before returning to my gaze. "I'm Roan DeWalt. And you, Allie…" he laughs softly and the sound makes my vagina do a Kegel. "You were seriously worth the wait."

I lick my lips and recover from my mini vagina spasm while noting his slight accent. "It's nice to meet you, Roan. Where are you from?"

His smirk reaches his eyes. "Well, I was born in England, but I grew up in South Africa…Cape Town. Ever been?"

I shake my head regretfully. "No, I haven't." *But if men look like this in South Africa, I definitely need to plan a visit.*

"Do we have time for a drink?" he asks, showing zero irritation over my tardiness.

"A quick one, yes."

He places his hand on the small of my back and guides me to the spot where he was standing. I noticed he hadn't ordered a drink for himself while he waited. I don't know why exactly, but I like that.

Drinks are ordered and I perch on the edge of the stool, sipping my vodka soda and feeling butterflies for the first time in…Well, perhaps my lifetime. I was attracted to Ghost Penis because of his confidence, but I've completely blocked it out if I ever felt this way when I met him. Maybe it's the vodka.

My eyes drift down to Roan's thighs stretched out wide and long as he sits on the barstool. They are so thick, they look like they might rip the seam of his tailored pants. He probably has to get special pants to fit around his muscular legs—casualty of the job.

"You play soc—um, football, right?" I ask and note that my voice has an odd rasp to it that I've never heard before. Maybe I'm taking this fantasy too seriously? *Dial it back, Allie. No need to go all Pretty* Woman *on him.*

Roan's smile grows, revealing stunningly white teeth. "We call it soccer in South Africa." He winks and adds, "But I'm surprised to hear you slip. People are crazy about calling it football here. I thought Vi said you are originally from England?"

I nod. "Originally, yes. I moved to Chicago with my dad when I was eight, so I've lived in the States much longer than I did here. But I was born here, so in my heart I'm still an English rose."

"With an American accent." He leans into me with a playful smile and the smell of his cologne is heavenly.

I return his smile. "When I was with Tanner and Booker earlier, they were giving me crap about losing my accent."

His brows lift curiously. "Tanner and Booker would be interesting cousins to have I'd say."

"Yes indeed." I exhale heavily because that claim is a cross to bear in and of itself. "I'm stuck with them by blood I'm afraid."

"Well, because of that, I'll be a perfect gentleman tonight." He smiles kindly.

"What do you mean?" I ask with a frown.

He shakes his head. "I need to get in good with the Harrises is all."

"Why do you say that?" Annoyance prickles my skin. "Because their dad is your team manager?"

"Well, that, and because I recently took Camden's position with Bethnal Green after he signed with Arsenal. Tanner is my fellow striker. We need to play well together or I'm sure they'll get rid of me faster than I can unpack my bags. Tanner and I haven't exactly clicked yet."

I don't know if it's the alcohol or the crushing disappointment of my mission being thwarted, but a low growl comes from somewhere deep inside my throat. "This sucks."

"What sucks?" Roan asks, confused. Even the way he says "sucks" in his South African accent is sexy. *Damnit.*

"Nothing," I sigh dramatically, already hating what I'm about to say. "Look, Roan, you seem like a nice guy, but I think we should just end our night now." I look over my shoulder to find a clock and see that it's almost time to head to the ballroom for the reception. Maybe there'll be a single guy I can pick up there.

Roan's warm hand cups my wrist. "Why would you want to end this? It's barely started."

Goosebumps ripple on my skin around his touch, and it's frustrating. He would have been so perfect for my plan...If only he wasn't trying to be so perfect.

My exasperated eyes find his. "Can I be blunt?"

He nods. "Please. I'm more than curious."

"I'm getting past a monumentally fucked-up breakup. Like, imagine the worst thing that could happen and times it by a million. My mind is a wreck and I am not at all ready for a nice date."

"So, what are you ready for exactly? Vi said you wanted a date for tonight."

"I wanted a one-night stand," I blurt out unapologetically, my inner Harris Ho stretching out her feminist wings proudly. "Sorry to be so candid, but I'm looking for a rebound. A fling. A no-strings-attached night of sex. But, in all honesty, we're probably doomed from the get-go because my cousins won't let us frolic along all night if things are tense between you and Tanner. They'll be prying in my business and wondering why I'm with you of all people. And if you're worried more about kissing Harris Brother ass instead of kissing mine, this won't work."

He rises with me as I stand, gently gripping my forearm. "Lis, just wait. I need a minute to think—" He releases me and begins fumbling for his wallet.

His face looks tormented, like he's conflicted about what to do, and even though I know he's not trying to be cruel, it hurts. It hurts because this entire night is uncharacteristic of me, and this small form of rejection is shining a big bright light on how out of control I am right now.

Those fucking unwanted tears rear their ugly heads again. I don't know if it's his urgent touch on my arm or the sympathetic look in his stunning light brown eyes, but I can feel bitchy little salt droplets forming around my irises and it's not happening. Not now. Not ever.

I begin walking away knowing I should have paid for the drinks, especially after blowing him off. But if I stay too long, these tears could form rivers and I refuse to give them the satisfaction.

When I approach the bar exit, I see my cousins walking in to the lobby. There's a gorgeous red-headed woman walking hand-in-hand with Camden and a coppery blonde-haired man with his arm wrapped around Vi and her baby bump.

For Christ's sake, I can't deal with them right now.

I take a sharp right toward the kitchen, hoping for a rear exit. As I push into the smelly, noisy room, two hands snake around my waist and twirl me on my feet.

I glance up into Roan's urgent eyes as the kitchen door swings closed behind us. He's tall. Perfectly tall because I'm over five-seven in these tall heels and he still has a good four or five inches on me.

He pins me with a steely look as he gazes down at my lips like he found exactly what he was after. Before I can catch my breath, he grips my chin firmly with one hand and presses his silky-soft lips to mine in a claiming caress. His tongue invades my mouth swiftly, like an expert seaman navigating an ocean, searching for buried treasure. My surprise turns to lust as his free hand brazenly reaches down and cups my ass, pulling me against his hard body. Pulling me right into his bulge. And what a bulge it is.

I moan loudly for no reason other than I absolutely have to. Nothing about this kiss is gentlemanly and I don't remember the last time I've experienced anything like it. The thought makes my body weep with sorrow and gratitude. To be taken…kissed…acquired. No manners, no polite chitchat. No asking! Just two people, tongue-dancing and enacting exactly what we wish our bodies were doing.

Fuck. Yes.

I give as good as I get, but he still won't let me move my head. That's more than okay, though, because I like it this way. I like the ravishing hold he has over me. I like that he took what he wanted and wasn't polite. It makes me feel desired for nothing but sinful pleasure.

A voice cuts into our intense make-out session. "Holy shit."

We break apart and discover a young female standing on the other side of a long, stainless steel counter with a knife in one hand and a sack of onions in the other.

Her wide eyes are fixated on us as she drops the onions and says, "Seriously. That was bloody hot."

I feel a shaking sensation and turn to find Roan attempting to stifle a laugh, but his eyes are still on fire when he looks at me. "Sorry about that. This woman evidently makes me do unusual things."

I bite my lip and smile, pushing his hefty frame toward the door we entered. Maybe this night can work out after all.

"Okay, so does this mean you're not on a Harris Brother ass-kissing mission anymore?" I ask as he walks beside me down the kitchen hallway. I pause to glance around the corner into the lobby and see the coast is clear of Harrises.

"It would appear so," Roan murmurs, the deep timbre of his voice like an instrument playing notes on my lower belly. He leans in close and lowers his voice to add, "But if it's all the same to you, I'd rather not make that fact obvious to your cousins."

"Um, same," I reply, barking out a nervous laugh. "Is it weird for me to thank you for doing this?"

I can feel his gaze on me, so I look over to see him staring at me with humour in his eyes. "It is weird, but there's a lot about this night that's already weird. I seem to have hit the literal gold mine of women, who happens to be related to a family that can make or break my career. But something tells me I would regret it forever if I decided to exchange a night with you in that sexy fucking dress for a team-building exercise with the Harris Brothers."

"Glad to hear it," I reply, unable to hide my delighted smile as we walk through the lobby and toward the hotel ballroom that's already overflowing with people.

"Are you skipping?" Roan asks out of nowhere, his gaze glancing down at my legs.

"No!" I exclaim, my voice louder than I intended it to be. "I'm, um, just hurrying because we're late." I turn my attention toward the doorway but can feel his sexy, curious eyes on me. "Let's do this."

Roan pauses our momentum as he hooks my elbow and twirls me into him so our lips are a mere whisper apart. His voice is low and urgent when he says, "Yes, but first tell me how long we have to stay down here, because all I can think about is the fact that I felt a goddamned garter belt through the fabric of your dress."

I inhale sharply, unabashedly staring down at his lush lower lip that I really want to sink my teeth into. My eyes are still focused on his mouth when I answer, "Two hours. Tops."

He closes his eyes as if in pain. "I'll try to manage."

"Good," I reply, my voice high-pitched because of the overwhelming butterflies happening in my belly. "Now, let's play a little game I like to call Avoid the Harris Brothers."

I turn to look into the ballroom and both of our gazes land on something terrifying. A murderous-looking Tanner is storming right toward us.

Roan grumbles, "Ag, I'll be at the bar fetching us drinks." He squeezes my hand in a reassuring way before leaving me to fend for myself against my very pushy cousin.

A moment later, Tanner reaches me, his eyes laser-focused on Roan as he walks to the bar before he turns back to me and barks, "Allie, a word."

"What's up, cuz?" I smile brightly.

"Don't you 'cuz' me. What the bloody hell is going on?"

He looks pissed, so I do the doe-eyed blink just to piss him off more. "Whatever do you mean?"

"Why are you here with my fucking teammate?"

"Vi didn't tell you?" I ask innocently.

"Tell me what?"

Vi's voice cuts in to save the day. "Tanner, I'm having some cramps. Would you mind getting me a water? The doctor says it's good to stay hydrated when this happens."

Tanner's jaw muscles clench. "I don't like what's going on here. It feels like you're trying to distract me."

"Don't start, Tanner. It's a family affair," Vi replies casually. "Allie needed a date, so I found her one. Roan will be a perfect gentleman. End of. Now stop upsetting me. It's not good for the baby."

"I'm upsetting you?" He watches Vi's hands stroke her belly and then closes his mouth, stifling any further argument. I almost feel guilty when his brow furrows with worry. He murmurs, "I'll get your bloody water," and is off without another word.

As soon as he leaves, Vi straightens as if she feels perfectly fine. "Give me a hug! I've missed you, Allie."

"Likewise, Vi!"

We hug and she tugs on my golden strands. "Look at how long your hair is now. It's gorgeous. And your big blue eyes are as stunning as ever!"

"You're one to talk," I reply, looking her up and down in her red, floor-length maternity gown. Her blonde hair is pinned off to one side and draped over her shoulder. "Your body looks exactly the same except for that perfect little basketball right here." I touch her belly because I can't help myself.

Vi laughs affectionately. "We call it a football in the Harris family, Amie."

She winks and we have a giggle over how easy it was for her to manipulate Tanner. "I promise I'll take care of Booker, Camden, and Garet, too. Don't you worry."

Roan approaches us with drinks in hand, and Vi lifts her brows appreciatively. "Nice to see you again, Roan."

"Nice to see you, too, Vi. Do you need a drink? Water?"

"No, thank you. Tanner is getting me some." She rubs her hand down my arm and waggles her brows. "I'll give you two some privacy."

She strolls over to the table where the rest of the Harris family is seated and I can't help but notice them all shooting daggers in our direction. One might have thought that Vi would have found me a date who wouldn't get her brothers so bent out of shape, but I'm not complaining one bit after that kiss we shared in the kitchen.

Roan hands me a glass of champagne and smiles pleasantly at our audience. He leans in and whispers in my ear, "Don't let me forget, I want to show you something when we're done here."

I'm intrigued, but his comment is completely forgotten when we get pulled into about ten different extended family circles. The Harris family isn't large or close, so there's a lot of catching up to do whenever we do see each other.

The bride of the night, Aunt Fiona, makes her way over to us in all her grandiose glory. She's tall like my father and uncle, and her lace dress is understated elegance, which I suppose is fitting for her second marriage.

My father never had much to say about his younger sister. Only that she followed her much older and wealthy husband at the time to Japan when she was only nineteen years old. The family didn't approve of the match and grew apart as a result. Husband number two is also a good decade older, so my father said he didn't care to watch history repeat itself.

She sets her wide brown eyes on me and gasps. "Is that little Alice Harris all grown up?"

"In the flesh," I reply through a forced smile.

"When Vi told me you were coming, I nearly fainted!" She scoops me up into a hug before turning me in a circle. "It's been years since you've been back, and I cannot believe my brother had the nerve to not come with you!"

I tilt my head regretfully as I come to face her again. "It was a last minute decision for me to be here."

"I should say!" She turns her assessing eyes to Roan. "And who is this dashing young escort beside you?"

"Roan DeWalt," he replies, holding his hand out to hers. "It's a pleasure to meet you."

She smiles playfully and yanks him into her arms for a hug. "Another footballer, I presume?"

He pulls back with a smirk. "You presume correctly."

"I can spot them from a mile away." She gently coifs her updo. "Footballers have an air of confidence that is unmistakable. It can also be perceived as over-confidence if you're my brother Vaughn, who, shockingly-enough, also could not bother to attend his own sister's wedding."

"Second wedding," I want to mumble, but I don't.

Roan's eyes narrow. "I think the manager of a football club has a lot on their plate."

She scoffs and flicks her hand in the air, dismissing Roan's comment as she gazes at me again. "My God, Alice, when I met you as a toddler, I never would have expected you to turn out like this." She turns to Roan and adds, "She was such a chubby child and had the most horrible teeth. Truly an ugly duckling."

My mouth opens to reply with something snotty, but Roan's hand reaches around my waist and rubs my side reassuringly. The affection is so surprising, it stops my knee jerk reaction.

He smiles a slow smile and says, "In my experience, ugly ducklings are swans in disguise, trying to give the other birds a chance at feeling special." He turns his head and eyes me curiously. "Because they haven't figured out that they're the most special of all." He tips his head and pulls me away. "Excuse us, please."

When my back is turned, my body instantly relaxes. "Holy shit, that was smooth!"

His shoulders shake with silent laughter. "I'm good at defusing female conflict."

My brows lift in appreciation. "That's a strange skill to possess, but it came in handy tonight. I was about to chop her head off so I could watch her flail around like a dead chicken."

His face twists in amusement. "Somehow I'm not surprised. You don't seem like the type of woman to go down without a fight."

"You can say that again," I reply and my brows furrow as I realise he's pulling me toward the dance floor. "I'm a horrible dancer," I state, pulling out of his embrace and freezing on the edge.

"Nonsense," he replies, wrapping his firm arms around me and hitting me with a smouldering look. "You just haven't had the right partner."

Before I know it, I'm in his arms and we're gliding across the dance floor. And we look good. Better than good, maybe even awesome. Roan's hand is firm on my upper back as his other hand holds mine level with our shoulders. We are legitimately dancing.

When I've recovered from the shock of my first twirl, I press into his body and ask, "Roan DeWalt, you can dance?"

He touches his lips to my earlobe and whispers, "In more places than one."

I laugh and shake my head. "I'm not joking! Where did you learn to dance like this?"

He gives me a sheepish smile. "My mom runs a ballroom dance clinic in Cape Town. I grew up in the studio."

My eyes fly wide with interest. "How fun! And you made the jump from dance to soccer because—"

A tap on Roan's shoulder has us both looking sideways at my tall, dark, and scary eldest cousin, Gareth, who's standing over us in all his brooding, narrow-eyed glory. "Mind if I cut in?"

Roan looks to me for an answer, clearly not easily intimidated.

I sigh and nod as Gareth swiftly takes Roan's place.

I watch Roan retreat with patient understanding and turn to find my cousin's eyes glaring down on me in judgement. "You okay, Allie?"

I nod and wink playfully. "Of course I am, cuz. Why do you ask?"

He huffs, "Because last I heard, you were on your way to getting engaged, and now I see you with Tanner's new teammate looking a bit cosier than I'd prefer."

I tense in Gareth's arms and divert my gaze toward Roan as he finds a seat and ignores the glowers from Tanner, Booker, and Camden. They aren't even being discreet.

"I need to know the truth, Allie-Cat. Are you really okay?" Gareth's voice is soft now, warming me up in a place that I'm not ready to defrost yet.

I steel myself and reply, "I'm not, but I will be." I meet his dark hazel eyes that are watching me anxiously, like I'm a time bomb about to blast. "Look, Gareth, I'm going to come back to London when I have more time so we can all have a laugh like the old days. Get some good quality bonding in…I mean it. But right now, things for me are just—"

"Too fresh?" he finishes my sentence.

I close my eyes. "Like a gaping wound."

"And you think Roan DeWalt will make better company than us? We're your family, Allie. You should let us be here for you."

I smile, but it hurts. These over-protective cousins are the closest thing to brothers I'll ever have. I don't want to trample that, especially since my idea of family has already been crushed and I need some sign that not all families are bad.

"I love that you want to be there for me, Gareth. But with where my head is tonight, a stranger is the only company I can handle. Roan's being really sweet. I promise."

He cuts a glare in Roan's direction and murmurs, "I just hope you know what you're getting into with him."

I exhale heavily because if Gareth knew what I have planned for tonight, he wouldn't be shooting daggers at Roan. He'd be shooting them at me. I pull him down for a hug because, damnit, these Harris Brothers really are pretty awesome. And at this point, they are the closest thing to siblings I have. "It was great to see you again. I promise I'll call when I come back to London."

Gareth kisses me on the top of my head and says, "You're always welcome with us."

With a resigned smile, I turn on my heel and stride toward my date, who's standing by the bar and watching me with great fascination. I grab his hand with determination because I'm not going to let the emotions my cousin stoked interfere with my plans for tonight. "Where was it you wanted to take me?"

A smirk plays on his lips as he leans in and whispers, "Somewhere that will make you very *wet*."

My insides convulse at the words that run off his tongue like liquid heat. I push my hair back in a vain attempt to come off cool and collected and reply, "If it's away from the Harris Shakedown, let's dive in."

CHAPTER

Allie

ROAN GUIDES ME THROUGH THE SIDE EXIT OF THE BALLROOM, out onto a gorgeously lit patio, and down several steps to a courtyard surrounded by a swarm of manicured bushes.

His eyes look positively evil as he says, "First, tell me this…Do we need to go back into the ballroom again?"

I frown and shake my head. "No. I'm actually wondering why we're outside and not upstairs getting naked in my hotel room."

His soft laugh is music to my nether regions. "I wanted to get you wet first, mooi."

"Mooi?" *Wait, did he just say wet?*

He looks down at his watch and smirks up at me while counting down his fingers from five. There's a slight delay when he gets to zero and then…

WHOOSH!

Water is everywhere. Up my skirt, in my face, freezing my back. I squeal as the various fountains shoot up from the ground in random places all around our feet. How did I not notice the little holes?

I had sex on the brain. That's how!

I glance up to find Roan is getting equally drenched—maybe even more—and I giggle as he yanks me into his soaked, suit-covered arms. "This was my plan to sabotage your night."

I squint through the onslaught of another spray and we spin a few times, laughing as we unsuccessfully attempt to find an area that won't pelt us with water.

"By soaking me so I couldn't go back to the reception?" I try to cover my head with my hands.

He licks his damp lips and nods as beads of water drip down his trimmed hair and over the curves of his face. "Ever since that kiss, I can't stop thinking about how much more I want."

Our eyes lock, and between the laugh lines, and the water, and the noise of the sprayers shooting up all around us, I'm definitely wet... in more ways than one.

We collide into each other at the exact same time with a hungry, frantic need. My fingers bite into his thick arms, wishing his clothes were off. Our mouths connect like starved animals, and I take the opportunity to bite down on his lower lip like I've been wanting to do since the moment I laid eyes on him.

Suddenly, Roan pulls back from me, breathless. His light brown eyes are now black with lust. "I'm going to take you upstairs and fuck you now."

More perfect words have never been uttered.

We hurry out of the fountains and up the steps to the front entrance of the hotel. Thankfully, our water-drenched walk of shame through the posh lobby goes unnoticed by the Harris clan, but not many others. And I know I'm fucking skipping, but I can't seem to help myself!

Roan's fingers play piano on my backside as we stand shoulder to shoulder in the elevator that is packed with strangers who are all gawking at the state of us. I use this time to clear my lust-crazed mind because I have a plan to execute and I can't get distracted. Going up to my room isn't only for sex. It's for payback. And while Roan may not be in on the details of my *entire* plan, he will serve the very basic role I need him for.

When we stumble into my room, Roan removes his suit coat

and begins working on the zipper of my dress, licking and nibbling my neck the entire time. I clench my thighs together at the sight of his white dress shirt clinging to his sculpted chest, showcasing absolutely every ripple of muscle on his body. *Focus, Allie! You have a job to do.*

We reach the bed and I turn quickly to shove him backwards before he can get my dress undone. He immediately pulls me down on top of him, but I hold up a finger and croak through my lust-filled brain, "Stop."

He stops. But the sexy look in his eyes is proof that his mind is still very much moving forward with whatever dirty plan he's coming up with.

I swallow a lump in my throat and force a sexy smile. "I want to do something, but I need you to close your eyes for a minute."

He eyes me like a lion that has been asked not to eat the raw steak right in front of him. But he complies, closing his eyes and yanking the tie off his thick neck. I pull him so he's sitting up on the edge of the bed, admiring his blatant trust in me as his eyes remain closed. I turn toward the TV, my knees trembling with anxiety as I try to blink away the fear of what I'm about to do, as well as the image of his chest in his now see-through shirt, and fumble with my phone.

You can do this, Allie. This is the plan that you've thought out completely. You're going to record yourself doing a striptease for Roan—a foreigner, a perfect stranger. Then you're going to send the clip to Ghost Penis and Rosalie and show them you're doing just fine on your own. You can do this!

I angle my phone downward to face the bed so both my upper body and Roan's face are cropped out of the top. All the frame shows is a man from about the shoulders down, but it's so darkly lit in the background you can't visualise much of him. What's more important is the foreground, which will feature my ass. Considering how possessive and immature Ghost Penis is, I'm certain this will send im into a blind rage. In turn, his jealousy will upset Rosalie. She'll end up throwing one of her epic tantrums and their budding new relationship will suffer the way I suffered. *They seriously have it coming.*

Before I can talk myself out of it, I click RECORD. Nerves instantly take flight deep in my belly. I awkwardly kick off my heels and turn to face Roan. "Okay, open your eyes."

His eyes open and blaze with arousal as he watches every move I make, like I'm a sex goddess sent straight down from Mount Olympus. The way his eyes burn into me makes me feel like I can conquer the world. He really has been so perfect tonight.

Maybe I should tell him about the camera? I think to myself as he licks his lips with excited anticipation. As his eyes rake over my body, I can't help but think maybe he'd be into it or happy to help out?

"*But what if he's not?*" The psychotic devil on my shoulder chimes in. It's the same voice that's been purring in my ear for the past two weeks. "*And now you came all the way to London for nothing?*"

I curse the guilt I feel for taking advantage of Roan and remind myself that my ex deserves this. Roan is simply a faceless male body. Nothing more. Ghost Penis and Rosalie will never know it is him in the video.

The last words I tell myself are, *Roan will never know.* Then his deep voice interrupts my warring thoughts.

"What's your plan, mooi?" he asks, his warm eyes mirroring the heat between my legs.

"What is mooi?" I ask, grateful for the reprieve from my sinister thoughts. I repeat the word back the way he pronounces it. It sounds like joy but with an *M* at the beginning.

He smiles a cocky smile. "It's South African for beautiful."

My body nearly melts to the floor. This guy has some serious game

"How many women have you used that term on?" I ask, biting my lip and reaching back for the zipper on my dress.

He shrugs. "Only the ones wearing garter belts."

I laugh and shake my head, feeling oddly touched. "Well, you're in luck because my plan is to show you the garter you felt earlier." He smiles knowingly, and I lower my voice to add, "The garter you felt when you kissed me so hard, I thought my legs would give out."

His hand moves to adjust the bulge in his pants. But instead of returning his hand to the bed, he unabashedly strokes himself over his trousers in slow, languid movements. *Holy shit, how is it possible for him to look so damn hot with all of his clothes on?*

I steel myself and slide the straps of my dress down to reveal my black, sheer bustier. My nipples are rock-hard as he takes them in. Before I have a chance to shimmy the dress down past my waist, he pulls my chest to his face and bites my right nipple over top of the sheer fabric. It feels so fucking good and so fucking surprising, I lose my mind for a moment.

"Oh my God!" I cry as he bounces his teeth on my tender flesh and then sucks hard. He runs a hand up my skirt to the area between my legs, and I let out a terrifyingly erotic moan when he finds my naked centre.

"No fucking broekies," he growls and burrows his face into my chest with a pained groan.

I pant loudly and my face falls when it occurs to me that I have no idea what he's talking about. "What the fuck is broekies?"

He stops his assault on my nipples and looks up at me. "Panties. You're wearing a garter belt with no panties. How is it that you keep fucking shocking me?"

I shake my head and realise that I've been so distracted, I haven't had a chance to finish my mission. Clearing my throat, I pull his face away from my breasts. "Sit back and see if I can shock you some more. I promise, it'll be worth it."

He does as he's told, propping himself on his elbows and

displaying an erection in his trousers so massive, it makes me nervous. I take a deep breath and slide my dress down the rest of the way. When I step out of the wet circle of fabric, I place my hands on my hips to feign confidence, like I do this all the time.

Black thigh-high stockings with black garter belts attached to the band around my hips are all that adorn my lower half. My freshly waxed pussy is on erotic display just for him, and I grow more and more wet with every passing second that his eyes are on me.

"Turn around," he demands as he slowly begins unbuttoning his shirt. I do exactly as he says because I did my striptease and I'm ready for him to take over. "Now, bend over," he adds.

My damp hair hangs nearly to the floor as I grip the dresser and look upside down behind me. Roan is perched at the end of the bed, his face eye-level with my ass as he opens a foil packet. When I catch sight of his hard dick springing out of his pants below his bunched abs, I remember my phone is still recording and instantly stand.

I hurriedly grapple for it, my finger stabbing out to the screen concealed behind the television set. Just as I touch the stop button…

Slap!

My left butt cheek stings from the blow he just landed on it. "Roan!" I squeal, shocked by the pooling desire his firm touch created in my lower belly.

His voice is controlled as he massages the area he just assaulted. "I thought I told you to bend over."

I glance back over my shoulder, and my eyes zero in on his dick. *Good-god, it's huge.* I mean, in all honesty, I was exaggerating about Ghost Penis because it made me feel better and he deserved to be mocked. In truth, he was average. Maybe on the smaller side of average, but he was passable as far as dicks go. Compared to Roan DeWitt's, though, it really was a micropenis.

Roan narrows his eyes, which elicits a nervous giggle from me. I dutifully resume my position, staring between my legs to watch him roll the Magnum condom over his length.

A cool trail slides down my inner thigh, causing my blood pressure to spike. Oh God, am I dripping down my legs? Is that water or my arousal? Either way, how mortifying. I close my eyes with embarrassment, but they fly wide when I feel a hot, wet tongue run up the path it has made on my inner thigh.

"Oh my God," I groan out so loud, I sound inhuman.

"Fuck yes, you taste as good as I hoped." His breath is like a feather against my skin. And without warning, he grabs my hips in his strong, meaty grip and buries his face in my centre. Just when I think my legs will give out, he flattens his tongue and swipes the entire length of me.

The *entire* length of me.

My knees buckle and I begin to wobble before he pulls me back against him.

"Spread your legs, mooi."

Mooi like joy...Please, God, bring me more joy!

I spread them.

He positions me over his lap and pushes his tip right where I want him. Right where I'm fucking throbbing to feel him.

"Now drop," he commands.

Reflexively, I comply.

A bizarre, animalistic noise garbles in my throat at the overwhelming feeling of him inside of me. It's too much but also not enough at the same time. I need to move to make it more comfortable. To find more room. I need to...

"That's right...Fucking ride me." Roan's voice is hoarse as his rough hands roam over my breasts, greedily groping handfuls at a time and tweaking my nipples while urging me to bounce up and down on him. And holy shit, I'm doing it. I'm doing it well. Too well, in fact. Everything feels too hot, too sensitive, too alive. He's rolling my nipples, driving me crazy. I feel like I'm losing complete control of all my senses because everything is rushing down to where we connect at my centre.

He moves his hands down to my thighs and then brushes harshly over my clit. I yelp. It's a weird reaction, but it wasn't consciously decided on. The area between my thighs feels like a live wire that I want him to ignite yet I don't want him to ignite. It's all too intense and my brain is too frazzled to tell me what I need!

Without warning, he pinches my clit. He pinches it so hard and so long that I scream. I scream and climax like I've never screamed or climaxed in my entire life. The orgasm catches me completely off guard and I feel a wet pressure explode out of me.

"Did I just fucking pee?" I exclaim more in shock and awe than embarrassment.

He bites my shoulder, his body shaking with silent laughter. "No, mooi. I think that's called a squirt."

"Oh my God," I groan as he thrusts into me while continuing to tease my clit.

My body must be on some sort of autopilot at this point because my mind is completely gone. I think I'm riding him, but maybe it's him riding me? I can't tell because I'm blacked-out and living inside my pussy where all I feel is our organs sliding against each other at rapid speed.

This is fucking. This is blissed-out, maxed-out, orgasmic sex to the nines. I've never felt sex like this. I've never felt an orgasm like this. Ioan is completely obliterating all penises that came before him.

He pulls out of me and I think to myself, *Thank God, I can't take any more.* But all he does is gently swat my bottom and turn me around so I'm lying on the bed. Holy shit, he's not even done yet? How has he not come yet? Can I take any more? My body is still recovering from that squirt!

Ioan slams back inside me, my centre still so wet, it's an easy entry. My garters snap off of me as my legs reflexively wrap around his waist.

I guess I can take more.

"Fuck me, Lis. You feel so goddamned good. Your ex is a moron."

I clamp my hand over his soft lips. "Don't talk about him while you're fucking me."

He chuckles against my hand and bites my finger, sucking it hard into the back of his throat.

Holy shit, I feel another climax building. This man is unbelievable. A guttural noise escapes his lips, and I can tell he's close because it's hotter than any other sound he's made all night. I shock myself again when my muscles tense in response. Roan swivels his hips and hits some magical spot inside of me that has never been touched before. Within seconds, I'm off again, silently screaming into his shoulder.

This orgasm is deeper and softer than the first, but still just as soul-shaking.

Roan flinches at the sensation of me pulsing around his cock before he finally drops his head to the crook of my neck and lets his own climax go.

"Holy shit," I inelegantly state as he breathes heavily on my collarbone with a shudder.

"Couldn't have said it better myself," he murmurs against my skin before licking a line along it and dropping a final kiss there.

He rolls off of me and we both lie on our backs, staring at the ceiling and replaying everything that just went down.

I'm the first to break the silence. "Roan DeWalt, you can fuck."

He huffs out a laugh at my bluntness and slides off the bed to quietly make his way to the bathroom. I should clean up, too, considering I fucking squirted! Good-god, I thought that was something only porn stars could do.

With that thought, my phone pops back into my mind. I'm desperate to look at the video and make sure you can't see Roan's face at all. Or heaven forbid, his dick. Things escalated more than I thought they would, so I probably need to delete whatever's on my phone right the fuck now.

I scramble up off the bed, my legs like jello and my stomach a ball of nerves as I grab my phone from behind the TV. My eyes fly wide when I see the screen is illuminated and the recording is still going.

"Holy shit," I whisper as I press STOP.

I swear I die a thousand deaths when I realise that I did in fact record our whole fucking session of fuckery and not just my little striptease. The thumbnail pops up and I cringe even though the image of me riding his lap reverse cowgirl style is kind of hot.

This is most definitely more than a striptease. It's the whole enchilada with guacamole and jalapenos, and faces, and pussies, and dicks and Magnum condoms slapped on like extras!

There's no way in hell I can send this to Ghost Penis even if I trim out the sex stuff. It's too much.

My thumb hesitates over the delete button because, quite perversely, I want to watch it first. I've never seen myself having sex before so I guess I just want to see how it looks. And if I press that button, it'll be gone forever. Boom. Not even a glance. Hitting delete means that Roan will become nothing more than a distant memory of a wild night I had in London when I had the best sex of my life. Meanwhile, the five shitty years I had with Ghost Penis will likely remain in vivid colour in the forefront of my mind until the day I die.

Roan clears his throat, and I look up to see him standing by the bathroom, light shining down on his erection. How is he hard again? He cocks his head. "Ready for round two of rebound fucking, Allie Harris?"

I squint at the glorious, delicious sight of him. I did this. I made this happen. This man, this moment, this wonderful night of passion is of my own making. Keeping the video for my eyes only is all the payback I need to move on with my life.

I smile at Roan and remove my finger from the delete button and click the power button instead. "Definitely ready."

And I'm definitely keeping this South African safely inside my phone for as long as I can. What's the worst that could happen?

CHAPTER 5

Allie

Two Years Later

> **Charles Harris,**
> **The honour of your presence is requested at the marriage of**
> **Rosalie Shay Dawson**
> **and Parker Lee Frost**
> **It's going to be an affair Chicago will never forget**
> **with cocktails, dinner, dancing, and above all...love.**

I close my eyes and my stomach rolls at the image of the wedding invitation I stumble upon in my father's apartment. I came over to meet him here after work because it's been weeks since we've spoken and months since we've actually laid eyes on each other. And with my father, if I don't put forth the effort to come over and say hello, he certainly won't.

Things have been off between us for the last couple of years. When he and my ex-stepmother found out about Rosalie and Ghost Penis, everyone became very distant. My father didn't raise a fuss, despite my battle cries. He simply retreated to his little corner of Chicago like the passive-aggressive, privileged asshole he is.

But it's been a year since he divorced Hilary, and I thought my relationship with him would improve once he didn't have other women vying for his attention. Apparently I was wrong.

When I let myself into his apartment, I found the offensive piece of paper sitting on the kitchen counter even though he knew I was coming over. Maybe this is why he's been so distant again lately?

My fingers glide over the embossed black calligraphy as I take in Rosalie and Ghost Penis' names stacked on top of one another, similar to the position they were in when I found them in my bed screwing. I'm not completely surprised by this news. I knew they were together because Rosalie sent me a ridiculous letter a few months after everything happened. All it said was that she was sorry that I was hurt but she and Ghost Penis were in love. I could barely stomach reading it because it was about as genuine as the time she apologised for turning in my essay instead of her own in our senior literature class.

Then I started getting text messages from her, asking me to take my name off our apartment lease so Parker could move in with her. It seems the apartment building has a policy about subleasing, and my name still being on that piece of paper was negatively affecting their plans. Admittedly, that tiny form of payback felt too good to give in, so I ignored her texts for months.

But seeing the invitation in my father's house does not feel good. Why are they inviting him to their wedding? Why does he need to be there when he is no longer married to Rosalie's mother? They don't even talk anymore, I don't think.

My fingers brush over a note stuck to the back of the invitation. I pull it off and see it's scrawled in my ex-stepsister's handwriting.

'*Daddy, will you do me the honour of walking me down the aisle and giving me away to the love of my life? I can think of no one else I want to hold my hand more." Love Always, Your Daughter, Rose*

I blink rapidly, feeling eerily like I've just been shot. My eyes shoot around the grey, sterile kitchen searching for hidden cameras, because I'm surely being Punk'd. This ridiculous note can't possibly be real! I mean, I know Rosalie has daddy issues since her birth father has been MIA, but that doesn't mean she gets to keep my dad forever.

But the note is real. And there's no question what she's asking.

Suddenly, the apartment door unlocks. I grab the invitation off the counter and rush over to meet my father at the entry.

"What is this?" I seethe, my voice shaking with fury.

Charles Harris is a tall man with a full head of dark hair that apparently is never going to grey. He stares down at me with his granite features as a wary look flickers in his eyes. "I didn't mean for you to see that," he replies crisply in his faint British accent.

"Are you going to the wedding?" I snap back as he shrugs off his jacket and hangs it on a hook.

He exhales heavily and strides past me toward the kitchen. "It's not that big a deal, Alice."

I follow in his wake. "It is a big deal. She's asking you to walk her down the aisle! That seems like a very big deal."

He pulls a glass from the cabinet and turns to face me. "It really has nothing to do with you."

"Nothing to do with me?" I shriek, my anger bubbling over. "He was *my boyfriend*, not hers! You're *my father*, not hers! And you keeping a relationship with her is a complete and utter betrayal toward me. If you walk her down the aisle and give her away to him, you're basically condoning everything they did to me!"

He rolls his eyes and fills his glass from the tap. "You know how Rosalie is. When she wants something, she's relentless."

"Who cares? She's not your problem anymore!"

He sets the glass down and takes the invitation from my hands. He tucks it into a nearby kitchen drawer, like concealing it will make all of this go away.

"You're being dramatic, Alice, and I won't talk to you when you're like this."

He picks up the glass to take a long drink again. I watch him as my eyes fill with tears that I could never seem to shed for the loss of my ex or Rosalie. But the tears for my father apparently fall freely.

"I don't even know what I'm doing here anymore," I croak, walking over to the table and grabbing my handbag.

He eyes me warily. "I thought you wanted to have dinner."

"Not here, in your apartment. I don't know what I'm doing in Chicago. In your life. We barely speak because you don't need me anymore. You have Rosalie. I don't know why I'm surprised. She always did have you wrapped around her finger." I state, knowing I sound childish but recalling all the times she manipulated my father into getting whatever she wanted.

"You're being unreasonable."

I nod thoughtfully before the image of my father walking Rosalie down the aisle in her white wedding dress flashes through my mind. The image makes me sick to my stomach because she has no right to take that moment away from me. And it's not because I still care about Rosalie or Ghost Penis. It's because my father's involvement in their relationship and his ambivalence toward me shakes the very ground I walk upon.

"I need to go," I state, turning on my heel and making my way out of the kitchen.

"Where are you going?" he asks, his tone flat and completely devoid of any emotion.

"I don't know," I call over my shoulder. "But anywhere is a hell of a lot better than here."

CHAPTER 6

Allie

A Couple of Months Later

V I GRABS MY HAND AND YANKS ME ONTO THE PITCH OF OLD
Trafford with the rest of the Harris clan to support Gareth during
his farewell speech to Manchester United. When I first agreed to come,
I thought I'd be watching the game from the stands with the rest of
the commoners. I didn't know I'd be involved in the final send-off.

The stadium lights are blinding as we approach centre field, where
Gareth is standing with a microphone. He's covered in sweat and is
decked out in his Red Devils gear as his spikes dig into the electric
green grass below his feet.

He smiles an easy smile and lifts the mic to his mouth. "Tonight
I bid a fond farewell to this stadium and the wonderful game of football." A swell of emotion catches him off guard as he looks up at the
seventy-five thousand screaming fans stuffed in the stands just for
him.

I look around at the Harris family standing beside him, who are
all equally as emotional regardless of the spotlights shining down
on them. This isn't just a final game for Gareth, it's a milestone for
their family. Gareth's career in professional soccer is known around
the world, and watching him say goodbye to it in favour of spending
more time with his growing family is special in more ways than one.

I glance around at the rest of the brothers and wonder how much longer they'll stick with the sport since their families seem to be growing, too. I once suspected all the Harris Brothers would end up as eternal bachelors, but here they stand with wives under their arms and smiles on their faces.

Shockingly, the twins were the first to commit. The two of them landed brilliant female doctors who also happen to be best friends. Camden's wife, Indie, is currently the team doctor for Uncle Vaughn's club, and Tanner's wife, Belle, is a prenatal surgeon who saves babies while they're still in the womb.

The youngest, Booker, married his childhood best friend, Poppy, about six months ago. I've only seen photos of their one-year-old surprise twin boys, Oliver and Teddy, and I can already tell those two adorable devils are going to grow up to be just as naughty as their uncles.

Gareth and Sloan's wedding was small since it was Sloan's second marriage. But they've clearly been busy as Sloan clutches their four-week-old little boy, Milo, to her chest. Gareth reaches down and lifts Sloan's ten-year-old daughter, Sophia, up into his arms. Sophia is from Sloan's first marriage, but she has the name HARRIS printed loud and proud across her back.

V and Hayden had a destination wedding with immediate family that was planned last minute. Their little daughter, whom they all call Rocky, was said to have been a perfect flower girl.

The group of them amaze me as they stand together with their new spouses and new babies. The Harris Brothers are mega, world-wide superstars, yet they are all still able to come together for this moment. This is what family should be about. Blood, commitment, loyalty, support. Not concealed invitations and ignored emotional reactions.

"I've been playing defence for over a decade, and it's time for me to play some other positions in life. A fan, a friend, a brother, an uncle, a husband...a father." Gareth's voice breaks at the end as he looks at his son in Sloan's arms. He gives Sophia an extra squeeze and finds strength in her beaming smile to go on.

"…there comes a point in your life when you have to start thinking with your heart instead of your head. And my heart is calling me home. To my family." Gareth finishes his speech to riotous cheers from the fans and wraps his family in his arms for a group hug. Vi pulls me over to her, laughing as Vaughn hoists Rocky up onto his shoulders for a victory lap around the pitch.

Tears find their way into my eyes as well. The inspiration behind why I'm here may be somewhat selfish, but I'm grateful those reasons made it possible for me to witness this up close. It helps me realise that there are still genuine examples of family in the world.

After we file out of the stadium, we head to Gareth's Manchester home just outside of Astbury. It's an incredible architectural, glass structure nestled in the stunning English countryside. He's in the process of putting it on the market now that he's retired from Man U. He, Sloan, Sophia, and Milo plan to live in their Hampstead house full-time so Sloan can be closer to the fashion boutique she runs with her best friend, Freya, and Hayden's sister-in-law, Leslie.

Dinner is a loud, typical Harris-style family meal, complete with arguments, *football* chatter, and loads of teasing. I laugh along with everyone as they catch me up on their lives, and I'm over-the-moon happy when Tanner informs me that his wife, Belle, is four months pregnant.

"Do you know what you're having yet?" I ask as I gaze over at Belle, who's a dark-haired, dark-eyed, bombshell with curves to match.

Belle smiles a secretive smile. "I do, but only because we did a scan at the hospital last week. Tanner doesn't want to know, though."

"Bloody well right I don't," Tanner crows. "I want to be surprised on the big day."

"Do you know?" I ask, glancing over at Camden's wife, Indie. I figured since she is best friends with Belle, she might have an inside scoop.

Indie shakes her head, her red curls falling into her face as she fiddle with her cheetah-print glasses. She is so adorable, and the fact that Camden's pet name for her is "Specs" makes me swoon a little how cute they are together. "I'm crap at keeping secrets, so I can't know. If I know, Camden will get it out of me. Then he'll let it slip to Tanner. It's a horrid domino effect."

Camden turns to his wife with a wounded look on his face. "That not fair! I'd say I'm pretty good at keeping secrets as of late, Specs."

Indie's eyes narrow behind her glasses as everyone at the table quiet down and turns their attention to them. "Camden!" Indie hisses a warning under her breath and then offers us all a nervous smile.

"No. I'm offended that you think I'm a horrible secret keeper." Camden tosses his napkin onto his plate and sits back to drape an arm over Indie's chair. "We snuck off to get married in Scotland without me spilling the beans. And you've been up the duff for two months now and I haven't told a soul."

"Camden!" Indie peals, her cheeks flaming red.

"You're pregnant?" Belle shrieks, her voice rising to a pitch that would send dogs running for the hills.

After a short, pregnant pause, Indie turns her attention to look past Tanner, who's sitting between her and Belle, and replies, "We were going to tell everyone after Gareth's big night. I'm only eight week—"

"Ahhh!" Belle screams and darts across Tanner to wrap her arms round Indie. "We're pregnant together! I can't believe we actually bloody-well pulled it off!" They continue screaming over top of Tanner as the rest of the table offers their congratulations.

Booker's wife, Poppy, fluffs her short blonde hair and mumbles to her husband, "They'd better ask for extra scans so they aren't surprised like we were."

He laughs heartily, but his eyes soften as they land on his

sister. My gaze follows his to Vi, and I see that her eyes are full of tears she's trying to hide. It's no use, though. They escape down her cheeks and she lets out a garbled laugh as she waves away our attention.

"Sophia, I hope you like to babysit!" Vi exclaims, glancing down toward Sophia at the other end of the table. "You could get rich off this fertile lot!"

Sophia sits up and nods eagerly. "Mummy said I can take babysitting classes this summer!"

Tanner's ears perk up at her response. "Does that mean you'll actually babysit *my* child, Soph?" He leans across the table and eyes her playfully. "The baby will be related to me, and we all know what you think of me."

Sophia rolls her big brown eyes in the typical tween fashion as she deadpans, "I figure if I can babysit, I'll be able to fix whatever you might do that could screw the baby up."

The table erupts into laughter, and Gareth's eyes twinkle with pride as he ruffles the hair of his very clever daughter.

Several more laughs are had throughout the night. It isn't until cheesecake and coffee that Vaughn turns his attention on me. "So, Alice, how long are you staying in London?"

I feel everyone's eyes turn on me as I pierce my fork into my dessert. "Um, a while actually."

"Oh?" he asks curiously.

"Yes," I state, lowering my fork and rubbing my palms along my jeans to dry the sweat off of them. I don't know why I'm nervous to tell them this bit of news, but I am. "I was going to tell you guys that I just moved to London."

"What?" Vi shrieks excitedly, grabbing my forearm. "When? For how long?"

I shrug. "I moved here a week ago, and I'll be staying as long as I like, I guess. My boss transferred here a couple of months ago, and I asked if I could join him."

"Oh my goodness, that is brilliant!" Vi squeals and pulls me in for a hug. "Where are you living? You told me you had a hotel."

"I am in a hotel for now." I force a smile because the hotel is not ideal. It's super old and small and smells musty. But it's all I could afford, and I certainly wasn't going to ask my father for money. "Once I find a place, the movers will ship the rest of my stuff from Chicago. I'm struggling to find an apartment I can afford on an assistant's salary, so I'm hunting for a roommate."

"A roommate?" Gareth barks, shifting Milo from one arm to the other now that Sophia has sat down in her chair to eat. "You're twenty-six years old, right? You don't need a *roommate*, Allie-Cat."

I blink rapidly at him. "Um, I absolutely do need a roommate because I know how much money I make."

Gareth eyes me harshly. "Who are you working for? Surely they should be paying enough for London cost of living."

I smile and turn my gaze to everyone watching me. "Well, the move was my idea, so I didn't get much for moving expenses. I think they only allowed it because I have dual citizenship."

"What's the company you're working for?" Vaughn asks, looking uncertain about my employer because this family has no idea what it's like to be part of the regular working class.

I plant on another smile. "That's the other surprise. I'm the executive assistant to Niall Capelle—the senior vice president for the new entertainment division at J&S Public Relations."

Vaughn straightens in his chair. "That's who we just hired for the team."

"I know," I reply, biting my lip and hoping that my uncle is as excited about this as I am. "I was working under Niall in the Chicago office before he left. I wasn't sure they were going to put me under him over here because of the family connection. But since I'm only an assistant and not your actual rep, they said it was fine."

"Wow!" Vi exclaims. "So, you'll be working for Dad's club?"

I shrug. "Probably more like fetching coffee. I'm still getting settled in the office at this point. I'm honestly not sure where I'll be in the grand scheme of things, but hopefully I'll get to see some of you in passing."

"You will," Vi says firmly, reaching out to clutch my hand. "We have Sunday night dinners at Dad's house in Chigwell every week, and we expect you to be there."

"Absolutely," Vaughn states, his face turning more serious than I've seen it all night. He clears his throat and adds, "What does your father think of you being back over here in London?"

I shrink in my seat because this is the first time Vaughn has brought up my dad. By the tight look on his face, I can tell it's not easy for him. The divide between Vaughn and my father happened after Aunt Vilma passed away and neither of them have made any sort of effort to repair the distance.

"He's happy for me," I state pleasantly, even though I don't believe it. The only thing he asked about was my salary increase and nothing of my emotional reasons for moving. "Of course, he still wishes I would have gone into law and worked at his firm in Chicago, but I'm enjoying what I do, even if it doesn't pay the greatest yet."

"I'll cover your flat," Gareth says from the opposite end of the table as he forks a bite of cheesecake into his mouth like he just told me what the weather is today.

"You're not covering anything," I argue, my spine straightening defensively. "Gareth, you're my cousin, not my father. I'm not letting you pay for me."

"There are a lot of nutters in London, Allie-Cat," Gareth snaps, his tone deep and firm. "You can't just swipe left for a flatmate."

"How do you even know what swiping left means?" Tanner interjects, his eyes narrowing in confusion. After all, before Gareth met Sloan, we never heard about him with any other woman.

Gareth shrugs. "I've heard the team talking about it…

What ver, Tanner. You know what I mean. She can't room with just anybo ly."

" Vell, I bloody well know that!" Tanner replies.

I lle chimes in next with a shrug. "They're kind of right. It took ears of friendship with Indie before I trusted her enough to let he move into my place."

" ecause you thought I was mental?" Indie peals, her tone hurt and s rprised.

" don't trust virgins," Belle states softly, and Vaughn's face pales in ho or. Luckily, Sophia is at the other end of the table and didn't hear er, and Rocky and the twins have been in bed for the past hour, o their precious little ears are safe.

" et's just announce all my private life to the table tonight, shall we?" Ier eyes widen as Camden's mouth opens, and she quickly claps er hand over it.

I ppy is undeterred by the spectacle and leans across the table to asl "Don't you have a friend from childhood you can maybe re-conno t with? That's what I did with Booker when I came back to town Poppy smiles a sweet smile at Booker.

I ooker lifts his brows and deadpans, "And it only resulted in one a cidental pregnancy, so things could have been a lot worse." Popp elbows him in the ribs, but he manages to add, "Well, two accid ntal pregnancies since they turned out to be twins."

" nd look how happy you are as a result," Vi states, shooting a wan ting gaze at Booker. "You cheeky bugger. Don't turn into a cocky sod just because your babies are in bed." Vi redirects her at-tentio i to me with her brows pinched together. "I'd say you can stay at ou place, but we don't have the room. Honestly, we've been flat hunti g for a while now."

I ayden looks at me regretfully. "You should talk to us about the n ghbourhoods you're looking at so we can tell you if they're safe."

" here's plenty of room at the house in Chigwell. You'll stay there until you find something suitable," Vaughn states matter-of-factly, not willing to listen to this conversation a moment longer.

"Guys! I'm not asking to move in with anyone!" I exclaim, holding my hands up to make sure they all still see me because they've been talking about me like I'm not here for ages. "My hotel room is working for now. I'm fine."

"We have room, though," Indie states quietly and looks over at Camden, who nods his agreement. "Our Notting Hill townhouse has three whole levels. The top floor even has its own kitchen and bath, so you really wouldn't be a bother. You could stay there as long as you'd like."

I exhale heavily because now everyone has weighed-in on my living situation, and I'm pretty damn sure I'm not getting out of here without moving in with one of the Harris Brothers. And since my other options seem to be unacceptable to them, I surrender to the lesser of all the evils.

"If you're sure, I won't be in the way," I respond to Camden and Indie.

"It's no problem!" Camden bellows cheerily. "As long as you ignore me yelling 'goal' from inside the shower, you'll be a great flatmate."

Indie flushes a deep red that brings a frown to my face. *I'm so not going to nibble on that dangled bait.*

CHAPTER 7

Rod

VUGHN HARRIS STANDS UP ON A BENCH INSIDE THE CHANGING room as we slowly strip out of our gear. It's mid-May and we just completed our final match of the regular season against Newcastle with a crushing four-nil victory, one of those goals being mine. Apart from a couple of friendlies we have coming up to promote our entrance into the Premier League, it's time for some much deserved downtime in the world of soccer. I can't wait.

"Great match tonight, gentlemen," Vaughn states, his voice gruff from all the yelling he did from the sidelines. "That's how you finish off the season for Tower Park!"

The team erupts into cheers, and Tanner grins over at me with a creepy look on his bearded face, which I have learned isn't anything unusual for the likes of him. A lot of Tanner's facial expressions resemble the look of a predatory stalker, but that's evidently just his face.

He holds out his fist to me and I bump it with pride. The Tanner Harris I've gotten to know this past season is a completely different guy than the one I met when I first moved to London. I don't know if it's because he's married and expecting a child, or if it's because his wife has his balls permanently locked in her handbag. Regardless, I'm grateful all the same because I finally have confidence in my position on the team.

Tanner suddenly stands up on his chair, grabs himself by the junk, and hollers over everyone's cheers, "Let's go balls deep in the Premier League next season, mates!"

Everyone hoots with joy, standing up and grabbing their own crotch in solidarity with their team captain. I glance over at Vaughn, who looks seriously unimpressed by his son's exploits but also not surprised.

Fuck it. I stand up and grab my balls, too. A balls deep chant begins echoing off the changing room walls, and I can't help but laugh at what a difference two years can make.

When I moved here from South Africa, I would have never expected our team to be promoted to Premier League this soon. Especially since Tanner couldn't stand me for the better part of my rookie season. I thought getting an assist from him would be less likely than him sharing his hot doctor girlfriend with me for a night. But after tonight's match, I've rounded off my season with fourteen goals and seven assists, making it my most successful season in my soccer career.

Suddenly, I catch sight of the new PR rep for the team walking through while all of us are grabbing ourselves and acting like idiots. Niall Capelle is a forty-something-year-old slick rick wearing an expensive suit and a pastel pink tie. He runs a hand through his greased blonde hair as he does everything he can to not brush up against any of our sweaty bodies. He sidles up next to Vaughn, who drops down off the bench and raises his hands to settle down the team.

"Oi, let's listen to what Mr. Capelle came here to say and then you can all go back to tugging on your trouser snakes."

The team chuckles and begrudgingly quiets as Mr. Capelle begins speaking in a smooth American accent. "Look, gentlemen, I know you don't know me very well yet as our PR firm just recently came on board, but you may as well get used to the sight of me now. I'm going to be pushing a lot of great publicity opportunities during your summer breaks. Getting promoted to Premier League next season means we all need to step up our game and present a clean front to the public. It's my hope that Bethnal Green F.C. will stick in Premier for years to come and we can grow this organisation to be even greater than it already is."

The team breaks into a cheer and a few of the guys high five each other. Mr. Capelle adds, "With that, I hope to see several of you at the charity event in West End tonight, benefitting the LGBTQ+ community centre expansion. You all should have received an email with the details. It's at Café de Paris. And perhaps since you just completed your last game of the regular season, your manager won't enforce a curfew?"

Vaughn scowls at Mr. Capelle and replies without pause, "Midnight is their curfew because anything that happens after midnight is a recipe for trouble." Vaughn smiles at the mixture of laughs and groans from the team and adds, "Have a good time. And great work tonight, gentlemen." Then he strides out of the changing room with Mr. Capelle hot on his heels.

"Hey, are you guys going tonight?" I ask Tanner and Booker, who are seated a little ways down the bench from me. "Or are you needing to get home to the twins, Booker?"

The youngest Harris Brother smiles at me. The gesture is so childlike that I have to remind myself the man is a beast as our team keeper and won the World Cup for England only a year ago.

He clears his throat and replies, "We're going out. We promised to take our cousin for a night out in London. She just moved here from Chicago last week, and we figured VIP access to a nightclub is probably the best welcome home party we can give her."

My blood runs cold. "Your"—I clear my throat—"Your cousin? Like a male Harris cousin I don't know about who's from Chicago?"

Booker frowns at my insanely specific response and shakes his head. "No, our cousin, Allie Harris. You know her, I thought? You were her date at Aunt Fiona's wedding."

My entire body goes stiff as I stammer, "Oh yeah, I remember her. I, erm, just didn't know she was moving here. We, erm, didn't keep in touch."

"Don't fuck with her tonight, all right?" Tanner barks out, narrowing his eyes at me. "This is her welcome to London night, and I won't have you stealing her away from us. I don't like the idea of bacon-sandwiching my own cousin, but I'll do it if I have to."

Booker's nose wrinkles as he stands up to yank off his shirt. "No, Tan. Just…no."

"What?" Tanner asks as he pulls the band out of his man bun and his long blonde hair falls down around his shoulders. "I'm not saying I'd lick her somewhere naughty."

"Stop," Booker says, making a face like he's going to vomit and turns toward the showers.

Tanner follows. "I'd just lick her hand or something. Like a knuckle maybe. Or her elbow? There's nothing sexy about elbows."

"You need help," Booker snaps over his shoulder.

"You know what, I'm tired of you twisting everything I say to be perverted…You're the one sexualising the Bacon Sandwich Rule."

Their arguing voices trail off, leaving me with a serious case of "what the fuck" after the bomb they just dropped on me.

Allie Harris moved to London?

I turn to face my cubby, my hands gripping the frame for balance. If I'm being honest, I've thought about her at least twenty thousand times since that night. She blazed in like a beautiful golden storm that I couldn't help but get lost in. Not only was she a fucking knockout, but she had such a sense of determination about her that seemed flawed somehow. On the surface, I saw power and poise. But there were times when she revealed glimpses of fragility that I desperately wanted to repair.

I'm not typically one for saving women because I have enough in my family who depend on me. But Allie was different. There was strength in her weakness, and that was a lethal combination for me.

It's why I made an exception to the rule I have about no one-night stand. I couldn't let her walk out of my life without tasting her at least once.

And fucking hell, that connection carried over in the bedroom in ways I never imagined. We spent hours fucking, and laughing, and talking. Maybe it was because we both knew there were no expectations beyond the one night. Regardless, Allie Harris was the best sex of my life, and I've spent the last two years comparing every woman I come across to her.

I had every intention of asking for her number, but she crept out of the hotel room before the sun was even up, like a thief in the night.

"What's your deal?" a voice booms behind me, causing me to jump about ten feet in the air.

Heart pounding, I turn on my heel to find my roommate and midfielder, Maclay Logan, leaning against a locker, watching me curiously. His heavily tattooed arms are crossed over his chest, offsetting the wild mane of childish auburn red hair on his head. The guy is built like a brick house and the largest soccer player I know who's not positioned as a keeper.

His eyes are laser-focused on me, so I quickly shake off my tense stance and coolly reply, "Nothing."

"Fuck that. You're shook," he growls back in his Scottish accent.

"I'm not shook," I snap defensively.

Mac's green eyes twinkle with challenge. "DeWalt, you're shooketh if ever I've seen a shooketh! Now get it telt what's crawled up your arse."

I roll my eyes and curse the day I ever let this pushy Scot into my life. We were both recruited to Bethnal Green F.C. the same year and ended up commiserating as newbies often do. This typically entailed moaning about the Harris family, doing workout sprints around Hyde Park, and playing Fortnite for an obscene number of hours like a couple of lame teenagers.

Mac awaits my response, so I do a cursory glance toward the showers to make sure Tanner and Booker aren't coming back yet. I lean in close and state in a low voice, "Allie Harris is back."

Mac's brows lift. "Fuck you."

"I'm serious, man. Booker and Tanner just told me."

"What's she doing here?"

"Evidently she lives here now."

Mac bursts out laughing, covering his mouth as he howls with way too much pleasure. "Fucking hell, you're doomed."

"Fuck you. Why are you saying that?" I snap, annoyed that he seemingly knows something I don't.

"Because you haven't stopped talking about the burd for two damn years," he booms. "You're as good as WAG'd. Mark my words. She'll be sitting in the wives and girlfriends section at our next match."

"Fuck off, you idiot. I barely know her. We had one night together that was just a bit of jol…a bit of fun," I state, explaining a term that's used in South Africa when referencing fun.

"One night you have every intention of repeating, am I right?"

My brows lift. "I mean, if I have any say in the matter, fuck yeah."

He laughs and shakes his head. "Future WAG."

"I told you, she's different. She didn't want any strings when I saw her last. I've never met a woman who blatantly admitted that she just wanted a casual one-night stand."

"You're not the type of lad who can handle casual," Mac replies knowingly.

I roll my eyes because it's somewhat true, but not exactly. I'm not like my teammates who easily roll from one bed to the next, night after night. It's not my style. I'm the type that if I find something I like, I like it more than once. But only for a month. Any length of time after a month is typically when women start to get attached, and attachment creates drama. I am a drama-free zone.

But I made a very happy exception to spend only one night with Allie Farris.

"So you're going to change her from a taste test to your usual flavour of the month?" Mac asks, tweaking his brows lasciviously at me.

I blow out a long breath. "Fuck knows. It's been two years since I laid eyes on the woman. Maybe that spark was something I imagined."

"Good point," Mac states with a serious look. "She could be married by now for all you know."

"Fuck you, man. Whose side are you on?" I'm not proud of the frustrated growl that vibrates in my chest.

Mac's eyes go wide as he holds his hands up defensively. "Look at you. Jealous already."

A chill runs down my spine. I turn on my heel to grip the sides of my cubby again, taking a deep breath to calm myself down. This is just like with any other woman, so why am I getting so worked up? Yes, I made an exception for her two years ago, but that doesn't mean she's some special, rare flower that is going to change who I am. I just need to find out some information on her. That's all.

I look over my shoulder at my best friend. "We're going to that club tonight to find out her status."

Mac smiles broadly and places his hand on my shoulder. "I'm here for you, lad."

Café de Paris is a cabaret nightclub, typically loaded with drag queens and performers. Tonight is no different. It feels a lot like walking into a circus when you're tripping on acid. Sequin costumes, makeup, colourful lights, and big personalities explode in every nook and cranny. Honestly, it's not a great deal different than what I grew up around at the dance studio where my mom, Diana, works. And since my mother's best friend happens to be a drag queen, the scenery actually makes me a little homesick.

I haven't been back home since my transfer and I know my mom misses me. But if I'm being honest, going home costs money, and I would rather send that money home to her to use on bills than pay to fly home for the holidays.

Mac and I follow the doorman through the packed club, and he guides us toward the split grand staircase that leads up to the VIP section. The elevated area is full of low-hanging crystal chandeliers and forms a circle around the dance floor. This section is loaded with London socialites and athletes from multiple teams. I'm not big on the social scene in London, though. I mostly stick to East London and small pubs where I can drink in peace and not find a photo of myself slapped up on some paparazzi site the next day.

We fetch a drink at the bar and find a spot along the rail that overlooks the dance floor. The place is packed shoulder to shoulder with people grinding against each other to house music as my eyes drift through the VIP section, hoping to find the Harris clan. They are typically easy to spot because they are the loudest crew in the room.

"Maybe we're too early," Mac says loudly into my ear to be heard over the music.

I nod slowly but then an unknown sensation pulls my gaze down to the dance floor near the front stage. A golden mane of soft curls sway along the bare back of a woman wearing a little black dress. She's dancing to the music, and I silently will her to turn around to face me so I can confirm what I suspect is true.

Suddenly, my fellow striker and teammate, Tanner, appears in all his man-bunned glory beside her. He grabs the blonde's hand, twirls her in an awkward motion, and completely blocks my view. Beside Tanner is Booker and his wife, Poppy, whom I've met a couple of times. She's dancing beside Tanner's wife, Belle, and our team medical trainer, Indie, who's married to Tanner's twin, Camden. Camden appears from the shadows and slinks his arms around his wife, his hands playfully stroking her stomach. She laughs and swats him away. Then I catch a glimpse of the oldest Harris Brother, Gareth, who is very recently retired and dancing nearby with his wife, Sloan.

I can't help but shake my head at the lot of them. This is how the Harris family rolls. Where one goes, they all go. Even with their busy schedules for their respective teams, they all manage to find time together.

A yellow burst of light illuminates the dance floor just as the blonde turns toward my direction and gives me a full view of her face. The first word that pops into my head when my eyes land on her is *nooi*.

How the fuck did Allie Harris manage to get even more beautiful than I remember? I suppose that dark, creepy photo I took of her when she was asleep wasn't necessarily a good representation of her. Especially as I see her now, swaying to the music and swivelling her curvier-than-I-remember hips.

She turns and I get a nice, clear sight of her voluptuous ass bouncing to the beat. Fucking hell, I don't remember her ass looking that lush either. Don't get me wrong, she was stunning when I met her. But I think she was thinner and a bit more on edge back then. Now she looks a hell of a lot more comfortable in her own skin.

She laughs at Tanner, who's dancing like he has a bee in his trousers, and I can already tell she's lost some of that intensity she had the night I met her. *It's a beautiful sight.*

What I'm seeing makes me realise with one hundred percent certainty that I am not done with Allie Harris. I really hope she doesn't have a fucking boyfriend.

Allie taps her cousin on the shoulder and gestures toward the direction of the hallway that leads to the bathrooms. She waves off the girls, whom I assume offered to go with her, and I watch her make her way away from the Harris clan. Without a word, I set my drink down and pat Mac on the shoulder as he continues ignoring me for the brunette who strolled up to him while I was distracted. I move past all the other VIPs to head downstairs toward the bathrooms because this is probably my only damn chance to get her alone tonight.

It's a long, dark hallway, illuminated by dim red sconces on the walls. The break in the thundering club music is appreciated as I prop myself against the wall outside of the ladies bathroom like a fucking stalker. Fuck it, I don't care. It's been two years since I've seen this woman, and I'm not going to miss the opportunity to talk to her.

When she strides out, she's busy tapping away at her phone and almost walks right by me. My words stop her in her tracks. "The infamous Allie Harris returns to London."

She stumbles at the sound of my voice, causing her phone to fall from her hands. I quickly squat down at the same time she does, and her hand lands over top of mine as I pick up her device. Our eyes lift and find each other with only a foot of space between us in the shadowy space.

Her gaze darts to my lips, and I inhale deeply because she still smells the same. Sweet and fruity with a hint of laundry detergent. Her electric blue eyes are blinking rapidly as a nervous flush crawls over her skin.

"Ro—Roan DeWalt," she stammers, her voice tight in her throat.

A knowing grin spreads across my face. "Hi there, Lis."

Her tongue slips out to lick her red-stained lips as she stares at my mouth. "You're…here."

"*You're* here," I repeat because I've been here since the day she ditched me in the hotel room.

She swallows slowly and I feel her grip tighten over top of my hand on her phone. "I, um, just moved back."

"So I hear."

"It's new," she adds by way of explanation.

My brows lift. "I like new things."

A moment of silence casts over us as her gaze drops down to her hand on top of mine. "Can I have my phone back?"

I turn my palm up to offer it to her. She grabs it, quickly clicking the screen off like she doesn't want me to see what she was looking at. Was she texting a boyfriend?

We stand up in unison, and my eyes drift down her body in a long, appreciative perusal. "You look really fucking good."

She takes a step back and runs her hands along her hips nervously. "Thanks." Her eyes seem to begrudgingly take in my body next. "So do you."

I chuckle because the woman before me is a hell of a lot different than the one who propositioned me for a one-night stand two years ago. This version of Allie seems guarded in a way that she wasn't on the dance floor a minute ago. She almost seems guilty for some odd reason. But guilty about what? Leaving me in the hotel room without a word? Returning and not telling me? Or maybe she doesn't want to see me? *Ag, this woman still intrigues me.*

"So, what are you doing back in London?" I ask, propping myself on the opposite wall and sliding my hands into my pockets.

She tucks a strand of her curly golden hair behind her ear. "My boss was transferred here to do PR for a soccer team in London. I decided to transfer with him last minute."

"Which club?" I ask, my curiosity piqued.

She gets an adorable guilty look in her eyes again. "Bethnal Green."

My jaw drops. "You're doing PR for my team?"

She bites her lip and nods. "My uncle's team, yes. But it's not a nepotism thing or anything. I got the job myself. Vaughn had no idea until I moved here."

I narrow my eyes speculatively. "Interesting…And you didn't think this news warranted a phone call?"

She runs her hands through her hair. "Well, as I said, it was sort of a last minute move…and…we didn't exactly exchange numbers."

Her cheeks turn redder as I imagine her thoughts have flickered to a knee-trembling memory that involves the two of us naked.

I drop my chin and eye her, trying to determine if she's embarrassed about our night together or if she's just not that into me. "I think you know how to get a hold of me."

She looks down and fumbles with her phone for a minute. "I didn't know if you'd remember me."

"Remember you!" I reply with a laugh. "How could I forget the woman who so ruthlessly stole my virtue?"

The cheesy line elicits a small smile from her, which feels like a major victory. "More like stole your time. I was such a mess back then. You were so kind to me."

"You were a fun mess," I correct. "And you were actually pretty great, all things considered."

She grins and chews her lip thoughtfully before pinning me with a serious look. "While researching the team, I noticed in some of the papers there was talk of a transfer for you last year."

My face falls at her shift in conversation. I grip the back of my neck and regretfully reply, "Yeah, I twisted my ankle pretty bad, and I was sure Vaughn was thinking about selling me to a lower team when a transfer window opened up since Tanner and I still hadn't found our rhythm."

"Yet here you are," she says, eyeing me like I'm a cat with nine lives.

"Yeah…It's all thanks to Camden's wife, Indie, though," I state. "She worked miracles on me during my rehab. She's unlike any team doctor I've come across, and whatever she did worked because I'm good as new."

Allie nods thoughtfully. "Indie is pretty brilliant. I actually just moved in with her and Camden until I find my own place."

"Oh, that's nice," I reply, but a woman diverts both of our attention as her heels clack down the marble hallway. Allie backs up against the opposite wall to allow the woman passage to the ladies bathr om. Once she clears through, I add, "Living with Camden and l die must be interesting. Whenever he stops by the training fa ility, he practically assaults his wife with public displays of affect on."

" hey are pretty into each other. And Indie is newly pregnant, so I t ink it might be even worse now," she says with a laugh and then er face pales. She covers her mouth in horror and mumbles again her palms, "Oh shit, I don't know if she's telling the team she's regnant yet."

" fo worries," I reply and wave my hand. "Her secret is safe with e."

, lie looks relieved. "Jeez, I've only been here a couple of weeks and I 1 already giving away family secrets."

" couple of weeks?" I ask, pinning her with an expectant look. "So it 'ou're all settled in, maybe I can get your number and we can go ou sometime."

I er eyes widen at my suggestion. "Um, I'm not sure that's a good lea."

" Vhy not?"

S e gets a cagey look in her eyes as she appears to be searching her b in for an excuse. "Because…my PR firm handles your team. I thin they'd frown on me canoodling with clients."

, pleased smile spreads across my face because her response didn' include anything about a boyfriend. Pushing myself off the wall, move so I'm standing right in front of her and can get a good look the freckle below her eye that I find utterly captivating. My voice s low when I reply, "But it's not like you're our direct representa ve. I've only ever met that Niall Capelle guy who evidently has a ing for pastel ties."

" le's my boss," she says by way of explanation.

" nd?"

S e swallows nervously. "And I'm pretty sure he'd say me spenc ng time with one of the players would be inappropriate."

"So he doesn't have to know." I tuck a strand of hair behind her ear and her cheek instantly turns into my touch.

Fuck yes, that spark is still there. Maybe even stronger than before. And Jesus Christ, she looks good. Healthy and lighter, even if my presence appears to make her a bit anxious.

"Where's the crazy rulebreaker who defied her cousins and danced in the fountains with me two years ago?"

Her jaw drops and she huffs out a laugh. "Um, she's fully recovered from her horrifying breakup and behaving more rationally now." A guilty look streaks across her face as she finishes her sentence.

"Rational doesn't sound like very much fun." I drag a finger along her waist and instantly feel a shiver run up her body.

She swallows slowly, the contact of my hand causing her to angle toward me like a cat stretching out in the afternoon sun. With a shaky breath, she gazes up into my eyes, and I can see the heat blossom inside of her. The warmth. The desire. *The memories.*

But she closes her eyes tightly, like she's forcing herself to bury those thoughts far, far away. She pulls her phone up and clutches it to her chest like a shield of armour. "I should get back to my family. They all got sitters so they could bring me out tonight."

"Are you sure you need to go so soon?" I ask, running my thumb in small circles along her hip bone. I lean in and murmur into her ear, "I think we had a bit of jol the last time we ditched them."

She exhales slowly and rubs her lips together while staring at mine with blatant hunger. "Maybe some things are better off forgotten."

"You wound me, Lis." My lower lip juts out in a childish pout. "Are you telling me you haven't replayed that night we spent together in your mind at least a dozen times? Because I certainly have." *More like over a thousand times, you pervert.*

I watch closely as her eyes turn hazy and I know she's recalling everything we did together as well. All the places on her body my li s touched. All the curves of her frame aligned with mine. The tightı ss of her wrapped around the firmness of me. It's not a night that's asily forgotten.

y cock stirs inside my trousers just thinking back on it. I lean in an whisper, "I'd be happy to remind you, mooi."

e lets out a breath and makes a little noise that sounds like a whin er. And just when I think she might touch her lips to mine, a loud ash of glass sounds off down the hallway, ripping us both out of ou special moment.

lie shakes her head and clears her throat in a formal way. "I really hould be getting back to my family." She pushes off the wall and s ips away from me just like she did the first night we met. The only ifference is she looks over her shoulder this time and adds, "See u around."

I mile at her parting remark. *Yes, you will, Allie Harris. Yes, you will.*

CHAPTER 8

Allie

SEATED AT MY DESK OUTSIDE OF MY BOSS' OFFICE ON THE WEST End of London, my finger hovers over the delete button on my phone for the fifty thousandth time in the past two years since I realised that I accidentally recorded a sex video of me and Roan DeWalt.

"Delete it, Allie," I murmur as I spin in my desk chair. "Just delete it and move on with your life! It's even more important now that he's back *in* your life!"

I exhale and have the same exact conversation with myself that I've had countless times before. *The video was an honest mistake. You were in a very vulnerable place in your life and maybe a little too focused on a crazy revenge scheme because you'd just had your heart broken by two people you trusted.*

Then another voice in my head says, *Don't delete it! You look beautiful and powerful! And whenever you feel like you might not be good enough and all those insecurities that Ghost Penis, Rosalie, and your father have inflicted on you come raging into your mind, the video reminds you that you're a total badass!*

My mind is a traitorous bitch who really needs to get her shit together.

What does my mind have to say about the fact that I touch

myself every time I watch the video? What ridiculous defence can I come up with for that in my corrupted, horrible conscience?

It's a hot video!

Shut up mind! You're embarrassing yourself.

Sort of like how I embarrassed myself at the club two nights ago when I ran into Roan. My body flushes from the memory of him leaning into me like he wanted to kiss me. Holy shit was I not prepared for that. I mean, I knew I'd run into him eventually, but I figured he'd ignore me like all the other jersey chasers whom I'm sure he's dicked and dismissed since he last saw me. In all honesty, I thought I had imagined the chemistry we shared or that I had inflated it in the past couple of years after replaying the video one too many times.

But then, there he was, waiting for me outside of the bathroom like he had to seek me out. That moment made me realise that there was a reason I knew I'd never do anything with the video the minute I walked out of that hotel room.

It's Roan.

He's not a faceless nobody, even if I could have edited the video down and clipped off all the offensive scenes that show his face. In the course of our glorious sex marathon that was so mind-blowing I probably would have thought it was a dream if I didn't have a horribly inappropriate and nonconsensual sex video on my cell phone, I sort of fell for the guy. And apparently I decided I needed to keep the video of him to remind myself of that fact. *Good-god, I'm going to hell.*

"Ellie, I have to head to Liverpool today for some meetings," Niall's voice booms as he strides out of his office.

I scramble to close the video and not look like the guilty sex offender I am. "Liverpool?" I ask, my voice high and official and maybe a tad squeaky.

He frowns curiously at me. "Yes, and I need you to do something kind of important for me."

"Okay, sure. What do you need?" I ask, shoving my phone into my drawer and quickly closing the employee handbook where I had been reading up on the policies of interoffice relationships. Annoyingly, there is no policy section on dating clients or possessing a sex video of said clients. *Shocking.*

I grab a notebook and pen and gaze up at Niall as he looms over me in his expensive suit. His spicy cologne invades my senses when he splays his hands out on my desk. "I received a call today from the Get Fit Britain charity, and they had a proposition for me I couldn't refuse."

I nod and pointlessly write down Get Fit Britain at the top of my notebook while Niall shifts to perch himself on the edge of my desk.

"They are in the process of raising funds for their nonprofit through a Win A Date Campaign, which features two athletes from select Premier League teams. They're asking viewers to donate for a chance to be their date for their formal charity gala happening in a couple of months."

"Oh, how cool!" I reply with wide eyes. "I've seen some of those videos circulating. People are going nuts for those athletes."

"Exactly," Niall confirms with an annoyed roll of his eyes. "I don't know why women go so crazy for athletes over here. In America, a nice suit and a high-rise office is what impresses. Apparently in England, it's muddy uniforms and low IQs."

I press my lips together, holding back the snappy response that is on the tip of my tongue. An argument with my boss is not the drama I need in my life right now.

Niall fiddles with his watch and continues, "Get Fit Britain thought that since the Bethnal Green club has recently been promoted, perhaps we'd want to have a couple of our players involved in the promotion."

"For sure!" I reply excitedly. "That'd be great exposure."

"Right…Well, I'm glad you agree because I'm leaving you in charge. The agency has selected Roan DeWalt and Maclay Logan to be our stars because they're young and single, but I want you to do some research on their backgrounds to confirm that they really are as squeaky clean as the agency believes them to be."

"Squeaky clean?" I ask curiously, trying to ignore the physical reaction my body has to the fact that we are talking about Roan.

"Correct. Look through their files, do some digging." Niall leans in closer to me, his voice taking on a lower tone as he adds, "Those players whore themselves out to anything with legs. The last thing we need is to feature a player with illegitimate children scattered all over the world."

My face cringes at his response and Niall huffs out a laugh. "Did that offend your precious virtue, Allie? What's it like to be so young and innocent?"

I swallow a knot in my throat because I'm certainly not that innocent, but that's not something I wish to discuss with my boss. Instead, I clear my throat and ask, "So, if the two players you mentioned are squeaky clean?"

He pulls back, that business mask returning to his face as he straightens his tie. "Then I need you to head over to Tower Park when they're done with their training at three o'clock and go over the script they need to say on camera."

"You want me to work directly with the players?" I can't help but ask this very obvious question because, since the moment I came to London, all I've done is organise the new office. This is the most Niall has spoken to me in days. Now he's tasking me with something this big?

He narrows his eyes at me. "Don't tell me you're one of those fangirls who goes gaga for athletes as well."

I shake my head defensively. "Of course not."

"Good, because they have a styling appointment for their wardrobe tomorrow that I need you at as well. The clothing boutique we're using has a personal connection to the Harris family, so they agreed to do a rush styling job."

"Oh, is it Kindred Spirits Boutique?" I ask knowingly.

Niall frowns. "Yes, that's the name of it. How do you know it?"

"That's Gareth Harris' wife's boutique in East London. She owns it with Leslie Lincoln, who would be Gareth's sister's husband's brother's wife."

Niall blinks back at me with a stunned look on his face. "I have no idea what you just said."

I swallow nervously. "Sloan does menswear and Leslie does womenswear?"

Niall continues to blink.

"Do you remember that my last name is Harris?"

He tsks his teeth and nods slowly getting a severe look across his face as realisation sets in. "I nearly forgot about your connection." He stands up and buttons his suit coat. "Well, I don't need to know about any family drama. I just need this boutique not to fuck things up. These two athletes need to raise a lot of money, which means they need to look fuckworthy, all right?"

I practically flinch as flashbacks of Roan's muscles flicker through my mind. "Fuckworthy. Got it."

Niall eyes me for a moment and then nods. "I'll be back on Wednesday to help you with the shoot. See you then."

He walks out of the office without another word. Once the coast is clear, I press my forehead to my desk. I just willingly signed up for multiple days in a row of doing publicity stuff with Roan DeWalt. Roan DeWalt—the man whom I currently have a sex video of on my cell phone, which I still watch on a regular basis.

Jesus fucking Christ.

Later in the day, I make my way to East London toward Tower Park—the home of Bethnal Green F.C. The team's training grounds are attached to the park, and that's where I'll find the two men responsible for my visit today. Roan DeWalt and Maclay Logan.

My uncle has been the manager of Bethnal Green F.C. for over a decade now. It isn't surprising because my father still talks about Vaughn's glory days as a *footballer* for Manchester United and how he used to cheer on his big brother all the time. But when Vaughn's wife fell ill, he quit the sport and everything changed. Dad and Vaughn grew apart and spoke a lot less. The only reason I even got to know my cousins is because of Vi's insistence that we get together for my birthday every year.

Then, shortly after I moved to America with my father, I heard whisperings from my mother about how difficult things were back in London for my cousins. Vaughn didn't want anyone's help raising all five of his children after my aunt Vilma passed away, no matter how hard they tried.

Despite all those sad times, looking at the Harris family now, you'd never be able to tell the struggles they all must have gone through. They still get together for weekly dinners, for Christ's sake. That's a hell of a lot more of a connection than I have with my parents. Although, maybe Dad has weekly dinners with Rosalie and Ghost Penis Heck, I wouldn't put it past him to pay for their damn wedding.

That's why moving to London and facing my awkward one-night stand paled greatly in comparison to staying in Chicago and being surrounded by my fucked-up past life.

A security guard checks my credentials at the Tower Park media entrance and then instructs me to wait in a holding area for someone to escort me to the players. I glance at myself in a nearby mirror, quickly smoothing out my black pencil skirt and straightening my cobalt blue blouse. Footsteps echo off the walls, so I look over and see my uncle striding down the darkened hallway toward me.

"Alice," he says with a smile and opens his arms to me.

I adjust my satchel and smile sheepishly. "Uncle Vaughn, you didn't have to come escort me. I know you're a busy man."

He scoffs. "I'm a lot less busy now. Just a couple of friendlies and the boys will finally get a few weeks off."

I nod knowingly. "Soccer is a crazy long season."

"Football," he corrects and chucks my chin playfully. "I know you've been in America most of your life, but don't forget you were born British, darling."

I laugh politely as I stare up at him. He's the spitting image of my father—tall, fit, handsome—but Vaughn has a lot more fine lines and grey hairs. Probably the difference between raising five kids versus one.

"I'll call it football from now on," I state with a nod, even though I will likely forget.

He smiles and gestures for me to follow him through several hallways. "Are you all settled at Camden and Indie's place now?"

"I am," I reply, adjusting my bag on my shoulder. "They have a beautiful home. I basically have my own apartment, so I really feel like I'm taking advantage."

"That's what family is for," he states firmly. "And with their schedules, those two likely only catch each other coming and going, so it's good to have someone there to actually use the house."

"I'm doing an excellent job of feeding their fish while they are away if I do say so myself," I state with a laugh.

Vaughn frowns, clearly unaware of their precious fish's backstory. Indie told me all about little Snowflake's existence when she helped me unpack one night. Apparently when she found out she was pregnant, she was terrified that she and Camden weren't capable of keeping a living being alive, so Cam went out and purchased a betta fish to prove her wrong. The poor thing was almost dead when I moved in.

"I can't believe both Camden and Tanner are going to be fathers," Vaughn states with a huff. "Do you think the world is ready for their offspring?"

I laugh because it's a very good question. Based on all the background information I had to read about the team, I learned that

Camden and Tanner's reputations greatly preceded them. Camden's most notable offence when he was still playing for Bethnal Green F.C. was kissing his surgeon in the operating room. Tanner's involved being caught naked on a London street corner by paparazzi. Thankfully, since settling down with Indie and Belle, those days are seemingly long behind them. Our PR company shouldn't have to worry about cleaning up any Harris Brother scandals anytime soon.

The one teammate who had a surprisingly squeaky clean track record was Roan DeWalt. When I laid eyes on him at the bar the night of my aunt's wedding, I thought he looked like a player through and through. But it seems he's lived a PG life. Only a handful of committed relationships that ended amicably and rarely photographed with groupies. He even has half of his paycheques automatically routed to his mother in South Africa. It's surprising.

Without warning, Vaughn pushes open a set of double doors and leads me into a changing room full of…

Naked. Soccer players.

Butt naked, wet or sweaty—I can't quite tell—soccer players.

I catch sight of one guy flicking a towel at the bare ass of another so I duck my head and shield my gaze. Good-god, if I'm caught ogling several hanging members being swung about all willy-nilly, I'll be sure to lose my job! *Be cool, Allie. Be cool. You're one of the guys! And you've seen penises before!*

I stumble behind Vaughn, who doesn't miss a step as he continues marching on, walking past loads more of naked soccer players positioned at their lockers. Seriously, why are they all completely naked? *Don't they get cold? I thought shrinkage was a real thing! Nothing in this room is shrunken. Shranked? Whatever…I can't grammar right now, there's dicks everywhere!*

He rounds a corner to another set of lockers and states firmly, "Here we are."

I look up just as my high heel catches on something beneath me. I make a move to extract myself, but my foot hooks on to whatever it is, holding my leg hostage while my body continues propelling forward. Letting out a yelp, I brace myself for an epic tumble.

But instead of falling down on the concrete flooring like I thought I would, I end up face planting into a chest. A very manly chest. A very manly, naked chest, whose pecs feel like two smooth boulders tensing beneath my twitching fingers that are currently clinging on for dear life.

"Ag, careful…That bag's a biter," a familiar voice murmurs on the top of my head as two very large hands wrap around my waist.

I look up and every organ in my body does a somersault as I stare up into the gorgeously pale brown eyes of Roan DeWalt.

Who's apparently not worried about shrinkage.

Reflexively, I glance down. Thank the good Lord that he has a white towel wrapped around his waist because, if my uncle had to bear witness to his niece twisted up in the arms of a very gorgeous, very naked athlete, I think I'd die a thousand deaths.

With a flirtatious smile, Roan props me back up on my feet and lowers himself to the ground to untwist the strap of the bag from my stiletto. His hand clutches my ankle, sending shivers up from his point of contact to the spot between my legs that I really, *really* don't want to be thinking about with my uncle standing only a few feet away.

As he rises, he stares brazenly into my eyes. "All right now?"

I roll my lips into my mouth and nod woodenly.

"Roan DeWalt, this is my niece, Alice Harris," Vaughn states grandly, clearly unaware that Roan and I went on a date two years ago. "She's the assistant of our PR rep, Mr. Capelle."

"Nice to meet you," Roan states with a secretive smile as he reaches out to shake my hand. The shivers return as our hands touch and our eyes lock. Flashes of our night together burst inside my head like they did when I saw him at the club on Saturday night. All the blood in my body begins whooshing up to my head.

"That's your cousin's duffel bag," a Scottish voice sounds off from the bench across the aisle, breaking the eye contact I'm experiencing with Roan. "He's such a fucking slob."

A giant, tatted, redheaded man still dressed in his practice gear, stands up, towering over me as he grabs the bag up off the floor. He places it inside of a cubby with the name T. Harris scrawled on the top and turns to face me when my uncle says, "Alice, this is Maclay Logan, one of our midfielders. Everyone calls him Mac."

Mac offers up his big paw to me, and I reluctantly pull my hand from Roan's to accept Mac's. He smiles a playful, boyish smile, looking like he knows all too well what my current nerves are about.

"These are the two men you were needing to see today, correct?" Vaughn asks, folding his hands behind his back.

I clear my throat and reply, "Yes, that's correct. I have a script I need to run through with both of you for the Win A Date Campaign?" I say it like a question, which makes me sound stupid.

Roan's smile grows knowingly. "That's no problem. All right if I get dressed first?"

My eyes drift back down to Roan's naked chest and linger on his washboard abs. "Ye—yes," I stammer, the heat returning to my cheeks. I turn to my uncle. "Is there a meeting room where I can wait? *Far, far away from naked soccer players and knowing smirks?*

Vaughn nods. "There's a small conference room across the hall. Why don't you guys finish up and meet Alice in there in five."

I turn on my heel, attempting to skip away only to end up smacking into another bare chest. This one is peppered with several tattoos.

"Cousin!" Tanner's loud voice booms as he cinches the towel around his waist. I see Booker standing in the background with a rueful smile on his face. "If you want to see some trouser snakes, I recommend finding some you're not related to by blood."

"Tanner!" I exclaim, my cheeks heating with embarrassment.

"Or better yet, just set up a profile on Porn Hub. The free stuff you find on there is not bad."

Vaughn sighs heavily and pinches the bridge of his nose. "Ignore him, Alice." He gestures for me to follow him.

As I pass by Booker, he offers me a sympathetic eye roll that does nothing to quell the humiliation his brother so casually inflicted right in front of my one-night stand.

CHAPTER

Alice

I ONLY HAVE A FEW MINUTES TO OPEN UP MY LAPTOP AND CATCH my breath before the conference room doors swing open to reveal the South African soccer player who has been occupying way too many of my thoughts the last couple of days.

Roan strides in wearing a pair of sporty joggers and a Bethnal Green T-shirt. The white fabric of the shirt is tight around his large biceps and contrasts nicely with his tan skin. He has a Mediterranean look about him that's like a more exotic version of tall, dark, and handsome. My eyes drop to admire the glorious V-shape of his athletic body. If anything, Roan has grown hotter since that night we spent together. A career in soccer certainly agrees with him.

I straighten my posture and plaster on a professional smile. "Roan, thank you for coming. Have a seat." I point to the chair at the opposite end of the table because space seems like a really good idea.

"So formal, Lis," Roan says with a lazy smirk. He ignores my request and lowers himself into the seat right next to me. "Do I need to remind you that I've seen you naked?" My face flushes as he brazenly winks at me.

"No, you do not need to remind me," I reply with an awkward laugh. "Though I prefer you forget that ever happened."

"Forget it ever happened?" he exclaims with a wounded look. "Fat chance, mooi. It'd be impossible to forget the best sex I've ever had."

Goosebumps explode all over my body. I look up expecting to see a joking expression on his face. Instead, his caramel eyes are dead serious as they blaze into me with an electrified energy that moves between us like an invisible current. I quickly divert my attention down to the papers strewn out all around me in hopes of hiding my body's reaction. Best sex he's ever had? What a smooth-talker! He's an athlete who has beautiful women throwing themselves at him every day, so there's no way I'm the best sex he's ever had.

Thankfully, his friend, Mac, decides to make his loud entrance. "I'm ready for my close-up!" Mac booms as he walks over to us and slaps his big paws on the table. "Please, for the love of Christ, tell me there are going to be cue cards. My memory is shite."

"We can use cue cards if needed," I reply as Mac takes the open seat next to Roan. "But practicing the script will give you a more natural feel, so I want you guys to try your best to memorise it before the shoot on Wednesday."

Mac nods seriously. "I shall give it my best effort…What do we have to say exactly?"

I clear my throat and thumb through the papers, handing them both their individual scripts. "The wording is pretty straightforward. Like, 'Hi, I'm Maclay Logan, and I've teamed up with LaFaze to raise money for the Get Fit Britain gala coming up in a couple of months. Your donation to this cause gives you a chance to be my date for the special evening.'"

Mac shoves Roan in the shoulder. "Fancy that. People will actually pay money to date us."

Roan nods, his eyes scanning over his script. "How do you pick who wins? Is it truly random?"

I nod slowly. "Random-ish…We do background checks on everyone so we don't accidentally pair you with someone crazy."

ye, but the crazy ones can be a right good time, though!" Mac exclaims.

I smile at his optimism. "We just want to make sure you guys are safe and comfortable."

Roan gets a wicked look in his eyes as he drops the script on the table and says, "If I do a good job at this, will you give me your number, mooi?"

"No!" I reply, my shoulders tensing as I flick a glance at Mac, who doesn't seem the least bit surprised by the remark from his friend.

"Why not?" Roan volleys back.

"Because we're working together. Because that would be inappropriate." I give a pointed look to Roan that basically tells him to shut the fuck up.

Roan leans in. "Ag, don't worry about Mac here. This guy is my best friend. He's heard me moaning about you for two years, so I think we have a well-wisher beside us."

Mac nods enthusiastically. "It's true. This goon hasn't spoken about any other burd for two years."

Embarrassment floods all of my senses as I place my head in my hands and let out a groan. This is not how I expected my reunion with Roan to go down. It was one thing when he was a stranger and a sexy memory in a video. It's another thing when he's gazing at me with his gorgeous eyes and calling me mooi right in front of his friend.

He puts his hand on mine. His voice is deep and smooth when he whispers, "I'm not one to walk away from a challenge, Lis."

"I'm gathering that," I retort, goosebumps exploding up my arm from his touch.

He smiles like he knows his effect on me. "Do I have to ask your cousins for your number?"

I slap my hand to my forehead because I can just imagine how horribly that would go down. My eyes meet his one last time. "Why are you so persistent about this?"

Pinning me with his smouldering eyes, he lifts his brows know-ingly. "Because I know anything worth having is worth working hard for."

My mouth turns to cotton as I attempt to figure out how the hell to respond to the most perfect comeback in the history of all comebacks.

I pull my hand from Roan's grasp and grab his script. With a shake of the head, I scrawl my number down, trying to decide if this is a crazy good idea or a crazy bad one. I look at Roan's wickedly sexy face and realise it's both. It's definitely both.

Jesus, take the wheel!

I push the paper over and stare seriously into his eyes. "Don't make me regret this."

He lifts the paper and presses it over his heart. "I don't believe in regrets."

Mac sighs from beside us, and I look over to see his twinkling eyes taking in our exchange with great delight. He smirks a naughty smirk and whispers loudly, "It's like I'm not even here."

CHAPTER

Rod ⱱ

I RE ST THE URGE TO CALL ALLIE THE SECOND I ARRIVE BACK AT my flat, and it's a gut-check moment when I realise that I haven't been is eager to pursue a woman in years. What is it about her that I find so alluring? Is it because she seems completely uninterested in th fact that I'm an athlete? Is it because she's adorably clumsy arou me and her awkwardness makes me smile?

I more likely because the one night we had together was so mem rable that I need to find out if it was all in my head or not. Or mayb it's because she acted so tense around me, I want to make it my m ssion to see her let her hair down?

en again, I've never had a one-night stand before, so some of th is probably a personal goal for me to keep my track record intac Thankfully, I'm going to see her tomorrow at the wardrobe fittin so I can do my best to pursue all of my curiosities.

I park my car on the street outside of the Georgian house that I share with Maclay. When the two of us joined the team, we both ad families back home who depended on us for support, so becol ing roommates seemed like a reasonable idea considering the c st of living in London. Championship League wages are decel as a whole, but the difference is night and day when you comp re my earnings of one hundred eighty thousand pounds per year to what Gareth Harris was making at Manchester United before he retired.

Regardless, the money I make per game affords me a comfortable life here in London and allows me to send at least half of my earnings to my mom to help out with my two younger sisters.

Mine and Mac's place is located slightly north of London in Islington Green. It is a bit more central than where we train in Bethnal Green, so getting to clubs and nightlife isn't too big of a jaunt.

I unlock the navy front door and jog up the creaky wooden stairs to the main level which features a cosy living room that opens up into the kitchen. The house is definitely a bachelor pad with our black L-shaped sectional sofa and a big screen TV stuck up above the old fireplace that we never use. The kitchen is small with black cabinets, brass finishings, and a tiny, old table that Mac found at a second-hand shop the day after we moved in. It's not much, but we like it.

Mac took the master bedroom located off the kitchen, claiming he needed it because of his penchant for midnight snacking. I ended up with the bedroom upstairs that has the bigger bathroom in the hallway.

Both of us had our fair share of houseguests when we first moved to London, but once we became well-known as soccer players in the area, we realised quickly that bringing women back to our place only made it that much easier for them to show up unannounced. Now, we're both a couple of lonely bachelors who honestly haven't seen much action as of late. Hopefully when I see Lis tomorrow, that will change for me.

My phone lights up and I glance over to see MOM on the screen. I answer as I drop my duffel bag on the floor by the washing machine. "Hey, Mom."

"Roan…How are you, sweetheart?" she coos into the line in her part British, part South African accent.

" ;ood. Just got back from training. How are you?"

" raining?" she tsks, and I can visualise her furrowed brow with very little effort. "I thought you had your final match of the season last week."

" Ve did, but we have a couple of friendlies coming up."

" nd then you'll get a break?"

I nod. "Yeah, but I still have to work hard to keep in shape durin the off-season."

S e tsks again. "That team works you too hard."

I pinch the bridge of my nose. My mother has always been supportin of my career, but she's also been very ignorant about the work takes to maintain it.

" 's only going to get harder with our premiership promotion next ason. It's a big deal to move up a level, so it's going to mean more matches and more training…But that's all good, Mom. It mean more money as well."

" Ve don't need more money, Roan." Her voice is sharp and brisk 'You already give us too much."

" re you still living in the same flat above the dance studio?" I ask k owingly.

S e sighs heavily. "Yes."

" hen we need more money."

I n met with silence on the other end of the line until she finally ays, "Did you hate growing up here that much?"

" Io, Mom," I volley back, agitation coating my throat. "But Mia and A a are seventeen now. They need their own bathroom, and you deser e to have a laundry room you don't have to put coins into."

" Iia and Ava are fine, and so is our laundry. That money needs to be aved for their education more than our comfort. You don't have o take care of us, Roan. We make do the same way we did when ou were a child."

I y jaw clenches at her words because making do is all my moth r has ever done. My father's sudden passing surprised everyone and we were not in a good place financially at the time. But my mother was too independent to accept help from his family or her own back in England. Despite her beliefs that less is more, I know my sisters feel differently. I've overheard them talking to each other about ways they can prevent their friends from coming over because they are ashamed of the small space. It's a big reason I moved out at eighteen when I started playing for my team in Cape Town. Moving out meant they could both have their own bedrooms at the very least. *And yet it's still not enough.*

"How's the studio?" I ask by means of changing the subject to something that doesn't make me want to grind my teeth.

My mom rattles on for twenty minutes about a new date night dance class she's teaching for couples looking to spice up their love lives. She always comes alive when she talks about dance, which I'm grateful for because she's really had some bad luck in love. Dance is her passion now. She tried to make it mine, too, despite my resistance. Now that I'm older, I can look back and say that dance made me a better soccer player. It certainly didn't hurt my skills in the bedroom either.

We end our phone call just as Mac strolls into the house.

"Was that your wee mum?" he asks with a lascivious smirk on his face that I don't like.

"It was," I reply through clenched teeth.

"Did she ask about me?"

I exhale heavily and shake my head. "No, she didn't fucking ask about you, Mac. Would you stop, please?"

"Stop what?" he asks, his green eyes wide and innocent. "It's not my fault she thinks I'm handsome."

Mac is referring to the one time my mom made me FaceTime with her to show her the house I'd bought. She got one look at his red hair and gushed about it so much, the idiot has decided she must be in love with him.

"I'm hitting the hay early. I'll see you in the morning."

"Aye, you do that, lad. You need your beauty rest for all the wooing you're planning on doing with blondie."

I eye him seriously. "Don't you be noticing her hair, all right?"

He hoots with laughter. "Don't you be getting possessive of a burd who's not yours yet. You got her phone number, lad. You still have to win her over."

I make my way upstairs, hoping that is exactly what happens tomorrow. My thoughts earlier about not calling her right away are forgotten when I flop down on my bed and pull her number up on my phone.

Me: Drinks after the fitting tomorrow?

Callie: Who dis?

I laugh at her humourous response and get a flash of her bright blue eyes as we laid in bed together two years ago. She started that night as a woman on a mission who was tense and nervous and completely focused on her goal. But after we had sex, there was a lightness in her eyes that I'm desperate to see again.

Me: This is the best sex you ever had…obviously.

Callie: Jake! I haven't heard from you in ages!

Me: I don't know who Jake is, but I'm certain my cock is bigger than his.

After a minute delay, she replies.

Callie: Just drinks?

I sigh heavily because she is not going to make this easy for me.

Me: For now, yes. Because I evidently need to remind you how much fun we can have together.

Callie: I do remember a little something to that effect.

Me: I remember everything, mooi. Let me remind you.

Callie: Okay. See you then…Jake.

And there it is—a glimpse of that sarcasm I remember so fondly.

85

After training the next day, Mac and I head to Kindred Spirits Boutique to get styled for our Win A Date shoot tomorrow. My muscles are tense as I drive behind Mac's jeep down the narrow Redchurch Street, and it has nothing to do with the road being narrow. It's because I'm going to see Allie and I need to get her beyond the "just drinks" mindset.

I slide into a parking spot behind Mac outside of the clothing boutique located on the corner. It's a red painted brick building with a large graffiti-style logo splashed across its window.

Mac smiles broadly as I hop out of my vehicle and approach. "Are you ready to woo your lass?"

I roll my eyes. "I don't woo."

"What do you do then?" he asks, genuinely curious.

I pin him with a serious look. "I impress."

He laughs as he pulls the door open and gestures for me to walk in first.

Kindred Spirits is as colourful inside as it is outside. When I walk through the door, my eyes are hit with an array of clothes, accessories, jewelry, and art intricately placed in every nook and cranny.

A woman in a fifties-style yellow dress and auburn hair strides out from behind the front desk when she hears the chime of the bell on the door. "You must be the footballers!" she states with a bright smile.

"What makes you say that?" Mac asks in an accusatory tone.

She sniffs the air in front of him and replies in her American accent, "The scent of balls and Icy Hot gives you away."

Mac's face falls and he lifts his arm to smell his armpit. "I showered after training."

The woman laughs. "Relax, I'm just giving you shit. My name is Leslie. I'm one of the owners." She shakes both of our hands. "You'll be working with my colleague, Sloan, today. She does all of our menswear styling. And our seamstress, Freya—"

" here to give you both a right poking!" a voice giggles from up above.

Mac and I glance up to the open second level to see another redhead finishing what she's currently working on. This one's hair is more fiery red, like Mac's. She glances down at us and I can see a smattering of red freckles all over her round face, even from where I stand.

"Please excuse Freya," Leslie says with an affectionate smile. "She's been binge-watching the American version of *Shameless* for three weeks now, so I'm afraid she's been more inappropriate than usual as of late."

"What season are you on?" Mac asks.

"Five," Freya answers. "Fiona just found out her fiancé is using again

"For the love of Christ, woman! Are you trying to ruin my life?" Mac bellows, covering his ears. "I'm only on season four!"

"You didn't say no spoilers!" Freya yelps down, her hands propped indignantly on her round hips.

"That's an unspoken rule! Common decency in the world of television." Mac shakes his head. "Hell, though, I never liked that Sean anyway. He's too old for her!"

"Agreed! I'd rather she be with Steven—the criminal—than that old g"

"I'm with you all the way! Though I must say the American *Shameless* pales in comparison to the UK version."

"That's exactly what I think," Freya states, her eyes wide in agreement. "I was only watching it to compare them, and I feel like I'm cheating on my home-country."

The two smile at each other for a few awkward seconds, but the moment is shattered when footsteps approach from the back of the shop.

"Hi there, I'm Sloan Harris. I'll be styling you today." A striking woman with brown hair walks toward us with several clothing options draped over her arm. She reaches out and shakes our hands and then states, "If you guys will just follow me, I'll show you to the changing rooms so you can start trying these on."

She turns on her heel, revealing a baby that's attached to her back in a cloth baby carrier. A smile instantly spreads across my face as I take in the dark hair swept over his forehead.

"You have a baby on your back!" Mac says with a finger pointing accusingly at the cute little squirt.

Sloan stops walking and slaps a hand to her forehead. "I wondered where I put him!" She winks at Mac. "This is my son, Milo."

"Hi, Milo," I say and reach out to hold his finger. He stares at me, completely unimpressed. "He looks like his dad."

Sloan nods knowingly. "The Harris genes are strong, but that's okay. My daughter is my mini-me, so it's nice to give Gareth something to stoke his narcissism as well. I mean, let's face it, that's all procreating really is, isn't it?"

I laugh at her very candid response. "I honestly wouldn't know."

She shrugs her shoulders and hands off two separate outfits to me and Mac. "Put on one of these and come out when you're done so we can have a look at you."

She points to the four changing rooms concealed behind purple curtains and then spins with Milo to head back to the shop. Mac grabs the first room and I move down to the third. When I pull back the curtain and walk into the small space, I run right into—

"Roan!" Allie exclaims, her eyes wide and alarmed.

"Lis," I reply with a surprised smile and glance down at her body that is currently clad in only a black bra and broekies. My cock makes himself very well-known inside my jeans as I take in the ample curves of her body that look better than ever. I shake my head and stare unabashedly at her breasts as I say, "I thought I'd have to buy you drinks before I got to see you like this again."

"Get out!" she squeals, grabbing a dress that's hanging on a hook to hold it in front of herself.

I ift my hands up and laugh. "I'm sorry, all right! I was told to try th se on." I make a move to leave but look back over my shoulder. " Vhat are you trying on?"

S e rolls her eyes and blows a piece of hair out of her face. "A dress or the gala if you must know."

I glance down at the dress she's clutching to her body. "I don't think t'll beat what you have on right now."

S e fails to conceal her pleased smile, which only makes my cock row harder. Then, like she's angry at herself for her response, she b ks, "Out."

\ ith a chuckle, I leave and murmur loud enough for her to hear, Still hot as ever, mooi."

M inutes later, I pop out of the changing room in a pair of fitted tweed trousers and a slim black button-down. The fabric feels xpensive and a hell of a lot nicer than the clothes I buy for myse . My eyes move to Leslie and Freya, who are standing by a three way mirror, fussing over someone standing on the podium. I wal a little closer to see it's Allie wearing a bronze, metallic eveni g gown.

" t's too tight," she whines, tugging at the chest, her breasts pushi g up from the low-cut neckline.

" t's supposed to be tight," Freya tuts around a pin in her mout as she grabs another needle off the pad on her wrist and secures spot by Allie's waist. "It's a corset bodice."

" 'm supposed to be working today, not trying on dresses," Allie rgues.

")h, hush," Leslie scolds, stepping back and admiring Allie like a wor of art. "I'm following orders from Vi, who said you need a dress or the gala. Haven't you learned by now that you can't resist order from the Harris family?"

" 'm a Harris," Allie retorts with an indignant tone. "Why won't you li ten to me when I say this dress is too expensive?"

I slie shakes her head. "It's taken care of, Allie! You get the family discount! And even if you didn't, I'd be giving this dress to you anyway." She runs her hand along the waistline appreciatively and adds, "It's like I made it for you!"

Allie lets out an exasperated breath and then looks up at herself in the mirror, almost like it's the first time she's truly allowed herself to do so. It's then that she sees me in the reflection, staring at her like I've just laid eyes on the queen. I nod in appreciation, my eyes drinking in every luscious curve of her body that the dress clings to. Allie's long blonde hair is tied up in a bun on top of her head, revealing her beautiful shoulder blades that I've touched with my tongue. I want to touch them with my tongue again right now.

"Fuck me, I look hot!" Mac booms, ripping me away from the eye candy I was shamelessly gawking at.

I turn to see him in a vest, a green button-down, and a brown pair of trousers. The guy doesn't look half bad for a tatted Scotsman with questionable table manners.

"You're done," Freya states, abandoning Allie at the podium and bustling over to Mac, who's smiling proudly with his arms outstretched like he's expecting a round of applause.

"Tell me I look good, woman," Mac says, smiling down at Freya, who's almost half his height.

"I don't think your ego needs any help from the likes of me," she replies crisply and begins tugging at the seams. "Hop up on the podium so I can see about lengthening the trousers."

"Your wish is my command." Mac shoots Freya a flirtatious wink, and she seems confused by his attention.

Allie and Sloan makes their way over to me. The two of them walk around me, grabbing and pulling at the clothes on my body. I'm not even embarrassed about the fact that I'm semi-hard from staring at Allie in her sexy dress.

"Did I pass inspection?" I ask, looking down at Allie.

It's Sloan who answers. "Not quite. I want to see the other ensemble. This one isn't doing it for me. You?"

Allie shakes her head, her eyes lingering on my crotch for a little too long. "He needs something that makes his eyes pop."

Sloan giggles and whispers barely loud enough for me to hear, "His eyes are up there, Allie."

Allie's eyes shoot up to my face. She flushes with embarrassment while barking out, "Let's try the blue shirt next."

Sloan giggles again and turns to walk away.

I take a step toward Allie. "Care to help me change?"

She takes a step back. "No. I'll, um, be struggling to get myself out of this dress as it is."

I move in closer yet. "I can definitely help you with that."

She presses her hands to my chest for a gentle shove and skips past me to hide behind the curtain.

You can run, but you can't hide, mooi.

Allie

Four outfit changes later, we find a fuckworthy look for Roan. In all honesty, it's so fuckworthy, I start to stress over who his date is going to be for the gala and how painful it will be for me to watch the winner drool all over him the entire evening. I'm certain she'll want to have sex with him. Good-god, the man is charming without even being dressed to the nines.

The way Sloan and Freya were laughing with him made me feel twitchy and hot. They even giggled to each other about how they were going to have to let the groin of his trousers out to make room for his "unit."

A unit that I can recall with great detail.

And when he looks at me with those dazzling eyes of his, he

makes it really easy for me to forget about what a horrible human I am for having a nonconsensual sex video of him on my phone.

Roan, Mac, and I say our goodbyes to the ladies at Kindred Spirits. Then Mac makes a quick exit to his car, nearly tripping over himself in some bizarre attempt to give Roan and me some space.

"There's a decent pub down this way called The Owl and Pussycat," Roan says, walking backwards and gesturing for me to follow him around the corner.

I purse my lips together and nod nervously.

You agreed to this, Allie. You said yes, even though you know this is a bad idea! So just get over it and hope he moves on quickly to the next girl who will most likely throw herself at him.

We walk side by side in comfortable silence to the pub. When we arrive, it's overflowing with patrons having a pint outside after a long day of work. Roan presses his hand to the small of my back as we move through the crowd, toward the beer garden in the back. We snag an open table in the corner before Roan asks what I want to drink and takes off for the bar.

Nerves erupt in my belly because, here we are again, having drinks. We may not be going to a wedding, but something tells me if I wanted to sleep with Roan tonight, I could. But I shouldn't want to sleep with him. Wanting to sleep with him would mean he's more than a one-night stand and I should tell him about the video.

He returns and sets my red wine in front of me, watching me curiously as I take a sip to brace myself.

"Why do you suddenly look like you have the weight of the world on your shoulders?" he asks, tilting his head and eyeing me speculatively. "You're reminding me of how you were the night we met, but you seemed lighter and more relaxed when I saw you out with your cousins at Café de Paris."

I swallow nervously. "I'm, um…I'm just not sure you and I are a good idea."

"Not this again," he groans and props his muscled forearms on the s all table, leaning closer to me so I can smell his freshly showered ent. "I thought you giving me your number meant there were good hings to come."

" Vhat kind of good things?" I ask pointedly. *Please don't say sex. F ase don't say sex!*

I ₹ shrugs. "The kind that involve you and me hanging out, I guess

I uff out a laugh. "You hardly know me. How do you know you want ） hang out with me?"

I ₹ drops his chin with a pointed look in his eyes. "Shall I remind ⁄ou of everything I learned about you that first night we had togetl ₃r?"

" pparently!" I volley back with a laugh, thinking he can't possibly member anything other than the multiple orgasms.

I ₹ clears his throat and pushes his sleeves up on his arms before ⅽ unting off his list on his fingers. "Number one, you occasionally s ort when you laugh, but you turn it into a cough because you think hat hides it. It doesn't." He winks and I have to cough back a snort

" lumber two, you get a crease between your brows when you're think ₁g about something else and not living in the moment... Some ₁ing I'd really like to make stop right now."

I elax my browline and do my best to give him my undivided atten ₃n.

" lumber three, you have no idea how beautiful you are, probably ｜ ⅽause you grew up with a father who didn't value beauty as mucl ⅼs intelligence. Not the worst thing he ever did, if I'm being hone ."

" nd number four..." He pauses and loses all humour on his face ｜ fore stating, "you were trying to hide your heartbreak from me tl night we met, but I could see it when you didn't think I was looki g. And what attracted me to you that night wasn't actually your ｜ rface-level beauty, even though you were fucking hot in that

93

garter belt. It was the fact that most women would have been crying and eating chocolates, but you were brave enough to put on a pair of heels and not let life knock you down."

My breath catches in my throat and I swallow the knot I feel rising. "Is that all?" I husk, still stunned by what he just said.

He gets a wicked glint in his eyes. "That and I know what your face looks like when you come. That should be worth something."

A zinging sensation shoots between my thighs from the overwhelming reaction I'm having to all of his words. Meanwhile, he sits back in his chair like he's just casually talked about the weather.

I touch the backs of my fingers to my hot cheeks and reply, "I feel like an asshole because I know so little about you."

Roan shrugs his shoulders. "What do you want to know? I'll tell you anything."

He takes a drink of his beer, so I take the opportunity to do the same before replying with the first question that comes to mind.

"What's your family like?"

A broad smile stretches across his face. "You want to meet my mom, mooi?"

I shake my head nervously. "No, that's not what I meant. This is such a bad idea. I haven't dated anybody in two years—"

Roan leans across the table, cutting me off. "I was raised by a strong, beautiful, single mother after my dad died when I was three. My mom found a new husband when I was about eight, which resulted in my twin sisters. He was a decent guy when he was sober, but he turned out to be a mean drunk toward her. It sucked. But after years of emotional abuse, she finally divorced him, only to fall back in love with her true passion in life…Dance. Ballroom dancing to be more specific."

I blink at him, surprised by his candid response. "I remember you mentioning the dancing thing at the wedding."

He nods around a drink. "We lived in a flat above the dance studio where she works, so I was always around it."

The image of a younger version of Roan dancing with his mother in a studio brings a small smile to my face. My smile falls when I think about growing up without a father, though. "I'm sorry to hear about your dad. Do you remember him at all?"

He gets a tight look on his face. "Not really. He was South African and met my mother when he was going to med school in England. He was evidently a brilliant man because it was no easy feat to get out of South Africa for education in those days. After apartheid ended, they made the decision to move to Cape Town and open a medical clinic. He barely got the clinic open before he had a heart attack."

"I'm so sorry, Roan," I state quietly, staring down at my wine glass and feeling guiltier than ever for not seeing what a unique person Roan was when we first met.

"That's life sometimes," he replies and drums his fingers on the table. "So, what about you?" he asks, diverting my focus from my drink to him.

"What about me?" I volley back.

"I shared. Now it's your turn. I know you're related to the Harrises, but what's your family like back in America?"

This question makes me cringe.

"That bad?" he asks.

I shrug. "Well, let's just say that I feel more at home with the London Harrises than the Chicago Harrises."

His eyes soften as I take another drink. "So, it is that bad."

I nod my confirmation around my glass, feeling horribly insensitive for complaining about my own family when his father isn't even here anymore. "It's fine."

He watches me for a moment, taking in my body language. "Is this not something you want to talk to me about?"

"Not really."

"Fair enough," he replies and slaps his hand on the table. "Let's make out instead."

"Make out?" I bark out an unexpected laugh at the sudden shift in conversation. He pins me with a flirtatious look as I ask, "What are we, sixteen?"

"I'm twenty-seven," he replies with a lift of the brows. "How old are you?"

I narrow my eyes. "Twenty-six."

"Look at how much we're learning about each other already." He reaches over and wraps his large, warm hand around mine in an intimate way that I feel in several more intimate parts of my body.

I swallow nervously, feeling bad for how little I've shared after he opened up so easily. I steel myself before stating, "My father is an emotionless workaholic who has been divorced three times and has still not called me once since I moved to London."

"Ouch," he replies, his brow furrowing. "And your mom?"

I shrug. "She's nice enough, but she's currently backpacking through Europe so her cell service is dicey."

He exhales heavily. "My mom calls me too often. She worries about me up here in London, but I'm more worried about her in Cape Town."

I nod and don't think about the words that fall out of my mouth next. "Is that why you send part of your paycheque home to her every month?"

Roan releases my hand and sits back. "How the hell do you know that?"

I sit up and splay my hands out on the table. "It's, um, in your file."

"What file?" he snaps, agitated by my knowledge.

"The file we have on all the players at the club. It's sort of a rap sheet so we know who has the potential to cause the most trouble."

"Jesus," he replies glumly and shakes his head. "I had no idea PR companies would know that kind of shit."

I shrug. "It's our job to know. You and Mac are two of the cleanest players on the team. It's why they selected you two for the Win A Date Campaign."

Ian rolls his eyes, clearly not enjoying the fact that I have this intel. He hits me with a steely look. "What other information do you have on me that I don't know about?"

God-god is that a loaded question. "Nothing," I chirp back innocently. "From now on, it's only whatever you decide to share with me."

My reply seems to relax him because he leans forward and resumes fondling my hands. "Do you think your cousins will kill me if you and I start spending more time together?"

"Time?" I croak, my voice catching in my throat. "In what capacity?"

"In the type of capacity where I buy drinks or food and you drink the drinks or eat the food…Then we kiss at your front door."

"That sounds like dating."

He grins at me. "You're skipping a couple of steps, Lis, but ag, you've been a fast mover since the day we met, so I'm into this."

Have I mentioned how much I love it when he calls me Lis?

I glance down at his drink. "You've had one beer with me and you're already wanting to commit to future time?"

"You forget that I spent the better part of twelve hours with you naked in a hotel room. I'm basing our dating status on more than tonight. Tonight was just the confirmation I needed to make sure that all the fantasies I've had about you are built on some semblance of reality." He winks and downs the rest of his beer in one gulp, his neck contracting in a really attractive way as he does. He wipes the top of his lip and adds loudly, "That and I've seen you naked."

I reach across the table and plant my hand over his mouth. "Will you please stop telling the entire pub that you've seen me naked?"

The smile in his eyes is panty-melting. Once I'm certain he's done humiliating me, I release his mouth and shake my head at him. "Most soccer players would take a one-night stand and never look back."

He lifts his brows and shrugs. "I'm not like most soccer players."

Roan and I have a few more drinks and lose track of time chatting about silly things like our favourite foods and hobbies we both dabble in. Mine is fake trip planning. I always felt like I would have been a good travel agent. I get vacation ideas in my head and research flights, hotels, Airbnb's, sight-seeing locations, the works. Roan's curious if I've ever fake planned a trip to South Africa, and I regretfully have to say no. With that said, I know that as soon as I get home, I'm going to be Googling Cape Town.

Roan's hobbies are a little less eccentric. He plays video games with Mac and loves soccer. He did say that when he's done playing professionally, he can see himself getting back into ballroom dancing because he always enjoyed learning with his mother.

The entire time we talk and laugh, I can't help but notice that the connection I felt with Roan the first night we met is still there, like it never left. And when I think back to that night, I'm surprised by how much I can remember because I think I was suffering from post-traumatic stress disorder. It's the only reasoning I can come up with for why I did what I did. Everything about that night was so wildly out of character for me. I've only slept with a total of five men in my entire life, so recording a sex video with a one-night stand is certainly skipping a few steps in regard to my sexual experiences.

For now, I'm putting that crazy, jet-lagged night behind me and focusing on Roan in the present. It's interesting to hear more about his experience as a soccer player because my cousins make it look so easy. His career has been anything but easy. He's worked hard to get to where he is now, and I can tell by the way he talks about Bethnal Green F.C. that he looks at it as his ticket to the big time. And maybe it will be. He'll be getting a lot more coverage with their promotion to the Premier League, so perhaps it's only a matter of time before a larger, better soccer team scoops him up.

It's dark outside when we leave the pub, and Roan offers me a ride home since I was planning to take the Tube. During our drive to Notting Hill, I marvel over the fact that he holds my hand on his lap like it's the most natural thing in the world for him to do.

Roan parks in front of Camden and Indie's quaint, white townhouse with a charming red front door. He shuts his car off and turns to look at me. "Can I walk you to the door, or do you think Camden will come me out and kick me in the balls?"

I giggle because I have a feeling that's dangerously close to the truth. "I think it's best if you stay safe inside your car."

He nods slowly and eyes my lips. "They'll have to know about us eventually."

"What's with this 'us' you keep talking about?" I ask with an exasperated shake of the head. "We've had one night out together and you're already saying 'us'? Did you come on this strong to all the women you've been with?"

"Only the ones that I let get away, which adds up to..." He pauses and raises his hand to count on his fingers, dropping all his digits down one by one except his pointer finger. "One."

I roll my eyes. "You're laying it on thick, DeWalt."

His chest vibrates with silent laughter. "Why don't you shut up and kiss me already, Lis? You've been staring at my lips all night, and it's getting kind of pathetic."

"I have not—" I exclaim, but my voice is cut off by those wonderful lips of his. *Okay, maybe I was staring at them all night.*

A flood of images from our first kiss hit me out of nowhere as he combs his fingers through my hair and cups the back of my head to fuse our mouths together. Our first kiss was aggressive and punishing in some ways. It was done in the heat of the moment as an answer to an obvious plea.

This kiss, however, is different. It's still firm and commanding like before but with a sweeter, more appreciative cadence to it that my body is reacting to very strongly.

I grip his bicep, holding on for dear life as he parts my lips and sweeps his tongue gently into my mouth. When he hears the sound of my soft moan, his grip on my hair tightens and the kiss turns more fervent.

The black leather makes a loud noise as I mindlessly move over the console. I don't sit on his lap by any means, but I offer up more access to whatever he wants to take from me.

Because kisses like this from Roan are clearly meant to be taken freely and without hesitation.

A stirring begins in my lower belly as we make out for several glorious minutes. This is a sensation in my body that I haven't felt in ages, so I'm letting myself enjoy it. I tried to have more rebound sex after Roan. For two years, I went out with my coworkers and attempted to flirt with men at bars, only to go home and watch that stupid video on my phone. I realised quickly that I would never have sex that awesome ever again.

Maybe that's why I never deleted the video. Heck, maybe he's why I returned to London. Maybe there was a part of my brain that thought if I came back here, I could get back what I walked away from.

Roan's large, warm hand releases my hair and slides down my neck and over my collarbone, his lips continuing to devour me. In one forceful grip, he grabs my breast over top of my blouse and squeezes it so hard, I rip my mouth from his and cry out in plea-sure-filled pain.

"Oh my God," I croak, my voice hoarse and filling the car with desire.

My gaze lands on Roan's lap, and I see the very large outline of the erection he has inside his jeans. It's bigger than it was at the bou-tique, and I bite my lip as I reach out to touch it. The ridiculous firm-ness of it causes a stirring between my legs that I want to be stoked.

"Look what you fucking do to me, mooi," he murmurs, running his tongue along my pulse in the most delicious way possible. "Are you want for me?" he asks as he bites down softly on my flesh. "Show me."

I release a pained moan because, Jesus fucking Christ, I want to show him. I'm already mentally chastising myself for wearing leggings instead of a skirt because it makes this moment a bit more tricky.

Suddenly, an urgent rapping on the car window tears my focus away from the dampness of my panties. I whip my head around to see Indie's curly red hair blowing in the wind.

She makes a hurried motion for me to roll down the window. As soon as I do, she rushes out, "You might want to stop whatever it is you're doing because Camden is coming out any second. I'm not sure he's going to appreciate the image of his cousin shagging his brothers' teammate."

"We're not shagging!" I exclaim defensively, pushing my hair away from my face and darting my gaze up toward the front door of the house. "We're not shagging."

Indie gets an awkward look on her face. "Right. I'm just warning you. As you were." She chirps the last bit and turns on her heel to walk back over to the steps leading up to their front door.

I run my hands down my thighs as I try to clear the lust-filled fog out of my brain. I know we weren't shagging but, holy shit, were we just on our way to it? What the heck am I thinking?

I look sheepishly at Roan and exhale regrettably. "You'd better go."

He caresses my face before asking, "Do you want to come home with me?"

I swallow. I swallow a lot. My feelings, my nerves, my hormones. I have to swallow them all down to the deep, dark vortex of my body because I know what it's like to be with Roan. I've been there before, and it sort of makes going there again seem like an easy choice. But with what I've done, getting close to Roan is a *really* bad idea. "I think I'd better head inside."

His eyes narrow. "Because of Camden? I'm not afraid of your cousin, Lis. I'll talk to him and tell him we're spending time together."

He makes a move to get out of the car, but I place a hand on his arm to stop him. "Please don't."

He frowns at me, clearly confused by my sudden change in direction. Of course he's confused. I was just stroking his penis and practically crawling onto his lap. Now I'm acting like a complete nut-job.

"I'll call you later?" I ask as a means of a peace offering.

He nods his reluctant acceptance. "All right."

He leans over and kisses me softly on the cheek before I slide out of the car and watch him drive away.

Indie winces at me from her seat on the front steps. "Sorry about that."

I exhale heavily. "I'm the one who should be sorry."

She straightens her glasses, perplexed by my reply, but Camden chooses that moment to stride out of the house.

"Snowflake is fed. He is alive. All is right in the world. Let's get you and our baby some ice cream, Specs." His gaze shifts from Indie as he notices me standing by the curb. "Allie! You look flushed. Want to come for some ice cream, too?"

"Sure," I reply with a polite smile. "I could use some cooling off."

CHAPTER 11

Roan

THE VANITY LIGHTS ARE BRIGHT ON MY FACE AS I SIT IN THE hair and makeup area at the East London studio where we're doing the commercial shoot. Mac is seated in the chair beside me, frowning nervously at his makeup artist, who is a handsome man with blue eyeliner on his bottom lids.

"Are you going to put eyeliner on me?" Mac asks with a wary look.

The guy shoots Mac a wink. "Only if you want me to, sugar."

"Pass," Mac replies.

Sloan and Freya bustle into the room a few minutes later. Freya points accusingly at Mac's shirt. "Would you look at the state of him?"

Sloan's brown eyes widen. "He's had that shirt on for two minutes!"

"I know! He's a complete mongrel!" Freya tuts and then hustles over to the clothing rack along the wall. "Just tell me which one of these you want to replace it, and I'll get it fitted on him in a jiff."

"What the hell did you do?" I ask as Mac looks back at me with wide, puppy-dog eyes.

"I might have snuck one of those jelly donuts they had sitting out when we came in. I was just going to have a wee bite. Our season is over, so I figured there wasn't any harm in it."

103

He turns to show me the enormous red stain smeared across his chest.

"Jesus Christ!" I bark out a laugh in shock. "It looks like you've been shot!"

Freya returns with a shirt in hand. "And I'm going to be the shooter if you don't get up and let me fit this shirt on you."

She grabs Mac by the arm and yanks him away from the hair and makeup team. He hurriedly fumbles with the top buttons on his shirt and pulls it off over his head.

This appears to exasperate Freya even more as she mumbles under her breath, "Can't even take off a shirt properly."

Mac just smiles down at her, not the least bit put off by her huffiness.

"Need me to run lines with you?" A familiar voice chimes in from behind me, and I look up to see Allie's reflection in the mirror.

I take a deep breath because this is the first time I've seen her since I arrived on set and, fucking hell, she's always so beautiful. It's an effortless beauty, too. She's the kind of pretty that doesn't even need the makeup she puts on her face.

I shoot her a lascivious smirk. "Don't I get a kiss hello?"

"What?" she snaps with a forced laugh as she looks over at Mac and Freya beside her. "Why would you get a kiss hello?"

"Because we're dating now," I reply with a shrug just to get a rise out of her.

"We are not dating!" she retorts, her voice high-pitched and overly defensive as she completely loses the crisp, professional façade she attempted to approach me with. She looks back at Sloan, who's fussing with the clothes and pretending not to listen. Then she repeats, "We're not dating."

"I'm going to wear you down, Lis," I reply casually as the makeup artist dabs the brush on my nose and tries not to smile. "Maybe I'll bid a ton of money under your name for this Win A Date Campaign."

She crosses her arms over her chest. "It doesn't work like that."

"That's what she thinks," I state to the man who's currently coming at me with mascara.

Allie lets out a frustrated squeak and turns on her heel to walk away. Her obvious frustration isn't what I was going for, so I leap out of my seat before the man can put that horrible makeup on my face. With a tug, I rip off the cape around my neck and toss it onto the chair, hurrying after her to try and right the wrong I've just done.

"Allie, I was joking!" I state, jogging to catch up to her as she strides down the hallway as fast as her thin black skirt will allow.

"It's not funny. This is my job," she retorts and gets that furrow in her brow that I hate so much.

"I'm sorry. Let me make it up to you." I kick myself for pushing too hard, too fast. "Where are you running off to right now? You are scary fast in that tiny skirt."

"I'm going to check in with my boss," she snaps and looks at me briefly, her eyes zeroing in on my lips.

"Why are you in such a hurry?"

"Why are you so…you?" she volleys back, and I can't help but smirk at her adorable feistiness.

I casually slide my hands into my trouser pockets. "What was that all about last night?"

"What was what about?" she asks, hanging a right and making her way toward the studio entrance.

I lower my voice. "Your kiss and run show." I'm only slightly embarrassed by how much I wish she would have come home with me. We wouldn't have even had to have sex. I would have been happy to watch a movie with her. Fucking hell, I kind of started to miss her last night.

She stops midstride and turns to pin me with a warning look, her blue eyes fierce on mine. "Last night was a mistake. I let things go too far, and I'm sorry for"—she gestures down toward my cock—"leading you on."

She makes a move to leave, but I press my hand against the wall to block her path. My shoulders tense as I lean in and hit her with a sincere look in my eyes. "You didn't lead me on, Lis. I'm not mad that things stopped. Jesus Christ, what kind of man do you take me for?"

Her hard expression softens. "I didn't mean that."

"Good," I state and my shoulders relax. "I would hate for you to think sex is the only reason I'm chasing you down a hallway right now."

She licks her lips, her eyes dancing from my eyes to my mouth. "Why *are* you chasing me down a hallway?"

The corner of my mouth tips up in a smirk. "Because you have this uncanny ability to always leave me wanting more."

My response obviously flusters her since she brings her hand up and rubs her forehead. "You have to stop saying stuff like that because I don't think we're a good idea. My cousins would flip out if they knew I was dating their teammate. And you and Tanner are finally playing well together. Us dating could totally mess that up."

"I'm not worried about the Harrises. A couple of years ago, yes. But they love me now. I'm practically one of the family." I lower my hand from the wall to touch her cheek. Her skin is like silk as I slide my thumb along her cheekbone. "I'm not afraid of them, Lis."

"I am!" she exclaims, her eyes wide as she bites her lip and tilts her face into my palm. "They're the only decent family I have left. If being with you hurts them, then I don't think we should go any further."

Her words and everything she is saying is a dagger to my heart, but what's even worse is that her body language is saying something completely different. She leans into my touch, and I can feel her drawing closer to me as she stares at my lips with a thirst in her eyes that I desperately want to quench.

"Are you sure about that, mooi?" I ask, sliding my fingers through her hair and knowing deep down that whatever comes out of her mouth is going to be a lie.

She clears her throat and nods, pulling away from my embrace. "I, um, need to go into the studio. I think you should go back to hair and makeup so they can finish prepping you."

Defeated, I take a step back and lift my palms to her. "You're the boss."

She scans my entire body one more time, regret painting her stunning features before she turns and walks away just like she does every damn time.

When I return to the changing room, I'm practically vibrating with frustration. I drop down in my chair and spin around so I'm facing Mac.

"What's eating you?" Mac asks as Freya pulls on the fabric of his shirt and pins it in the back.

I throw up my hands. "I can't figure Allie out."

Mac frowns thoughtfully. "What do you mean?"

I run my palms down my trousers and reply, "She's hot and cold. Her body and eyes say one thing, but her mouth says another. It's really confusing. I just wish I knew why she's fighting so hard to keep me at arm's-length. Hell, maybe she's not over her ex."

"How long has it been since she broke up with the lad?" Mac asks, his brows furrowed tightly, like he's solving a math problem.

I scoff. "Two years, I think."

"That can't be it then," Mac states.

"I know," I reply with a groan. "It doesn't make any sense. I feel like she's holding back from me, but I don't know why."

Freya makes an odd noise that turns both mine and Mac's eyes to her.

Mac watches her as she tugs on the front tails of his shirt and his eyes suddenly light up. "Hey! You're a lass!"

"Oh, thanks so much for clearing that up!" Freya barks defensively around a pin in her mouth. "I wasn't aware it was up for questioning."

"Well, of course you're a lass," Mac laughs and then moves his

107

hands to gesture toward Freya's ample breasts. "You can't have a chest like that and have any doubt on the matter. Am I right, lad?"

Mac waits expectantly for me to confirm his assessment while I do my best to look invisible.

"What?" he asks, diverting his attention from me to Freya, who's glowering up at him. "It's a compliment. I just meant that since you're a woman, you might have some advice!"

Freya slowly pulls the pin from her mouth. "I'm holding a needle and thread here, Maclay." She narrows her eyes at him. "And I'm a very skilled seamstress, so I'm quite certain that if you decide to talk about my breasts like that again, I could artfully stitch you in a place you'd never want to be stitched."

Mac's face contorts in fear. "Noted. Sorry about that."

She exhales and turns her focus to me. "Look, I don't know Allie that well, or you for that matter, but two years is plenty of time to get over a breakup. Even the worst breakup of all time."

"So that must mean there's something that is causing her to stop the momentum between us," I reply with a huff. "Because it's clear she likes me. Every time I'm near her, she looks like she wants to devour my face, which I wouldn't mind."

Mac leers over at me with a look of solidarity while Freya's nose wrinkles. She clears her throat and replies, "I don't know what she wants to do to your face, but if you want to know what the real problem is, ask her when she's at ease and relaxed. Maybe over a glass of wine. The truth always comes out of me whenever a tiny bit of alcohol is involved, whether it's served in a kitten coffee mug or not."

She begins fussing with Mac's shirt again but then turns to point a finger at me. "Just don't take advantage of her when she's drinking. That would make you a bigger pig than this sorry lad, and I promise you that I can get a hold of something much bigger than a needle and thread to make you pay."

I lift my hands up in surrender and turn in my chair to contemplate her surprising advice. In order to be around Allie when she's

drink ng, we'd have to be in a social setting where she feels com-
fortal e. Probably with her family. And odds are I'm not going to be
invite to any Harris family gatherings anytime soon. I exhale heavily ov r the fact that figuring out Allie Harris is proving to be more
diffic lt than figuring out her cousin Tanner.

CHAPTER

Roan

OPPORTUNITY STRIKES A FEW DAYS LATER WHEN I'M ON THE Tower Park pitch warming up for our friendlies match against Norwich City on a glorious sunny Saturday afternoon. Tanner stands five feet away from me as we do short warm-up passes back and forth to each other. He stops the ball under his boot and starts fidgeting with the sweatband he wears around his forehead.

As he does so, he says, "DeWalt! After the match tonight, we're taking the ladies out and we need another man."

"What for?" I ask, my face furrowing at his odd request. Tanner normally isn't inclined to let me near his wife after he caught the two of us flirting at a pub before they started dating a couple of years back. That unfortunate history may have also been part of the reason it took us so long to get along with each other.

Tanner kicks me the ball. "Some date night thing that my sister set up for all of us. She says just because our brides are up the duff doesn't mean we should stop romancing them or some nonsense."

I roll the ball under my boot and stare back in confusion. "So, what exactly do you need me for?"

I pass it back to him and he stops it to juggle between his feet for a few seconds. "To be Allie's date of course. The poor girl still doesn't know anyone in London, so Vi told me to ask you since you two know each other from that wedding."

Tanner passes the ball back to me and it rolls right between my feet. I've never wanted to kiss a Harris Brother more in my life.

With a shake of the head, I jog after the ball, amazed by how easy this just got. I return seconds later and casually reply, "Yeah, I suppose I can do that. What do I have to wear?"

Tanner's face contorts as he catches the ball with his foot. "Clothes if it's not too much trouble." He turns and passes to Mac, who's warming up beside us with another midfielder. "You need to come too, Scot."

"Come where?" Mac asks, bending over to adjust his shin guard.

"To this couples thing my sister is forcing us all to go to. It'll be a big group of us."

"Who's my date?" Mac asks, his eyes bright and way too damn excited.

"Gareth's wife's friend, Freya. She said you two are acquainted."

Mac deflates. "We are, but I don't think she likes me."

I roll my eyes and give him a shove. "Maybe stop talking about her breasts. That might get you back into her good graces."

Mac nods in agreement, intrigued by the prospect of a second chance. I'm intrigued by mine, too. Tonight might just be the night that I'll be able to take Freya's advice and figure out what's going on with Allie once and for all.

Allie

It's a Saturday afternoon at the Tower Park stadium and everyone is buzzing with excitement. I follow Vi down the concrete steps to our front row seats where Hayden is standing with Belle and Poppy. They're all decked out in green and white Bethnal Green F.C. gear, and I'm feeling like an idiot in a yellow blouse because it's apparently the other team's colour.

However, I'm not stressing too much because I'm too busy taking in the splendour of Tower Park on a game day. The crowd, the lights, the smells, the grass. It's all practically vibrating with enthusiasm even though this is a somewhat casual friendlies match. I can't imagine what an experience it would have been to watch all the brothers play together in Russia for the World Cup last year.

Hayden, Belle, and Poppy all say hello but quickly turn their focus back to the pitch. I glance over at the three empty chairs beside me.

"Camden has a team meeting and will be joining us later, but Gareth, Sloan, and Freya should be here any minute," Vi says, leaning over my shoulder. "I told Sloan to stop at the shop and grab you something decent to wear."

I cringe down at my banana-yellow top. "Sorry, I had no clue what the other team's colours were."

She shakes her head. "It's fine. They're getting Sophia a new shirt anyway because she was really upset she couldn't come to this game on the account of tonight being a grown-ups-only night out."

"Where are we going?" I ask curiously. Vi was quite cryptic on the phone when she told me to pack a sexy dress to change into after the game.

"It's a surprise!" Vi says, her blue eyes twinkling with an evilness that's at odds with the innocence of her blonde features. "But we all got sitters for the night, so prepare for some fun!"

I look over and see Belle and Poppy snickering between the two of them, and I suddenly feel like I'm missing out on a joke.

"We're here!" a voice says from behind me.

I swerve my gaze over to Sloan, who's moving down the row to the open seat beside me. Freya shuffles in after her with Gareth bringing in the rear.

"Hi, Allie-Cat," Gareth says, shooting me a wave. "Are you surviving at Camden and Indie's all right?"

I nod earnestly. "I'm doing awesome, thanks! Good to see you guys again. Hi, Sloan. Hi, Freya."

"Hi, hi!" Freya beams, looking delighted about being at a soccer stadium right now. "This is my first football game ever!"

My eyes brighten. "Exciting! I haven't been to many either, so we can fangirl together."

Sloan smiles at the two of us commiserating before handing me a Bethnal Green shopping bag. "Throw this on over your blouse." She smiles and waggles her eyebrows.

"Thank you for picking this up. What do I owe you?" I ask, pulling out a white official-looking jersey from the bag.

"Don't bother. I already tried to pay for mine and was shut down," Freya states with an eye roll.

Sloan helps me put the jersey on over my hair, and I smooth out the expensive-feeling fabric over my hips. Gareth frowns curiously at the back of it.

"Did I get something on it?" I ask, reaching around but my attention is completely diverted when loud music erupts in the stadium.

The Bethnal Green F.C. team marches out onto the field, and the first person I spot is Uncle Vaughn. I feel a sense of pride at the sight of him down there looking all serious in his buttoned-up polo as he walks alongside the coach. Off to the side of them is Indie, who is impossible to miss with her neon green glasses and curly red hair piled on top of her head. She smiles and waves at our section, and we all wave right back.

My eyes scan through the players as they spread out on the field for their final warm-up before the match starts. I feel a pang of guilt when I realise I'm not looking for my cousins.

I'm looking for Roan.

I finally find him, his bronze skin contrasting beautifully against his crisp white uniform as he nods at something Mac says. His muscles are flexed and on full display beneath the tight fit of his jersey. I can even see those enormous quads of his peeking out from under his shorts.

I thought he looked fuckworthy for the shoot the other day, but I was wrong. In his uniform like this, with an intense look in his eyes and his focus on the match he's preparing for…This is Roan's fuckworthy look.

He takes a warm-up pass, and I can't help but notice how powerful he looks out there, like he's ready to take on the world. As if he feels me staring at him, his eyes move through the crowd and land right on me. He doesn't wave or give me any physical indication of noticing me. He just stares at me with a look that says, "I see you, mooi."

I do my best to hide the flush I feel all over my body from my family. Although, it's not the girls I'm worried about noticing. It's Gareth, who seems to be watching me very closely.

The players line up on their spots for the start of the game, and it's that moment that Vi yells over all the loud cheering, "Oh, Allie, did I tell you?"

"Tell me what?" I ask, angling my ear so I can hear her better.

"I set you up with a date for tonight."

My face falls and I turn to look at her in confusion. "With who?"

She smiles at Sloan before turning her attention to me. "With Roan."

"Roan?" Gareth barks in unison with me. But all of our attention is diverted because kickoff has just happened, and Tanner is driving up the field, fast and furious.

I do my best to calm my heart that's pounding in my chest like a jackhammer over the idea of being up close and personal with Roan again. I just started feeling like I could breathe for the first time since the night we went out for drinks. Now he's going to come in and turn me inside out.

That's a problem because the more time I spend with Roan, the more time I *want* to spend with Roan. He's funny, and sexy, and charming in a way that's so utterly believable. And he's ten times more perceptive than I ever took him for the night we met. Frankly, it's frustrating because I know we're a bad idea. I know that after the awful thing I did, getting close to him isn't wise. Any relationship that starts off with a lie like the one I'm hiding is doomed to fail. But he and my family seem bound and determined to shove us together at any available opportunity, making it really hard for me to resist him.

I put Roan in the back of my mind to focus on the match, which is a real nail-biter, and not only because of what happens on the pitch.

The most interesting spectacle to watch is what happens in the stands.

Gareth, Sloan, Vi, Hayden, Belle, and Poppy all morph from normal, society-functioning humans into rabid beasts that are being teased with a slab of bloody, fresh meat. Even Freya seems to be losing her mind along with them. I begin to wonder if it's a British thing, a Harris thing, or if I've somehow missed out on some sort of Incredible Hulk green elixir that everyone shot up before the match. Whatever it is has turned them all from loving, supportive people to vicious, I'll-cut-a-bitch, terrorists.

I'm so terrified of getting my hand bitten off that I remain completely silent through the entire game as they scream obscenities at the ref and call out the players who should be passed to. At one point Vi stands on her chair and screams at her dad to have the coach put Lionel in the game. I don't know who Lionel is, but according to Vi, he's the best centre back they have and Booker is getting riled out there.

During the second half, Vi starts a chant that the entire stadium joins in on. It's such a powerful sight, I actually get tears in my eyes. It's even more awesome because it was all started by this little blonde powder-puff of a woman who is *that* passionate about her brothers' soccer careers.

With only a couple of minutes left in the game, Roan takes a bad tackle to the leg. Luckily, he gets right up and is seemingly unharmed, but Indie isn't pleased. She's flailing at the ref like another adorable little psychopath, and I begin to grow worried about her blood pressure.

The game finally ends in Bethnal Green's favour thanks to Roan's successful penalty shot at the end. Watching him celebrate his game-winning shot with Tanner and the rest of his teammates gives me the most intense goosebumps of my life.

After the game, Vi leads us all through a door that's guarded by security. "Let's go congratulate the boys and then there's a place where we can all change," she says as we grab our bags from the security officers and make our way through the hallways.

The smell of sweat becomes strong as we meet head-on with the other team that is slinking into their changing room. One of the players stops Gareth to say hello, but I continue following the rest of them, who have found the boys, talking to the press.

"Booker!" Poppy squeals when she lands eyes on him. She runs in full-force toward him, and he breaks away from the video camera to wrap her in his arms. He lifts her up to his tall stature and plants a kiss on her lips.

Tanner's boots clack along the concrete as he approaches Belle. Before he hugs her, he leans down and rubs her protruding belly. "What did my baby think of the game?"

"Your baby thinks you made a killer goal," Belle replies with a sexy smile. He looks up and grins at her, then grabs her face, pulling her in for a very socially inappropriate kiss.

Vi interrupts Tanner and Booker's reunions by diving into details about the game while congratulating them over and over. I try to follow along, but soccer chatter isn't one of my strong suits.

Suddenly, a chill runs up my spine like I'm being watched. When I turn around to find Roan standing there tall, broad, and sweaty, the butterflies I had when we first met return with vengeance.

His mouth spreads into a wicked smile as he looks me up and down, his eyes lingering on my shirt as he states, "Nice to see you again, Lis."

I swallow a nervous lump in my throat and do my best not to stare at the drizzle of sweat sliding down his thick neck that I have the strangest desire to lick. "Nice to see you, too," I croak, my voice sounding uncomfortably hoarse.

God-god, is he emitting more pheromones when he's all sweaty like this? I'm feeling a really embarrassing amount of dampness between my legs that wasn't there a moment ago.

"How'd you like the match?" he asks with a knowing smile that makes it seem like he can see exactly what's going on in my panties right now.

I brush back a piece of my hair and try to look cavalier. "It was quite an experience, that's for sure."

He cocks his head to the side. "What do you mean by that?"

"Oh!" I exclaim, thinking I must sound unimpressed. "The game was amazing. The stadium really comes alive like I never realised. But what was really interesting was experiencing how this group behaves during a game." I gesture behind me toward my family.

"What's that supposed to mean?" Gareth's voice booms out of nowhere as he comes up from behind Roan and throws an arm over his shoulder. "Nice penalty shot, DeWalt. You and Tanner look bloody good out there together."

"Thanks, Gareth," Roan says with an easy smile. "It took some time, but we found our rhythm."

Gareth nods slowly. "I just hope you don't do anything to screw it up before your big move to the Premier League."

Roan loses all sense of humour on his face and turns a serious look at Gareth. The two seem to exchange silent words for a few seconds before Tanner's voice bellows, "Not a chance, Gareth! Roan and I have a bromance that cannot be broken."

Belle's eyes fly wide. "You better not let Camden hear you say that. He'll get all awkward and start sending you chocolates."

"Lucky for me, my wife loves chocolates, so it's a win-win." He wraps an arm around Belle and kisses her temple.

"So, what did your comment mean, Allie-Cat?" Gareth asks, pinning me with his hazel eyes. "What was so interesting about us watching the game?"

I flush and shake my head. "I didn't mean anything by it. You guys just really get into the game."

Vi moves to look at me, her brows furrowed. "How do you mean?"

I look around at all of them staring at me like I'm speaking in a foreign language. "You have to know how crazy of fans you are, right?"

"Everybody goes crazy for football in England," Vi volleys back.

I laugh and glance over at Roan, who has crossed his arms and appears amused by the image of me squirming under the Harris scrutiny. "I get that. But you guys have to be a special brand, right?"

They all blink back at me in confusion, so I look to Hayden, or Belle, or Poppy, or Sloan to confirm my assessment because they're outsiders like me to a degree. But apparently they've been infiltrated for too long in this bunch. Their opinions have been compromised.

Finally, I roll my eyes and say, "Never mind. Everything was completely normal, like any other Saturday afternoon."

They seem satisfied by that answer, so I quickly take a step out of the middle of the group so they can resume their post-game chatter.

Roan follows my retreat and props himself on the wall while shaking his head at me. "You can't call the Harris lot crazy. They just go crazier."

I shrug his comment off. "I can call them whatever I'd like. I'm a Harris, too."

His shoulders shake with laughter. "I give you three more months in London with them. You'll be just as crazy and blind to it as well. This is a preview of your future."

A huge smile spreads across my face at the notion of truly being one of them because I quite like the idea of being completely entrenched in this family. It's a nice change from what I had back in Chicago. Even if I do think they're nut-jobs, I have a fond appreciation for them.

Vi motions toward the door at the end of the hallway. "Us girls are going to go change in Dad's office. You guys need to go hit the showers!"

I look over my shoulder at Roan and sort of wish he wouldn't shower because I think his sweaty scent could be bottled up into a cologne.

I clear my throat and state, "So I hear you're my date again."

He lifts his brows victoriously. "I hear the same…It's funny because it would appear that even your family wants us to be dating."

I roll my eyes. "It's not a date. It's a setup."

He bites his lip and looks down at my jersey. "Whatever you say, DeWalt."

I frown at his bizarre reply and then Sloan grabs my arm to pull me down the hall.

As I depart, Roan calls out, "My name looks good on you, moon."

He winks a sexy wink and I turn around with a confused look on my face. "What's he talking about?"

Sloan looks ahead at Vi and the other girls, who all erupt into laughter. "The back of your jersey says DEWALT."

"I what?" I exclaim and then grab at it like a maniac.

All this time, I've been worried about the Harris Brothers interfering when, in reality, it is the Harris ladies that I should be keeping an eye on.

CHAPTER 13

Roan

MY DICK FUCKING TWITCHES THE SECOND I LOCK EYES ON Allie as she strides out to the limo in the player parking lot. Evidently whatever we have in store for the night requires limousine transportation, which seems a bit ostentatious to me. But considering the net worth of this family of athletes, it's probably just another drop in the bucket.

I drink in Allie's appearance, starting with her sexy black heels. I have to bite back a laugh because there's a little jolt in her step as she does everything in her power not to skip. It's probably the cutest, most endearing goddamned quirk that I've ever seen in a woman. A flowy, pale pink skirt with black lace lining the bottom ripples in the light breeze. On top, she's wearing a tiny black crop top that reveals a few inches of her waistline and more cleavage than the cock in my trousers can handle. Thank fuck most of this lot is related to her because I'd be really damn jealous watching her flounce around like this near a group of single guys. Especially single soccer players.

The rest of the women are dressed remarkably as well. I'm suddenly grateful that I had a button-down in my garment bag or I'd be feeling really underdressed right now. We all compliment the ladies before filing into the limo to head to our destination that is still a mystery. It seems only the women know where we're going, but Allie and Freya are just as clueless as me and Mac. Allie slides down to the end of the limo to sit beside me, and I have to swallow my tongue as her asymmetrical skirt reveals a good deal of thigh. There's champagne in a nearby bucket, so I offer drinks to everyone in the vehicle in an attempt to focus my eyes on anything other than the stunning woman beside me.

Freya is seated next to Allie, decked out in a black lace dress. Mac smiles sweetly at her, but she narrows her eyes at him while doing a cheers with Lis.

"Here, Allie. Drink my champagne and describe it to me in great detail," Belle says, handing over her full glass of bubbly.

Allie laughs as she double fists two drinks. "Are you serious?"

Belle's dark eyes grow ominous. "As a heart attack."

Lidie passes her glass to Freya. "Same goes for you."

The two women look at each other and laugh as they do the Harris wives' bidding, and I start to think this might help my chances of getting Allie to open up to me tonight like Freya advised.

We drive for about an hour around the city, drinking and laughing and making guesses about where we're headed. Allie seems extra giggly as she and Freya bond over some television show called *Heartland*. I even see them exchange numbers so they can hang out outside of work-related meetings.

We end up in SoHo at a building that houses a dance club. I assure that's where we're headed, but Vi leads us to the door right beside it and we head up a rickety flight of stairs. It isn't until I see the familiar wooden floorboards and mirrors that I realise we're in a dance studio.

A woman with short, white blonde hair that reminds me of my mother comes out to greet us with a man who's dressed in a purple silk shirt, black dress pants, and dance shoes.

"Hello to you all. I am Francesca De La Rosa, and my husband here Ricardo De La Rosa. We will be your dance instructors this evening."

I glance over at Allie, who has a stunned look on her face, along with Mac, who looks like he might actually vomit.

"Tonight we will be teaching you the basics of the Viennese waltz!" Belle lets out a double whoop and Francesca smiles at her shared enthusiasm. "I know you are all beginners, so please, do not worry about your skills. We are here to have fun and help you all connect with your partners."

At that moment, I lock eyes with Allie, who is shaking her head in fear? Excitement? I can't quite tell. But what I do know is that this is the perfect setting for me to impress her.

"There is champagne for those of you who need a little liquid courage," Ricardo says in a thick Spanish accent. "Please, have a drink and get comfortable. We will begin in five minutes."

We make our way over to the table that's lined with flutes of champagne, and I can't help but notice that Allie is drinking hers in large gulps.

I sidle up next to her and whisper in her ear, "Nervous?"

"Um, yes!" she barks out and takes another large gulp.

"Why?"

She laughs and shakes her head, refusing to answer.

My brows furrow. "What? What aren't you saying?"

Belle appears next to us and hands Allie a flute. "Again, please."

Allie rolls her eyes. "Are you trying to get me drunk?"

Belle places her hands on her swollen stomach. "Are you trying to deprive me of the simple pleasures in life?"

Allie's face softens. "Of course not. But why can't Tanner help you?"

"He hates champagne," Belle replies with a wave of the hand. "And unless it's something perverted, his descriptive skills leave a lot to be desired. Come on, just one more glass."

Allie exhales in defeat and takes a drink of Belle's champagne. I wrinkle my nose as she describes the fizzy bubbles and dry finish because champagne is definitely not my drink of choice either. After she's done and Belle walks away, I resume my questioning.

"Tell me why you're nervous," I repeat, placing my hand on the small of her back and letting my fingers rub along her exposed flesh.

I see her shiver from my touch as she takes another drink and replies, "Because you're going to be awesome at this."

I laugh at her response. "Are you that competitive?"

She licks a drop of champagne off her dark merlot-stained lipstick. "No."

"Then what are you worried about?"

She looks at me with wide, heavily mascaraed eyes. "Because I remember what happened after the last time you and I danced together." She covers her mouth and gets a guilty look in her eyes like she didn't mean to say what she just said.

I open my mouth to reply, but we're interrupted when Francesca instructs the women to join her. Ricardo directs the guys over to his side of the studio and I smile broadly at Allie's parting words as I follow Mac. With one little sentence, she has given me hope.

Ricardo walks through the Viennese waltz steps with painfully slow directions. I'm not saying I'm an avid ballroom dancer by any means, but I know enough about counting that picking up choreography isn't hard for me. Sadly, no matter how much Tanner and Mac try, these two can't seem to tell their right feet from their left.

After several minutes of Mac screwing up, I get so frustrated that I grab him by the arms, force his hands around my waist, and dance the part of the female so I can lead him into taking the right steps. It's maybe a bit more aggressive than Ricardo appreciated because he asks to step in, using my same technique but with a softer approach.

When he does the same with Tanner, all I can think is, *Jesus Christ, these guys are supposed to be professional athletes. How hard is it to pick up a simple three-four natural step?*

The longer they struggle, the less time I get with Allie. And after seeing her down that champagne, I'm dying to get close to her to speak with her when she's less uptight.

Once everyone eventually gets enough of the choreography worked out, we're able to rejoin the women.

Allie's cheeks are flushed as I take her in my arms and slowly slide my fingers up the small of her back. I place one hand on her shoulder blade while the other hand clasps hers level with our shoulders. It's not where I want my hands to be on her body, but I have plans for this evening and I need to stay focused.

Allie glances down at our feet, chewing her lip nervously. "I hope you're wearing steel-toed shoes."

"It won't be necessary."

The guys look awkward as Francesca and Ricardo busy themselves, going from couple to couple and fixing their holds on the women. There's a lot of laughing going on, but my face is completely serious as I stare at Allie and try to get a read on her.

We go through the steps manually with the instructors, getting used to holding our partners with a strong gate and stepping in time to the sound of Ricardo counting into a microphone.

Finally, Francesca announces that she's going to play the music that goes along with the choreography. "Dance as many of the steps as you can remember. If you forget, just keep dancing anyway. This is not a test!"

A minute later, the studio fills with the song "At Last" by Etta James. With no effort, I begin waltzing us through a series of four natural turns and four side-steps. The Viennese waltz is a quick tempo dance, but it's smooth and the steps are simple. Once you have them down, it's just a matter of repeating them over and over.

Allie is staring down at her feet, fretting over the steps.

"Just watch me," I state softly into her golden hair that smells like flowers. She forces herself to look up as I add, "I promise I won't lead you astray."

She nods and bites her lip, and I wish it were my teeth sinking into that delicious piece of flesh. She feels good in my arms, responsive and alluring. Our bodies move fluidly together, even if she doesn't know what she's doing. As our heartrates increase with the action, I want to press myself harder against her so she can feel everything she does to me.

To give myself a break from the intensity of her eyes on mine, I twirl her into an underarm turn.

When she soars back to me, she has a shocked look on her face. "We didn't learn a turn," she exclaims, impressed by how easily she flowed through the movement.

"I needed some space," I say with a shrug. "You were taking my breath away."

Her eyes lower to my lips. "You can be really charming when you want to be, DeWalt."

"You can be really sexy without even trying, Lis," I reply. My thoughts take a dark turn as I glance down at her skirt flowing around her legs and think about how easy it would lift up for them to wrap around me instead. I shake away the image and add, "And you can be confusing and frustrating as well."

"Confusing and frustrating?" she asks, her brows knitting together.

"You act like your family is a barrier, but they've pushed us together twice now."

She looks around at the group, who are all barely dancing because none of them know what the hell they're doing. Ricardo has pulled some of guys to the side for another mini lesson, and I cringe when I catch sight of Mac stomping on Freya's foot. She howls in agony, so he drops down to his knees to rub the pain away. She whacks him on the head and yanks him back up to resume dancing.

In the corner, Vi and Sloan are sipping champagne and watching us with wide eyes as I continue moving us around the room.

Elie sighs and presses her head against my chest. "You'll come to find that I say and do the wrong thing a lot."

"Am I a wrong thing you did?" I ask, gazing down at her with a somber look, my gut twisting at the idea that, that is how she sees me. "Is that why you're trying to stay away from me? Because you regret that night we had together and don't want me to be a constant reminder?"

"No!" she exclaims, popping her head up to look at me. "I mean, it's true that night isn't something I normally do, but I don't regret it. I actually can't stop thinking about it."

"Good," I retort, a rush of relief washing over me. I turn her under my arm again, pulling her back into my embrace with my confidence restored. "Then stop using your family and your job as an excuse. None of them care about us being together."

Just as the words leave my mouth, I catch a glimpse of Gareth, who's pulling Sloan out onto the dance floor. Instead of focusing on her, he's watching Allie and me. I tilt my head in amusement just as Sloan grabs his chin and turns his attention to her.

Allie lets out a long breath, obviously not noticing the vibes that I'm getting from Gareth. "I'm just scared you don't know enough about me to know that you really want to be with me."

"Let me ask you this," I state, staring down at her to gauge her reaction. "Are you over your ex?"

She looks up at me with a confused look in her eyes. "What?"

"Are you over the guy who drove you into my arms two years ago?"

She whips her head from side to side in shock as she shrieks, "God, yes, I'm over him! I have no clue why I ever stayed with him as long as I did."

Her answer pleases me. It pleases me greatly. "Maybe it was all to lead you to me, mooi." With a deep breath, I release her from my hold and wrap my hands around her waist, hoisting her up in the air in a ballroom lift that my mom had me do with all the females in her class one time. When I slowly lower her back down, our bodies are completely flush, every inch pressing against one another. When she's back on her feet, I murmur into her ear, "Just give in already. You know you want to."

She pulls back and has a dreamy smile on her face. I can't help but offer up a silent "thank you" to my mom for teaching me how to dance. When the song draws to a close, I twirl her once more and end the move with a dip that has her long hair dangling to the floor. As I lean over her, our mouths only a couple of inches apart, I add, "This could be our wedding song for all you know."

Alice

Good god, there is not enough alcohol in the world to douse the attraction I have to Roan DeWalt. After our couples dance lesson, the group of us head downstairs to the dance club where the instructors encouraged us to test our skills. At first it is only us girls out on the floor flailing about, but the guys eventually join in. And when I see the hunted look in Roan's eyes, I retreat to the safety of the bar where Freya is also currently parked.

I smile at her as I sip my drink. "It's hot out there!"

She nods and sips her fruity cocktail. "Hotter than the wedding night in *Outlander*."

I giggle at her response. "Oh my God, Jamie Fraser is so sexy in season one!"

"He's sexy in all of them, but you're right. Season one was his prime. And that episode had the best foreplay in cinematic history."

My thighs clench together. "So true. What is it about delayed gratification that's so—"

"Fucking hot?" Freya finishes. "It must be something special because I've been delaying my gratification for twenty-eight years."

"Twenty-eight years?" I groan and spread my hands out wide on the sticky bar. "Fuck!"

"Fuck is right!" she says, fanning her face.

"Well, you should go back out there with me. Let's go dance and keep the sexy Jamie Fraser foreplay going!" I state in solidarity, thinking perhaps my new friend needs a shove from me like I need a shove from alcohol.

She shakes her head. "I can't. My bloody feet have blisters from these damn heels!"

I glance down at her feet and cringe. "They are really cute shoes, though."

She nods. "I'm just waiting for my medical escort to show up."

"Your what?" I ask, my face puzzling in confusion.

Suddenly, Mac appears beside us.

"Ready to go, lass?" he bellows, his eyes scanning Freya's curvy body like she's some sort of patient in a hospital.

"Ready," she replies with a curt nod and holds her hands out to him. "Now don't you make a big fuss when you carry me. You're Scottish and a footballer, so you should be able to handle my immense size."

He rolls his eyes and squats down so she can hop up on his back. "Has anyone ever told you that you talk too much?"

"All the time!" She reaches back to check that her dress is covering her butt and then waves goodbye to me. "Don't forget to call me sometime! I literally do nothing but watch Netflix and sew with my cat. It's pathetic and I'd love some company."

Mac turns and eyes me. "Aye, make sure my lad gets home safe and sound. Your bed or his…Makes no difference to me." He shoots me a wink and carts his dance partner out of the club.

I chew away at my lip and picture how good Roan would look in my bed. That's when I see him approaching, right behind Camden and Indie.

Indie sidles up next to me and states over the loud music, "We're leaving."

"Okay, I'm just about done with my drink." I tip the remaining contents to the back of my throat and smile at the lovely buzz I have going on right now.

"No, I mean Camden and I are leaving." She winks and then eyes Roan behind me.

Camden's voice cuts in, "Roan, can you get Allie home safely?"

Roan's posture straightens. "Of course."

"Great. I trust you, man." Camden pats Roan on the back and, without another word, takes off with Indie tucked under his arm.

Roan takes the seat that Freya vacated, and I can feel his large presence wrapping around me like a delicious weighted blanket.

He leans in and whispers in my ear, "They're basically giving us their blessing."

A riot of goosebumps erupt all over my body. I quickly shake my glass at the bartender, indicating I need a refill. Everything about this night is easier to handle with alcohol.

I turn toward Roan, our faces now only inches apart, and he's looking at me like he's seen me naked. I'm looking at him like I've seen him naked. And I'm suddenly starting to wonder why the hell we're not just seeing each other naked already.

Without pause, I grab Roan by the shirt and state, "Let's go Jamie Fraser on the dance floor."

He smiles and lets me lead him out to the swarm of people. He takes over our dancing and reminds me all over again why I haven't deleted that stupid video of him.

Roan

It's after midnight, and judging by the smudged makeup under Allie's eyes, I'd say she's good and drunk. We're dropped off at my car in the Bethnal Green lot and then I drive Allie back to Camden and Indie's. I had one drink all night, and I think it's safe to say Allie drank what I didn't.

She's fidgety on the car ride to Notting Hill, her hands moving up and down her thighs as she crosses and uncrosses her legs. The way she's squirming around in her sexy outfit and mussed up hair is driving me fucking mad. And the closer I get to Camden and Indie's place, the heavier the sexual tension grows between us, making it hard to breathe.

Freya's advice was spot-on. Getting Allie a little relaxed brought down all her walls, and now I get the sense that she is done trying to push me away. But as I park on the street in front of Camden and Indie's townhouse, I know that tonight isn't the time for us to reconnect.

I open Allie's car door and offer her my hand. She smiles up at me, her eyes slightly drooped as she wraps her fingers around mine. "Such a gentleman."

"Always," I reply as we make our way up the stairs. "Do you have your key?"

"I do indeed." She looks up at me seriously. "Do you have your key?"

My brows lift. "For my house? Yes, I have my key."

Her eyes narrow. "Do you want to see my room?"

I blink back in astonishment. "Erm, your room?"

"Yeah, you know…My room. Four walls, a closet, a bed."

The muscles in my shoulders tense at the thought of being in Allie's bedroom. I shouldn't. I know I shouldn't. She's drunk and probably horny. *And I know I'm fucking horny, so this could end very bad or very good.*

The prospect of very good is all it takes for my head to begin nodding in agreement.

She smiles with glee and places a finger over her lips. "We'll have to be really quiet and sneak you in so we don't get caught by Mom and Dad."

She fumbles with the key while I press my forehead to the side of the house and silently berate myself for being so fucking weak.

When the door opens, she reaches back and slides her fingers in mine to lead me through the corridor and straight for the large wooden staircase ahead.

I'm a fucking gentleman. I can handle this.

We take the steps one at a time, Allie giggling every time we hit a noisy board. Almost all the steps are noisy, though, since the house is so old, which means she giggles the entire time. My cock is obviously enjoying it, though, because I feel it thickening inside of my jeans with our ascent.

By the time we reach the third level, she rounds the railing and skips past a small kitchen and a bathroom. She opens the door at the end of the hall, which reveals her bedroom. It's a large, white-walled space with a giant four-poster bed covered in a pink floral duvet. There's a green armchair by the window with a book tossed on it, but the space is pretty bare other than that. Not even a stray sock to be found.

"I like your room," I say by obligation, curious as to why she wanted to show it to me so much when it has nothing personal of value inside of it yet. I walk over to the large window and pull back the lace curtains to glance at the view of the street. "It's cosy."

"I'm still waiting for my stuff to arrive from Chicago, but I like it here," she says as she kicks off her heels and closes the door, pressing her back to it and watching me with a pointed look in her eyes. "I never want to leave."

"Your bedroom?" I ask nervously because she's currently reminding me of the woman I met two years ago. A woman who knows exactly what she wants, and I know that's a hard woman to deny.

She nods. "And my bed. Feel it."

She tiptoes over to her bed and flops down, spreading her legs out wide so her skirt rises up. She pats the space beside her, and I know this is a bad idea. A really bad idea.

I join her because I evidently enjoy torturing myself. But I have the sense to lie myself a good two feet away from her, so there's still some fight left in me.

"Isn't it comfy?" she moans, making my cock twitch again.

I swallow. "It's comfy."

She turns on to her side and props her head on her hand to stare at me. "You look good in my bed."

I smile and turn my head to look at her, doing my best not to stare at the line of cleavage this angle creates. "Why is that?"

She shrugs. "Your dark skin against the pale colours. Kind of like how you looked in your uniform during your game today."

My brows lift flirtatiously. "Did you like how I looked in my uniform?"

She covers her eyes and drops her face into her duvet, obviously embarrassed by admitting that fact. "Maybe," she mumbles against the fabric.

I press my hands to my stomach as I chuckle. "No need to be shy."

I turn on my side to watch her as she twists her head to prop it on her flattened hands. She stares at me with a seductive gaze for a minute and then suddenly moves to sit up on her knees. With a coy bite of her lips, she crawls toward me.

I flatten onto my back, my hands shooting up by my ears in defence. "What are you doing?"

She throws a leg over my waist and begins unbuttoning my shirt. "What does it look like I'm doing?"

I reach down and still her motions. "You're drunk, Allie."

Her face furrows. "I'm not drunk!"

I jerk my head up and retort, "You're definitely not sober."

She scoffs and blows a stray piece of hair out of her eyes. "Well that's different than drunk, okay? I know what I'm doing."

I shake my head again. "Let's just talk."

"Talk?" she barks. "We talked all night. And we danced all night. Now it's time for us to fuck all night."

She giggles and squirms her heated centre down on my cock in a way that makes my halfy turn into a fully. I throw my arms over my eyes to shield myself from the very sexy image of her body gyrating on top of me.

I growl in sexual frustration. "You're making it really hard to be good right now."

"Maybe I don't want you to be good," she states, her face lowering to my ear as she adds, "Maybe I want you to be bad."

When she presses her tongue to my neck, I swear to Christ it takes every muscle in my body to not grab her by the waist, roll us both over, and fuck the ever-loving shit out of her.

My swollen cock slides along her clit as she pumps her hips in frantic need. "Oh my God, you feel good," she groans, and I want to kill myself.

"Ellie, please," I beg, my voice barely holding on as I stare up at her and try to determine just how drunk she is.

"Roan, I'm not drunk." She sits up and stares at me with extreme focus. "See? Now will you please shut up and kiss me?"

She reaches down and pulls her top off, exposing her naked breasts. I admit, I had a feeling she wasn't wearing a bra because I could feel her nipples through her top all night. But seeing her bare, pale pink nipples pebbled and only a foot away from my mouth makes everything in my body roar to life.

Her hands are back on my buttons, undoing every last one while I inaudibly whisper, "Grannies naked, baby ducks being murdered, Chewbacca on a holiday, bulldogs eating oatmeal."

"What are you doing?" she asks, spreading my shirt open and sliding her fingertips over my abs.

I prop myself on my elbows. "I'm trying to get control of my fucking cock."

"Why?" she asks, completely innocent.

"Because I want to fuck you right now, but I promised Freya I wouldn't take advantage of you when you are drunk. She may be a short woman, but I don't doubt she could maim me with very little effort."

Allie props her hands on her hips, losing all humour in her eyes. "Roan, this is me, completely topless, giving you my full consent. Seriously, why don't you want to fuck me?"

I tilt my head and stare up into her eyes, a seriousness to my expression that wasn't there before. "Ag, believe me, I want to fuck you, Lis."

In a rush, I grab her hip with one hand and wrap my other arm around her waist as I roll us so she's now beneath me. Her eyes are wide and excited as she reaches down to fumble with the waistband of my jeans. With a low growl of frustration, I wrap my fingers around her wrists and pin them above her head.

"What are you doing?" she asks, her voice breathy and needy as she arches up into me and spreads her legs wide to invite me inside of her.

I stare down at her beautiful body before lowering my lips to her chest to blow warm air all over her exposed flesh. I pause at her nipples, my tongue dying to taste the hardened flesh and suck her so deep into my mouth that she screams.

With great effort, I reply, "Good things come to those who wait." I gaze deeply into her eyes that look dangerously similar to the way I remember them looking when she comes.

She groans and wraps her legs around me, hooking her ankles on my lower back. "Don't tease me, DeWalt."

My body shakes with laughter. "You know from previous experience that it will be worth it." I detach myself from her body and stand to admire the view of her spread out half naked and expelling large, sexually charged and extremely frustrated breaths. Is it fucked-up that I like seeing her like this? Does that make me a sadist?

She begins kneading the tender flesh of her breasts as she rubs her thighs together. When her hand twists her nipple, I nearly give in. Nearly.

Jesus Christ, I'm not a sadist. I'm a fucking masochist.

Tearing my gaze from her, I yank my shirt off and remove my jeans.

She sits up in the bed, abandoning her breasts and staring at me while I adjust the raging hard-on inside my black boxer briefs. "What are you doing?" she asks, eyeing me excitedly like I'm getting ready to unwrap a fucking present for her.

I walk around to the other side of the bed and pull the covers back. "I'm going to bed," I answer and slide myself in between her pink sheets even though I'd much rather be sliding myself into her pink pussy.

"Here?" she asks, glancing at the door like her cousins are going to walk in any minute and shout at us for having the nerve to actually sleep.

"Goddamn right," I reply and pull the covers back for her to get in next. "And don't look at your door like that. If you were willing to fuck me with them under the same roof, you should definitely be able to sleep with me."

"Like…you really do mean to just sleep?" Her brows knit together as she finally accepts the situation.

I nod and pat the bed. "The sooner we get some sleep, the sooner I can fuck you."

She huffs out an annoyed noise before stomping over to her wardrobe. She pulls out a blue Chicago Cubs T-shirt and yanks it on over her head before sliding her skirt off her hips. My eyes drink in her creamy legs and I stare at her ass while she walks over to flick the lights off.

My head tilts curiously. "I'd forgotten how sexy your ass is."

She turns to look at me, her face flushing a deep crimson. "What?"

I point to her butt cheek. "I remember slapping your ass two years ago and, looking at it now, I have no clue why I didn't chain you to that bed so I could keep you forever."

She clicks the light off and tiptoes back to me. "You sure you're not remembering some other one-night stand?" She hops into the bed, turning her body away from me in one fluid motion.

I press myself up behind her, my hand resting on her hip as I murmur into her ear, "I don't have one-night stands." I kiss her shoulder and add, "You were my exception."

She rolls onto her back and stares up at me, her face illuminated by the faint glow of streetlights outside the window. "Why was *I* your exception?"

She puts extra emphasis on "I" like she can't possibly believe she's special. I fucking hate that shit. I hate that she doesn't see what I see. It makes me want to dick punch her ex because he's probably the one who put those doubts in her head.

I cup her face, gliding my thumb over her lips that ache to be kissed. "Because I like how you go after what you want, Lis. When I met you, you had a goal and you weren't going to stop until you achieved that goal. That kind of determination is sexy, even if you hadn't been wearing a garter belt."

She smiles and rolls her eyes, a line forming between her eyebrows as she thinks deeper about my reply. "I think you're putting me on a pedestal that I don't deserve to be on." She scrubs her hands over her face, and I can feel the anxiety in her body like there's a third person in bed with us.

I pull her hands down, lining my finger along the furrow in her brow. "What can I do to turn this frown upside down?"

She sighs and looks up at me like she wants to say something. Whatever it is can wait, though, because I need to taste her again more than I need to hear what she's about to say. I lower my face and press my lips to hers. She instantly opens for me as my tongue slides in to tangle with hers. I taste the faintness of alcohol and mint as her hands wrap around my neck and she holds me to her, propelling the kiss deeper and more intense than I originally planned.

This is what I like so damn much about this woman. She takes what she wants, everything else be damned. I grew up watching my mom cater to my sisters' father and apologising for shit she had no business apologising for. It was a reflex for her, ingrained in her bones at a young age. Allie is different, though. She's a fighter.

Allie shifts to wrap her leg around my hip, and I pull back with a laugh even though her skin feels like a slice of heaven against mine. "You're relentless."

"You're a tease!" she retorts, her brow still furrowed in frustration.

I kiss the crease on her forehead and then move back to my pillow. "Sleep, then sex."

With another huff, she rolls away from me, her body tense as I wrap my arms around her and nudge my cock between her beautiful ass cheeks.

"You only have yourself to blame for that situation," she mumbles in reference to my erection and then she inhales a big yawn.

I drop a kiss to her hair. "I know, mooi. I know."

The smile on my face feels permanent as we both let sleep do the time travel for us.

CHAPTER

Roan

I'M WOKEN THIS MORNING BY SOMETHING HOT AND WET ON MY cock, and the surprising sensation sends me flying to the head of the bed.

"What?" Allie exclaims breathily, throwing back the covers to reveal herself crouched on her knees at the foot of the bed and looking like she just had my cock in her mouth because she damn well did.

"Jesus Christ! Warn a guy, why don't you," I state, looking down at my wet, bare dick sticking out of my boxers. It looks veined and really pissed-off at me for waking up and ruining all the fun.

She sits up, looking adorable in her Cubs shirt and messy sleep hair. "If I told you first, you'd probably accuse me of still being drunk."

Her smart mouth brings a smirk to my face as I lunge across the bed at her. She yelps and tries to squirm out of my hold, but I overpower her and bind my arms around her waist. I turn us and splay her out on the bed so I'm on top of her, right between her soft legs.

"I don't remember you being such a brat when we met," I huff, my hands wrapping around her wrists and pinning them to the bed.

She unsuccessfully fights my hold, trying to hide the sexy smile on her face as she replies, "I don't remember you being such a prude!"

I growl and dip my head to bite her nipple over top of her shirt. She squeals in protest, but her legs find their way around my hips and she pulls me into her warmth.

I release her breast and press my cock against her pussy. "Can you stop pouting long enough for me to fuck you?"

"I don't know," she volleys back, her brows lifting in challenge. "Can you stop making up ridiculous excuses for why you can't fuck me?"

"That mouth of yours needs to be fucked, too, I think."

"Promises, promises." She giggles as soon as the words tumble out of her mouth. It's so cute, I think I want to fucking marry her.

With a huge smile, I dip my head down to hers and press our lips together to taste the sweet sounds coming from her mouth. The kiss heats up fast, so I release her wrists in favour of touching her body. I move my hands up the outsides of her thighs that are grinding around me. She skates her hands down my back, pausing to grab my ass and pull me in tight against her centre.

Christ, she feels good. And I haven't even been inside her yet.

My hand slides between our groins and under her panties. When my fingertips brush over her folds, I find exactly what I hoped to find.

"Fucking soaked, mooi. Is this from last night or this morning?"

She moans against my lips. "Probably both."

"Goddamn right," I reply, taking her mouth hard while plunging my middle finger deep inside of her.

Jesus Christ. So wet. So ready. So tight and soft and, fuck, I need to be inside of her. My cock is a rigid stone of granite as it pushes against my boxers, practically rooting for her hole like an animal in heat.

I break our kiss and murmur against her lips, "Next time you want to blow me, make sure I'm awake to watch."

Allie moves her hands down to my dick, grabbing it firmly in her fist. "Please tell me you have a condom."

I bite my lip and mourn the thought of leaving her soft body long enough to go get a condom. But I am a fucking adult and leave I must. Pushing myself off the bed, I stride over to my jeans and fumble for the condom in my wallet. When I turn around, I smile because Allie has ditched her shirt and broekies and is lying on the bed naked like a damn dirty magazine model.

"What? No striptease like last time?" I ask, my mouth tilting up in a half-smile as I admire her luscious curves. "I jerked off to the image of you slipping out of that wet dress for fucking months, mooi."

An odd look flickers across her face, but she shakes it off and replies, "I tried to give you a striptease last night, but you were too busy rejecting me."

I laugh at her bullshit response. But instead of arguing with her, I grab the waistband of my boxers and slide them off. My cock springs out, long, thick, and proud. I roll the condom over the head and notice the hungry look in Allie's eyes as she watches the entire process in great fascination.

I crawl over top of her on the mattress, holding myself a foot above her face. "Preferring sober consent is not me rejecting you. And trust me when I tell you that I will make up for lost time right fucking now."

My head dips low and I bite her nipple like a savage, growling against her skin. She gasps from the onslaught, and it's an incredibly sexy sound that makes the condom feel really fucking tight. I move over to pay lavish attention to the other hardened nub, and she lifts her pelvis up to feel my wrapped cock against her tender flesh.

When my tip slides along her clit, we both still and our eyes lock.

"You ready to feel me, mooi?" I ask, dropping a soft kiss on her lips.

"Yes," she breathes, tightening her legs around my hips.

"This isn't another one-night stand," I warn, staring deep into her eyes and pressing my cock deeper into her folds.

seriousness shadows her lust-filled gaze as she silently nods. Then he reaches down and holds me right where I need to be, begging me to enter her.

So I do.

I press inside her wet, soft flesh, moving so slowly that both of us have to hold our breaths high up in our chests. Our mouths hang open as we stare at one another and her body adjusts to my size. When I feel her muscles pulsating around my thickness, her channel so fucking tight it's uncomfortable, I want to fucking roar in delicious agony.

Thankfully, Allie's wet enough for me to slide out. When I push back in, I go even farther and she nods urgently, her brows knitting together as she encourages me to move more.

As I throb inside of her, she becomes a wave of motion beneath me, rocking and rolling with every one of my thrusts. It's sexy as hell. Soon, her breaths turn to gasps, her gasps turn to moans. All her noises feverishly propel my body to move faster and faster inside of her.

When her moans grow too loud, I kiss her, plunging my tongue hard and fast into her mouth while she clings to me for dear life. The slap of our bodies meeting with every push echoes in the room like two hands clapping in an empty stadium. Her breaths become erratic as her body tenses all around me.

This woman is too easy. It's barely been five fucking minutes and I can already feel her orgasm coming. It's like a high-speed train tearing through a small town with no signs of stopping. And right now, I want to beat that fucking train to the finish line.

I thrust in sharp, and I can tell when I've found her G-spot because she digs her nails into my back and lets out a garbled cry. I pull back to watch her and see her eyes roll into the back of her head before they close. When her jaw drops and she lets out a silent scream from somewhere very deep inside of her, it's then that I feel it.

Her wetness.

It releases all over my cock and everything in her channel tightens around me, freezing me mid-thrust and making it impossible for me to move. Without warning, my own climax erupts, obviously not used to the vice-like grip her pussy is creating down below. I drop my head to her neck and tense for several seconds as I explode into the condom and feel her heart racing beneath my chest.

When I come to again, all I feel is the sticky wetness of our bodies..

It's fucking hot.

What I do to her—how she responds to me—doesn't get any fucking better than this. Either this woman's body was made for my cock, or she could make a shitload of money doing porn.

Allie

Roan and I shower together.

Let me repeat that.

Roan and I shower together!

Meaning, I get to rub soap all over his muscled body. Halfway through the shower, I can't help but drop down on my knees and take his beautiful cock in my mouth. He's hard and long and it looks so powerful, I want to feel it on my tongue. I've never had such an urge to suck a man's dick before, but the appreciative expression on Roan's face when I swallow makes it completely worth it.

When he yanks me up from the tiled floor and kisses me senseless under the hot stream of the shower, I actually physically pinch myself to make sure this is all truly happening. Who moves to London and dates a sexy athlete with muscles in places I didn't even know muscles could exist?

Apparently me—Alice Harris.

This move is either the most epic comeback in history, or the other shoe will drop any moment now and all the good things happening in my life will cease to exist.

Once we're clean, Roan and I wrap ourselves in white, fluffy towels and make our way back to my bedroom. I search my closet and find a clean pair of sheets that I definitely feel the need to put on my bed.

Roan grins at me like he's king of the world as he helps me put the fitted sheet on the bed. "It's nice to know some things never change."

I feel my cheeks flush as I yank down on the elastic corner and smooth out the top. I stand up and run a hand through my wet hair as I stammer out, "I, um, thought the last time when I…" My face burns with embarrassment because I am pretty much mortified, even though Roan told me he thought it was sexy when we were in the shower.

"…squirted," Roan finishes, his face completely at ease.

I prop my hands on my hips in annoyance. "Why is it so easy for you to say?"

He shrugs a bare, muscled shoulder. "I watch a lot of porn."

I laugh at his response and then narrow my eyes curiously at him while I spread out the top sheet. "Do you make all girls—"

"Squirt?" he finishes with wide eyes. "Hell no! My cock is fucking magic, but it's only ever been extra magical with you, mooi."

We refocus our attention back on the bed, tucking the bottom under the mattress. He straightens and stares at me for a moment. "Have you squirted with other men?"

"No!" I exclaim, hating the word and wishing there was another term to use. "Can we stop calling it that, please? I seriously hate that word. Let's call it…lemons."

"Lemons?" he volleys back.

"Yes," I reply with a sombre nod. "They're fresh and pretty and they make me feel happy."

"Okaaay." He stares at me like I'm a nut-job.

"And the answer is no. I have not lemon'd with other men."

Roan pulls the duvet off the bench at the end of my bed. "Not even your ex?" He watches carefully for my facial reaction, which is a giant cringe.

"No…God, no! I nicknamed him Ghost Penis after our breakup because that's about how it felt when we were together…Like you know he's there, but you can't feel him."

"Ouch," Roan says, watching me with great fascination. "But you were with him for a long time, right?"

"Five stupid years," I answer and flop myself onto the duvet and drape my arm over my forehead. "I can only chalk it up to being young and naïve. I didn't know that I could want more in my life, you know?"

He lies down beside me on his side, propping his head on his hand as he looks at me. "What kind of more?"

His question provokes a swirling tornado of thoughts because this "more" realisation is relatively new, only having formed when I decided to move to London.

"Like, since I moved to the States with my dad, I always just accepted what was given to me, even down to the family he created when he remarried. My stepsister was my best friend, but I realise now that, that wasn't by choice. It was by convenience.

"And when it came to Ghost Penis, he just happened to be the guy who asked me out in college whom I said yes to. The thought of breaking up with him because I wasn't madly in love seemed overly dramatic.

"But since coming here, I've watched my cousins interact with their spouses and each other, and it's crazy all the time. When they're all together, it's complete madness. They're always arguing and talking over each other, getting in fights about stupid things like whose piece of pie is bigger. Even Indie and Belle, who are best friends, mercilessly tease each other." She pauses with a fond smile while thinking about her Harris family. Based on the warmth in her expression, I can tell she really loves them.

"They all have this love-hate relationship that is so wonderfully real, it's refreshing. They may be annoyed by each other at times, but that candour they have makes it possible for them to love and respect each other through the supposed flaws. It made me realise that I want that kind of *more* in my life. More goals, more connection, more sex, more laughter…more craziness!" I look at Roan to gauge his reaction. "Do I sound crazy?"

"It's what you're going for, so I vote yes," he replies with a laugh.

I shove his chest and he captures my hand with his. We watch our fingers slide in between each other's for a moment before he says, "I think you deserve all the *more* you can find in life."

I feel a warming comfort in his words that bring a contented smile to my face. "So, what do you want out of life?"

He purses his lips off to the side and, while playing with my hand, he answers, "I want to feel content, I guess. I want my mom to stop worrying about money. I want my sisters to stop worrying about appearances. And I want to stop worrying about my career."

"Do you worry about your career a lot?"

He nods. "I have to. That injury to my ankle was scary and I'm such a bubble player as it is. I'm no young buck anymore. If I want to make it in soccer, the time is right fucking now." He flattens on his back, staring up at the ceiling with a weighted look on his face.

"Well, the team moving to Premier League helps, right?"

"Yes," he confirms, his jaw muscles ticking along with his thoughts. "And I'm going to prove myself next season. I'm going to train harder and keep my head on straight. The next step for me is a brand endorsement. That's been my goal for ages."

"Is that why you look so good on paper?" I ask knowingly. I work in public relations, so I know better than most that the best way to get a big, well-known brand to sponsor you is to never have skeletons in your closet. And the fact that what I did to him could be completely damning to his career is in no way lost on me.

He nods. "I don't fuck up in my life because I can't afford to fuck up. People depend on me. That's why I don't hang out in clubs and take random women home. I stay out of the gossip rags as much as possible. I'm not saying I'm a saint. I do have needs after all. But typically, if I bring a woman to my bed, I've gotten to know her enough to know that she'll be staying for a few repeat sessions. And when we part ways after a few weeks, there won't be drama."

His words pierce through me because he has clearly worked hard his entire life to not put himself in socially dangerous situations, and one night of trusting me could ruin so much for him. He protects himself by being a serial dater with an end date. Judging by what I read in his file, I know that's true. He's dated some gorgeous models and even a sports reporter. High-profile people who would certainly seem like a long-term thing. But with every single one, they eventually parted ways after only a month. Always amicable. No drama. Just like he said.

So, why would I be any different? Relief comforts me a bit with that realisation. If this is in fact temporary, what good would come from telling him about the sex video? Surely one little secret can't hurt our short-term relationship that much.

CHAPTER 15

Allie

I T'S BEEN FIVE DAYS SINCE I STEALTHILY SNUCK ROAN OUT OF THE townhouse. Since then, he has stealthily snuck back in every single night with Camden and Indie being none the wiser. Granted, they are busy with their own lives and it's easy for me to go a few days without seeing them, but I like the exhilarating feeling of hiding everything. I feel like I'm living a double life this week.

I go to work and take orders from Niall like usual, I get home, take a shower, and make myself dinner before Roan calls and asks to come over. Some might say what he's doing is a booty call, but I'm one hundred percent okay with it because the orgasms I have are worth any crass label our situation might be considered. And telling Camden and Indie what's going on sounds like a horrible idea, so I continue on with the booty calls!

Today, though, while I was at work, Roan texted and said he wanted to cook dinner for me tonight. And since cooking at my place might raise suspicions, he invited me over to his. My belly is full of butterflies as I change out of my work clothes and into a flirty blue floral sundress. June is just around the corner and, like my semi-relationship with Roan, London is heating up. The humidity here reminds me of Chicago, but I marvel over the fact that I have yet to feel the least bit homesick since I arrived here a few weeks ago.

I freshen up my makeup and slip on a sexy pair of blue lace panties before heading downstairs to call a cab. Camden is walking through the front door from a run as I descend the final steps.

"Allie!" he states cheerily as he pulls off his phone that's strapped to his bicep. He pops his earbuds out and pulls the bottom of his white T-shirt up to wipe the sweat from his brow. "I haven't seen you all week! Where are you off to?"

My face flushes with guilt because I've been purposefully avoiding Cam and Indie for fear of them asking questions about Roan after Saturday night. With how much we've seen each other this week, I wasn't sure I'd have a very good poker face.

"I, um, was just going to go hang out with some friends," I stammer.

"Friends?" Camden repeats, gesturing for me to follow him through the living room. He pauses at the accent table by the fireplace and taps on the glass of the aquarium that houses Snowflake. "Hiya, mate. Have you been fed today?"

"Yes, I fed him earlier," I answer, hesitating in the foyer and desperately wishing I could ignore his request to chat and bolt out the door.

But I remind myself that I am a guest in his home. A guest living here rent-free even after I begged and pleaded for them to charge me. So, like the mature adult I am, I clunk my wedge sandals over the beautifully restored wood floor and follow Camden into the massive gourmet-style kitchen.

He opens the refrigerator and grabs a water bottle, offering one to me before propping himself on the white marble island. "Specs is out shopping with Belle for baby stuff," he states before taking a drink. "I don't think she's quite ready to buy nursery items yet, but Belle is apparently in her…Oh, what did Tanner call it?" He pauses and scratches his head as he tries to recall and then snaps his fingers. "Nesting period!"

I nod and smile, positioning myself on the opposite side of the island. "I don't know much about babies, but I have heard of that. Mother hens want to get their house ready for the baby bird on the way."

"Speaking of baby birds," he says in his best father-like voice, flashing me a warm smile. "Who are these friends you're meeting up with and what time will you be home? Since you are currently my ward, it's my job to keep a close watch on you."

I laugh at his serious face and reply in a mocking tone, "Are you my new daddy now?"

He chuckles and shrugs his shoulders. "Perhaps it's good practice for me since I'm going to become one very soon."

We both laugh but then the room goes silent and I realise that Camden is still literally waiting for an answer. "It's just some people from work." *I do work for the team, so it's not a total lie.*

He nods and eyes me curiously. "How did you get on with DeWalt the other night? Was he a gentleman when he brought you home?"

I blink rapidly for a moment because just hearing his name in the presence of Camden sends a physical reaction through my body. "Yes," I chirp, my voice tight in my throat. "Total gentleman." *Not so much of a gentleman the past few nights, though.*

He nods thoughtfully. "Good. Gareth has it in his head that you fancy DeWalt. I told him he is mental. You have better sense than that."

I frown at his curious response. "What's wrong with Roan exactly?"

Camden barks out a laugh. "Nothing in particular. He's a decent enough bloke I suppose. But you do PR for the team, and that makes things complicated. I can tell you firsthand how hard it is to date someone you're working with. Indie and I met in a doctor-patient situation, and what started off innocent enough soon turned into a shit-storm for both of us when real feelings got involved." He pins me with a serious look and adds, "Trust me when I tell you that no amount of professionalism matters when real love enters the picture."

"Love!" I sputter. "Camden, I appreciate your advice, but I can assure you that there is nothing like that happening between me and Roan DeWalt."

He gives me a skeptical look. "Good. I'd say you have enough footballers in your life." He winks and hops off the counter, glugging the rest of his water all at once before throwing the container into the recycling bin.

He moves to walk out of the kitchen but pauses as he stares at me for a moment. "You coming to Sunday dinner this week?"

I nod. "Yes, for sure. Sorry I missed the last one. I was just over-tired, I guess."

His mouth tips up into a half-smile. "All right. Love you a latte, Allie." He ruffles my hair before he leaves, and I exhale a huge sigh of relief when he's gone.

I appreciate the brotherly advice, but Camden is way off the mark here. Roan and I are definitely not on our way to love. We're just having a bit of fun. Nothing more.

Roan's house is adorable. Then again, I think everything is adorable in London. The charm and character of the older homes they have here are so different than the ones in Chicago.

I walk up to the navy front door and don't even have a chance to knock before it's pulled open. Roan is standing on the threshold, his light brown eyes wide and excited. My eyes drink in his sexy appearance, causing my insides to squeeze in on themselves. The past few nights, he has come over in joggers and a T-shirt. Not that I'm complaining. The man could wear a jumpsuit and manage to look amazing.

But tonight, he looks like he's put in some effort and it's certainly appreciated. His dark hair looks freshly cut and he's dressed in a fitted grey thermal Henley with the sleeves pushed up to reveal his tan, muscled forearms. His dark denim jeans are fitted around his thighs, revealing the outline of his quad muscles, and I'm not hating it one bit.

"Jesus Christ, Lis," his voice husks in his delicious South African accent as his eyes zero in on my chest. He looks around the street at a few people passing by and jerks me by the hand into the doorway. "Fuck the barbeque. I'm eating you for dinner."

He wraps me in his arms, his lips crashing down on mine as his hands move from my waist to my ass. He double squeezes each of my butt cheeks, pulling me against his groin as his tongue plunges deep into my mouth. It's a fast, needy kiss, full of passion and power, and I realise that this is what makes it impossible for me to stay away from Roan DeWalt. The way he just *takes* at the exact moments I want to give is the epitome of sexy.

And truly, giving back is the hospitable thing to do. I wrap my hands around his neck, wrestling my tongue with his and breathing in the fresh scent of his body that I'm quickly growing attached to. I just saw him last night, but in less than twenty-four hours, I somehow managed to miss him. Is that fucked-up or what? To have this desperate, frenetic need to unite our bodies on a daily basis surely isn't normal, is it?

As the kiss heats up, I contemplate wrapping my legs around him and begging him to take me to his bedroom for a quickie before dinner. Thankfully, reality crashes in with a loud, clearing of the throat.

Our mouths break apart and we look up the staircase to see Mac standing awkwardly at the landing. He's scratching the back of his neck with a sheepish look on his face. "I'm really trying hard to give yous some privacy, but you're kind of blocking the door."

Roan's body shakes with silent laughter as he releases my ass and pulls me into the foyer. "Get out of here, you big goon," he states jokingly.

Mac clomps down the stairs with a grin on his face, grabbing his keys off the hook by the door. He shoots me a wink. "Nice to see you again, Allie."

"Nice to see you, too, Mac," I reply, wiping at my lips because I'm certain that my gloss is smeared all over my face. "Where are you heading?"

A pleased smile touches his lips. "I'm going to see a film with Freya."

"Like a date?" I ask excitedly, thinking the two of them together is an unexpected pairing but kind of perfect in a lot of ways.

"No, we're just mates. I think she still mostly hates me, but we have similar taste in movies and telly, so she seems to be tolerating me for whatever reason."

I nod and smile knowingly. "Well, have fun then."

"You, too." He waggles his eyebrows at Roan and then leaves, closing the door behind him.

"Where were we?" Roan asks, moving in to assault my mouth again.

"Show me your place first," I state, pressing my hands to his chest for some space. "Or were you planning to keep me in the foyer all night?"

He purses his lips to the side and looks around. "I think I could fuck you against this wall quite easily."

I roll my eyes as he smiles and grabs my hand, leading me up the stairs. "Living room, dining room, kitchen." He points to a door just off the kitchen. "Mac's room." He rounds a corner and points up another flight of stairs. "My room. Let's have a closer look, shall we?"

I laugh and pull him back into the kitchen. "You're supposed to be cooking for me."

"I was until you showed up in that sexy dress with your nipples out for the world to see. Do you ever wear a bra when you go out, mooi?"

I frown and cover my breasts. "I wear bras…sometimes."

He points accusingly at my chest. "You haven't worn a bra on either of our two dates, leaving your breasts out for everyone to see."

My shoulders tense from his observation. "Well, it just depends on the outfit, and this happens to be a no-bra sort of dress."

He nods and leans himself against the counter with his arms crossed, the veins running up his skin on full display. "Believe me, I'm not complaining. Nor would your cab driver, people you pass on the sidewalk. Fucking Mac." He gestures toward the door.

"Are you *jealous*?" I ask, my posture stiffening as I position myself against the opposite counter like I'm preparing to face-off.

"Jealous of people seeing your nipples?" he asks, his brows risen like what I said is humourous. "Fuck yes, I'm jealous."

Trigger. Instant, bright red, and very angry trigger.

I cross my arms over my chest defensively and reply, "Then maybe we should stop all this now."

He pushes himself off the counter and stands up straight, rubbing the back of his neck in shock. "What do you mean by that? Stop us?"

I prop my hands on my hips. "I'm not looking for someone to be overprotective of me. Or possessive. Or jealous. I had someone like that for five years and it made me miserable. And it was total bullshit because the same rules didn't apply to me."

"What rules?" he snaps, dropping his hands to his sides.

I bark out a laugh as flashbacks of all the fucked-up shit in my relationship creep into my mind. "My ex went nuts whenever I so much as looked at a guy. He even quit inviting me to work parties because he didn't want other men to notice me. But apparently he could speak to or flirt with whomever he liked, even going so far as to screwing my stepsister. So I'm sorry, but if you're the jealous type, then you and I are a bad idea because I'm not putting myself in a one-sided situation like that again. I refuse."

"This isn't one-sided," Roan retorts, shoving the sleeves of his shirt up to ready himself for a fight. "If you and I are dating, you can absolutely tell me when something I do bothers you. Hell, you can tell me what to do if you'd like!"

"What are you talking about?" I ask, my voice wavering.

He shrugs. "If you don't want me to talk to women, I won't."

"That's stupid," I reply, rolling my eyes.

"It's not stupid," he says, taking a step toward me. "You've been burned, so I'm willing to do whatever it takes for you to feel comfortable with me, mooi."

I open my mouth to respond, but no words come out. He's just made me realise how awful I would feel if I saw him out with another woman after the last few days we've spent together.

"So if you need me to not speak to other women to help establish trust between us, I'll do that for you. Gladly. I can't imagine how fucked your head is after that kind of betrayal, so accept what I'm offering." He takes another step closer. "But if you think I'm not going to get jealous of people who get to see those beautiful nipples of yours, then you're dead wrong. I'm a man, and I have a right to be jealous of people who are undoubtedly having sexual thoughts about you."

He looks down and eyes my breasts with a hungriness that has me taking a step away from the countertop to stand up straight and meet his power toe to toe. I jut out my chin and open my mouth to reply with some sort of counter-argument that should be alive inside of me, but our close proximity seems to have sucked out all my good sense.

With a wicked look in his eyes, he reaches out and runs the tip of his finger along my breast. His digit swirls in a circular motion around my nipple, causing it to harden even more beneath the tight fabric. I inhale a shaky breath, hating how my body is reacting to his touch when I was trying to take a stand only twenty seconds ago.

His voice is deep and husky when he continues, "However, I don't have a right to tell you what to wear or hide you from the world, mooi. No one should. But I do have the right to calmly tell you how I feel about it. If I don't, it defeats the whole purpose." His finger slides over my other breast, teasing the flesh and eliciting more reaction from my traitorous hormones.

"What purpose?" I ask, my voice cracking with arousal.

"The purpose of turning you on." He slowly splays his palm out over my breast and squeezes me in a way that has my body arching into his touch. My pelvis is practically begging for his fingers to go lower. He leans in and whispers against my lips, "Jealousy is epic foreplay if used properly. Because if I tell you I want to fucking murder any man who lays eyes on you since you're mine, you can't tell me it doesn't make your broekies wet."

He pulls the strap of my dress down and presses a kiss on my exposed shoulder. Goosebumps erupt all over my skin and my insides clench at his naughty words.

"I can smell your arousal from here, mooi," he says, sliding his hand down my body and reaching under the hem of my dress. He slowly glides his fingers up the inside of my thigh. His bare skin on my bare skin causing my entire body to catch fire. "Jealousy can be fucking sexy when there's trust attached to it."

His touch reaches the apex of my thighs, and I let out a tiny moan when he presses his fingers over my panties along my centre.

He smiles down at me. "Damp, just as I suspected."

With a deep growl of desire, he presses his other hand on my belly and backs me up until I'm against the kitchen counter.

"What are you doing?" I ask, my voice breathy and uneven.

"I'm showing you that it's okay to like this."

He dips his head and captures my lips with his, thrusting his tongue deep into my mouth. At the same time, he grabs the crotch of my panties and slips his fingers past the barrier to touch my bare clit. The instant his skin touches mine, I have to bite back a cry of pleasure because it's exactly where I want him. I want him there and everywhere. I want his cock inside of me, and I want to come like I've been coming every day this week.

"Jesus, you're so wet for me," he murmurs against my lips, thrusting his fingers as deep inside of me as he can go. I gyrate against his palm with desperate need before he pulls out of me and begins to yank my panties down my hips. Then he hoists me up onto the counter and spreads my legs wide.

My eyes flicker open, remembering where I am and what we're supposed to be doing. "I thought you were making me dinner," I state nervously, my body feeling like a ticking time bomb, ready to explode. It's not normal to need someone this much.

Staring straight into my eyes, he replies, "I'm going to have you for my first course, if you don't mind."

Lowering to his knees, he shoves my dress up with his large, masculine hands. With one sharp inhale of breath, his mouth is on me, between my legs and on my tender flesh that is practically sobbing with need.

He licks and sucks and works my clit over to within an inch of my life. His tongue swirls and flattens, and he occasionally brings his fingers into play to fuck me so perfectly, I can't sit still. My wedge sandals prod into his shoulders, my hands are frantically grabbing at anything near me just to make sure that this entire act doesn't disintegrate me into nothingness.

My reaction seems to please him because I feel his rumble of approval between my thighs. He grabs my hips and jerks me harder onto his face, his fingers digging into my flesh like he wants to permanently mark me as his forever.

Maybe jealousy *can* be hot.

It was never hot with my ex. It was ugly, and it made him look insecure and weak. Roan is none of those things. He's strong and confident, and he's claiming his territory with his mouth.

When he sharply clamps down on my clit with a hard, punishing suck, my climax tears through me. My cries are so loud that I'm sure the neighbours can hear everything. But it's not something I could stop. The reaction my body has to his touch is involuntary and completely out of my control.

Roan does nothing to quiet me, continuing his assault between my legs until the spasms of my orgasm are complete. He pulls back from my aching pussy and stands up to look at me with his darkened, lust-filled gaze. Without warning, he kisses me, swirling his tongue deep in my mouth so I can taste the saltiness of my release.

His voice is hoarse as he breaks away and says, "That's what my jealousy tastes like."

"Point taken," I say, my head spinning in my post-orgasmic state. "Goal one goes to DeWalt."

Chuckling, he bends over to pick up my panties. "Since I won our first official argument, I get to keep these." He tucks the lingerie in his pocket.

When he moves to walk away, I reach out and grab his shirt, pulling him back and kissing him with need. I press my hand over his straining erection.

"Want me to go for a second goal?" He smiles a dirty smile against my lips.

"Um, yes," I reply and make quick work of his jeans.

Without another word, he tugs his shirt off and pulls down the straps of my tiny dress while I dig my fingers into his beautiful muscled chest. The tip of his cock presses against my bare body when he suddenly pulls back, shaking his head aggressively. "Fuck, I need to go upstairs for a condom."

My breaths are coming hard and fast, my orgasm buzz still coursing through my veins. All I want is to continue riding the wave. "When was the last time you were checked?" I pant, my voice raw with desire. "I had to have a physical before I moved here, so I know I'm good."

He blinks back at me, his tongue slicking out to wet his lips as he racks his brain. "I was checked a few months ago, but I've never not used a condom."

"Okay then," I say, nodding eagerly.

"Okay what?"

"I trust you, Roan. You're the most trustworthy player on the entire Bethnal Green team. I think we'll be fine."

He pauses for a moment, thinking over what I just said like he might not actually agree with it.

"Or go get a condom if that's one of your rules!" I exclaim, not sounding angry by any means. Just impatient.

"It is one of my rules…" His voice trails off as he eyes my breasts with a fiery look that I swear could burn me alive. "Fuck it, I want you," he growls and he's back between my legs, pulling me to the edge of the counter and thrusting into me hard, fast, and deep.

He stills inside of me, his head dropping down on my shoulder, and he groans out the sexiest sound I've ever heard coming from a man. "Jesus Christ, mooi. You're going to ruin me." He pulls out and pushes in again, making more noises and his muscles turning to granite stones beneath my hands. "You feel so fucking good."

"So do you," I gasp, my legs wrapping tightly around his hips, squeezing him to me as I adjust to his size, relishing how perfectly he stretches me. "So fucking good."

"So fucking good," he repeats.

Whatever is said after that is forgotten because most of it becomes unintelligible as we fuck like we've never fucked before. Angry, passionate, emotive, overzealous, wet, frantic fucking that has me seeing stars before another orgasm rips through me.

Roan is definitely right. Jealousy can be an awesome thing… when it comes from him.

We clean up and finally head outside to the small garden behind Roan's house. It's a cute little oasis of greenery and dim lighting that becomes really romantic once the sun begins to set. Roan looks sexy as he mans the barbeque and brushes the chicken with marinade while talking about the various foods that are made in South Africa.

I talk about Chicago-style pizza and how the sauce goes on

the top, and he says he hopes to visit Chicago someday to try it. It's nice. It's easy. It's impressive how we were arguing when I first arrived and now we're back on the same page, continuing to get to know one another.

Once the food is plated, we sit down at the small patio table and Roan pours me a glass of white wine. "So, when are we going to tell your family about us?" he asks.

I laugh and shake my head. "I pick never."

"Tomorrow then?" he asks, shooting me a wink and taking a bite of his salad.

"No. Jeez, what is with you?" I ask, my eyes wide. "Things are going awesome here. Why are you such an all or nothing kind of guy?"

He smirks, not the least bit put off by my refusal. "I don't half-ass things, Lis."

I swallow my bite of chicken and take a sip of wine. "But you don't know what you're asking by inviting the Harris family into our business. They aren't going to make it easy for you."

"I think the ladies are on my side, though," Roan says, sitting back in his chair with a pleased look on his face. "Didn't you say it was Sloan who got you the jersey with my name on it?"

I shake my head, still mortified that I was wearing Roan's name on my back and didn't even know. "I have a feeling Vi was the true ringleader there. She is like this adorable little demonic puppet-master, secretly pulling strings from behind the curtain."

Roan chuckles. "I think she wants us together. She's set us up twice now."

I shrug my shoulders but can feel Roan watching me. "What?" I ask, hitting him with an annoyed look.

"Are you going to Sunday dinner at Vaughn's this week?" he asks pointedly.

I roll my eyes. "Um, yes."

He nods curtly. "We can tell them then."

"What?"

"Bring me as your guest and we'll tell them then."

"That's a horrible idea."

"No it's not. They'll all be there, so we can tell everyone at once."

"Have you been to one of those dinners before?" I ask, sitting back in my chair and abandoning my food.

"I have not, but I'm not intimidated."

"You should be because they are complete and utter madness. Crazy, loud, over-crowded, and charged with way too much energy in a small space. It's a bad, bad idea to tell them about us at Sunday dinner."

"That's fine," he says with a nod, seemingly accepting my response. He tosses his napkin on his plate and adds, "We just won't have sex until we tell them."

My eyes fly wide. "What?"

He shrugs. "I won't have sex with you until you find a time when we can tell them we're dating."

"Why would you do that to yourself?" I ask, my face twisting up in confusion. "I think what we just did in the kitchen kind of took us to a new level that's worth exploring."

"Call me old-fashioned," he says matter-of-factly, "but I don't want to date my manager's niece or my teammates' cousin behind their backs. It's a respect thing."

"You're right. It's definitely more respectful for us to announce that we're fucking over Sunday dinner."

Roan rolls his eyes and chuckles at my phrasing. "I don't think we should use those exact words."

I push my plate away. "You're crazy. You wouldn't withhold sex. You're a guy. You thrive on sex."

"I think you thrive on sex with me," he states with a dirty smirk. "More than you realise."

I open my mouth to argue but promptly close it and turn to look away with a laugh. "I can go without sex from you."

"All right then. We're officially taking a break."

"Fine," I snap. "What an awesome night. Our first fight, our first makeup sex, and our first breakup!"

He laughs at my little outburst, and it irritates the living shit out of me. I get up and grab both of our plates and state loudly through clenched teeth, "We'd better clean up then because there apparently won't be any sex for dessert!"

I can feel him following close behind me as I take the plates inside. I set the dishes in the sink and suddenly feel his heat wash over my back as he reaches around and grabs the soap.

"Sorry. Just needing a bit of soap," he says against my neck, and a riot of goosebumps take flight as he presses his groin into me in an obnoxious way that is not at all conducive to doing dishes.

He turns on the faucet and squirts some soap into the warm water before his hands land on mine, which are currently splayed out on the edges of the sink.

"Mind helping me?" he asks, taking my hands and plunging them into the hot, soapy water.

Need pools in my belly as he uses my hands to wash the first plate, his fingers sliding between mine in sexy, slippery strokes. As he reaches down for the next plate, I feel his thick cock pressing against my backside.

I lie my head back on his chest. "See?" I husk, glancing over my shoulder and down at his erection. "You're already struggling."

"So are you, mooi," he says with a smirk, grinding against me. "And don't forget I have your panties, so pretty soon you're going to feel that wetness slide down your legs."

"Oh, am I?"

He nods and presses his lips to my shoulder. "It might even be a little bit of me."

That thought sends a shiver up my spine and the need inside of me grows.

His breath tickles my skin as he whispers in my ear, "I *could* help you with that feeling that's stirring inside of you. But instead, you're going to have to suffer through it all the way home tonight."

"I'm going home?" I ask, turning on my heel to face him.

He remains flush against my body, his hands caging me in. "I mean, you're welcome to sleep here, but you're not getting my cock out of these trousers again."

His dirty talk has my eyes flashing to his groin, which is literally straining behind his jeans. I clear my throat and reply, "Well that's good because you're not getting these breasts out of this dress again."

He bites his lip and glances down at my chest. "You're not going to win this battle, Lis. I'm an athlete. We're made of stronger stuff than most."

I roll my eyes, annoyed that he has me right where he wants me. Jutting out my chin, I press my finger to his chest and say, "Well, I'm a Harris. You don't even want to know what we're made of."

CHAPTER

Roan

"THIS IS ALL YOUR FAULT," ALLIE HISSES, GRIPPING MY HAND so hard it might actually hurt if I wasn't such a manly man.

"You agreed to this," I reply with a laugh as we stand outside of Vaughn Harris' house in Chigwell, where the infamous Harris Brothers grew up.

Allie turns her crazy eyes at me as the sun slices through her blonde hair, making her look like some sort of deranged angel in a pretty pink dress. "Well, I didn't *want* to agree to this! But being a Harris apparently means I'm a weak, sex-crazed, nut-job who gets one taste of a good orgasm and can't function in society without a daily dose of it."

I beam happily down at her and say, "This is going to be fun."

"This is going to be a nightmare!" she exclaims through clenched teeth.

God help me, her adorable manic state makes my cock twitch as I pull her up the gravel lane toward the brown brick mansion with a bright yellow double door entry. It doesn't look so scary. It looks kind of cheery actually.

I knock and Tanner appears a few seconds later, slurping jam out of something resembling a rolled-up pancake. He looks me up and down, zeroing in on my hand holding Allie's. "You are so fucked, DeWalt," he states flatly and turns on his heel to walk inside.

With an ominous feeling, we follow Tanner down a long, marbled hallway and turn left through double doors that lead into a huge gourmet kitchen.

Allie frowns, looking at the butcher block countertop full of empty barstools. "Where is everybody?"

"Warming up," Tanner replies and head nods for us to follow him toward the back door beyond the large kitchen table.

"Warming up?" I ask curiously, glancing through the wall of windows that overlook a garden.

Tanner lets out a maniacal laugh and steps back so we can walk outside first. I'm not sure I like what I see.

For starters, the garden chairs are pulled away from the patio tables and line the large, flat, grassy yard. Seated in those chairs are Vaughn, Vi, Sloan, Poppy, Indie, and Belle. They are all hunkered down with drinks and snacks, like they're preparing for a theatre show. I would guess the kids are going to put on a performance, but Vi's daughter, Rocky, is busy colouring with chalk on the patio and Poppy is busy bouncing her twins on her lap. The view of them isn't what's bad. It's what their chairs are facing that has my mouth going dry.

Situated in the middle of the yard is Gareth, Camden, Booker, and Hayden, and they are all wearing full-blown soccer practice gear. They're standing in front of a recreation-sized goal net and appear to be working with Hayden on his kicking technique. Tanner jogs past me to join them.

"What's going on?" Allie asks, her voice wary as her grip on my hand tightens.

"Oh my God, they're here!" Poppy squeals, shooting up out of her chair with both her twin boys. They look big enough in her arms that they could tip her over. "This is happening!" she peals in a sing-songy voice as the other women look up at us with wide, excited eyes.

"What's happening?" I ask, embarrassed as fuck by the tremble in my voice. It's not so much seeing the soccer gear that has me nervous. It's the fact that this is obviously going to be a lesson on how I'm to treat their cousin, or else.

The guys turn their icy gazes at me and stare me down like I've committed some sort of war crime.

Suddenly, Vi is in my face. "It's going to be okay," she says soothingly, rubbing my arms in an odd, motherly way. "This is just how they show their love."

They begin walking toward me, and I swear it's a ridiculous, slow motion movement like you see in movies. Tanner is staring off into space, so Camden gives him a shove to get him moving along with all of them.

"Are they wearing shin guards?" I ask, glancing down and seeing they aren't just wearing guards but their spikes as well.

"What do you mean by, 'it's how they show their love?'" Allie asks, her voice sounding terrified as she stares her cousin in the eyes.

Vi giggles nervously and looks over her shoulder. "Well, this is what you'd call a Harris Shakedown."

"A what?" I ask in confusion.

"A Harris Shakedown," Vi repeats with a playful punch to my shoulder. "You'll be fine. Just don't show them any weakness. They're kind of like sharks. If they smell blood, they'll go in for the kill."

"Vi!" Allie whines, her voice a shrill, high pitch. "You said you knew how to handle them!"

"I do!" she retorts, looking over her shoulder again. "This is them handled. I got them to do it football style, which is much better than the alternative."

"What was the alternative?" I'm almost afraid to ask.

"Well, I'm not sure. The last one that I recall involved some stalking and sort of a street fight threat. But this is much better because there are rules in football. They can't just punch you in the guts if you're playing football."

165

"Jesus Christ," I murmur.

The next thing I know, Vi is pulling Allie away from me to make room for her brothers to approach.

From left to right is Tanner, Booker, Gareth, and Camden. They all turn their eyes to slits and give me an intimidating head nod.

My gaze swerves to the left and my eyes land on Hayden, who lifts his hand cheerily. "Hiya!" he says and Tanner turns to whack him in the stomach. Hayden winces and then recovers, doing his best to give me the same menacing glower the rest of the guys are shooting me.

Gareth steps forward so we're toe to toe. "DeWalt." He says my name flatly, like it tastes bad on his tongue.

My eyes flicker side to side for a second before I smile back at him. "Hey there, Gareth. How's the wife and kids?" I ask flippantly.

He tilts his head. "I heard what you did to my cousin."

"What I did to her?" I retort, choking on a laugh. *If he only really knew what I've done to her.*

"He didn't *do* anything to me!" Allie says, shaking loose from Vi and coming to stand between us. "We're just dating! That's it. No crimes were committed. I didn't even want you guys to know about us, but he basically sex-threatened me into telling you."

Gareth, Tanner, Camden, and Booker all have murderous looks on their faces…and they are directed at me. Hayden still looks mostly ambivalent.

"That is not how it sounds," I state, lifting my hands innocently.

"No! Like…I mean he wouldn't give me sex until we told you guys!" Allie stammers, trying to right her wrong, but it's not exactly helping.

I wince and gently place my hands on her shoulders. "Thanks for the help, Lis, but maybe just go back over by Vi."

She nods, pulling her lip into her mouth and chewing on it nervously like she immediately regrets everything she just said. She retreats to Vi's arms, and Vi rubs her hair soothingly.

Gareth cuts warning eyes at me. "I don't know what sex threatening is, DeWalt, but it involves my cousin, so that means I don't like it."

I roll my eyes. "I would hope you don't like it. She's your cousin."

"Is this a joke to you?" Gareth snaps, his eyes glacial.

I huff out an exasperated noise. "Will you please stop acting like we're in the middle of some goddamned mobster scene right now? We're athletes, not criminals. I'm dating your cousin. So what?"

"So what?" Camden cuts in, taking a step forward to stand by Gareth. "You have to prove yourself if you want to date her."

"How?" I retort with a mocking tone.

"The only way we know how," Camden replies. "On the grass."

I eye their clothes. "I didn't bring my gear."

"We have gear for you," Tanner states, stroking his beard like he's a villain.

I shake my head, annoyed by how quickly things have changed between me and my fellow striker. I shrug my shoulders. "Fine. Let's get on with it then."

The ladies cheer victoriously, but Allie's voice raises above them. "Uncle Vaughn, are you seriously going to let them do this? What if someone gets injured?"

Vaughn adjusts the baby in his arms that I realise is Gareth and Sloan's little one whom I met at the boutique last week. "I'm just here in the Grandpa capacity I'm afraid. No coaching involved. Thankfully we have a couple of doctors in the family."

Belle and Indie clink their lemonade glasses as they continue to watch the scene and pop snacks into their mouths.

I turn my attention back to the brothers. "So, what are the stakes?"

"This is just a friendly," Gareth answers, his voice deep and ominous. "A little three on three."

"All right," I reply knowingly. "Who's on my team?"

Hayden takes a step forward and winces as he raises his hand. "Sorry, mate. I don't really play football at all, so I'm afraid they've set you up to lose."

"Great," I murmur, rolling my shoulders to loosen the tightness that has formed.

Booker walks forward next. "I may be a keeper but, unlike you, I know how to score properly."

"Twice!" Poppy peals from behind us, juggling their twins in her arms as proof.

Booker smiles a boyish smile at her that makes me want to punch him.

Hayden claps me on the back. "Cheer up, mate. If I could survive a Harris Shakedown, then so can you."

Several minutes later, I stride out of the house in borrowed soccer gear and make my way to the centre of the grass where the guys are standing in a circle. I clear my throat, and they make an opening to reveal a small brunette girl who can't even be twelve years old yet.

"And who are you exactly?" I ask, eyeing her collared referee shirt.

"I'm Sophia," she says with narrowed eyes as she sticks a silver whistle into her mouth. She points at Gareth and adds around the metal between her teeth, "That's my dad."

"How old are you?"

She drops the whistle out of her mouth. "Old enough to red flag you."

The sidelines erupt with laughter as I frown down at the little girl. "Fair enough."

"We're going to play a clean game today, gentlemen," Sophia

states, her eyes serious as she stares up at all of us towering over her. "No cheap shots and no offsides. We may be in the off-season, but your bodies are your temples. Remember that."

"And take your shirts off!" a voice catcalls from the sidelines. I look over to see Belle laughing hysterically with Indie.

Vi looks over at her, nose wrinkled. "Too far."

"What?" Belle asks with a shrug of her shoulders. "They're not *my* brothers. And by the way, I'm hormonal!"

"You heard my wife," Tanner says with a grin. "Let's give our ladies a show!"

Tanner ditches his shirt and, to my surprise, the rest of the brothers do, too. They all look ridiculous, but evidently being a Harris Brother means they don't give a shit. So, I follow suit and lose mine. My eyes connect with Allie, who's doing her best to hide her amusement as her eyes drink in my entire body.

I walk over to take my place on the sidelines near her. I point straight at her and say, "You're lucky you're worth it."

That makes her smile grow, and I can't help but think I'd do this and a lot more to see that look on her face.

Sophia blows the whistle and we're off.

Hayden kicks off the ball, directing a pass right away toward Booker like he can't get the ball away fast enough. Gareth flies in out of nowhere and instantly steals it away from Booker with very little effort. He turns to drive the ball back toward the net and switches tracks to play defence against Tanner, whose moves I am able to anticipate from playing with him on the pitch.

What I don't anticipate is how easily Camden gives Tanner what he needs. The two of them are always in the right place at the right fucking time. When Cam takes a shot that is blocked by Booker, Tan picks up the rebound and shoots it in the net with great ease.

The twins do a victory dance that involves Tanner busting into a rendition of the robot. He taps Camden on the head and, like an oiled tin man, Cam busts out his best robot moves, too. Their antics even carry over to Mr. Always Serious Gareth, who taps Sophia and she joins in as well.

"All right," I groan, pointing at Sophia, who's giggling and roboting. "That's obvious favouritism."

She shakes her head. "Score a goal and maybe I'll victory dance with you, too." She winks and takes off back to the middle of the grass.

"Hayden!" Vi screams from the sidelines as we get back into position. "You have to do something, love. You can't just run around out there with no purpose!"

"I'm trying!" he roars back, agitated. "I can't even keep up with them!"

"Well, run faster!"

"They're professional fucking footballers!"

Vi's eyes go wide and she presses her hands over Rocky's ears. "Language!"

Hayden stops jogging and props his hands on his hips. "Bunny, I love you, but you cannot sideline coach me right now or I am going to come over there and spank you."

Vi pulls her lips into her mouth to hide an amused reaction that is rather odd. Vaughn seems equally disturbed, and I hope he's not thinking about the nature of their bedroom antics like I am.

Speaking of which, I haven't spanked Allie in a while either. Now that that's on my mind, I'm struggling to focus on the task at hand.

I shake my head to clear away my wayward thoughts as we resume our match. The ball is mine this time, and Gareth defends me like we're at the World Cup instead of in a garden at a home in Chigwell.

Booker does his best to help me, but Camden and Tanner have double-teamed him, leaving Hayden wide open because they've given up all hope that he's worth anything.

Finally, when I can't seem to make any progress past Gareth, I pass the ball over to Hayden, who's standing five feet from the goal.

He stops the pass, his eyes flying wide in triumph. But his expression turns to horror when Gareth, Camden, and Tanner all tear after him in a dead sprint.

"Shoot it, Hayden!" I shout and hear Booker shouting the same thing. "Shoot it in the net!"

Hayden hesitates, obviously sorting through the limited soccer knowledge he has so he can make a clear shot.

"Just kick the bloody thing!" Vi screams.

Hayden snaps out of his thoughts and kicks the ball just before he's trampled by his brothers-in-law. The ball hits the back of the net and we erupt in cheers, running straight for Hayden, who is on his back in shock as Booker and I knee slide toward him. We both place our hands on his chest and make dramatic motions to shock his heart. His body jerks twice before coming back to life in full-on celebration mode.

The women and Vaughn laugh from the sidelines. Allie just places her hands on her temples, shaking her head in complete surprise over how fun this is turning out to be.

Unfortunately, the match ends in a five to three loss for me, Hayden, and Booker. We're all drenched in sweat and I'm flopped down on the grass. I stare up at the sky and wonder how the fuck training with a professional soccer team is easier than scrimmaging against the Harris Brothers.

Suddenly, shadows fall over me. I look up to see the four of them looming over me, dripping sweat all around me.

"I lost," I state knowingly.

"We know," Tanner replies with a chuckle and squirts a drink of water into his mouth.

"I'm dating her regardless," I reply. At this point, what more could they possibly do to me?

"We know," Gareth states and stretches a hand out to me. He yanks me up onto my feet and slaps his hand on my back. "But it still felt good to kick your arse today."

"You still got it, bro," Tanner states with wide, puppy-dog eyes.

Gareth smiles proudly and claps a hand over his abdomen. "Retirement hasn't made me soft yet."

I look around at the group of them and ask, "What now?"

Tanner throws his arm around my shoulders. "Now we eat."

Allie

It is completely impossible not to stare at Roan like he's some sort of complex painting in a museum that I have to figure out as I sit across from him at my uncle's kitchen table.

He just played soccer against my insane family for me! The grandest gesture I remember Ghost Penis doing to prove his affection was sending me flowers on my birthday. Even then, I'm pretty sure it was his father's secretary who had them sent because it was on her calendar.

Roan and I are only dating, yet he was willing to go that far. What does that mean? We were supposed to be casual, for Christ's sake!

I watch him spread lingonberry jam on Swedish pancakes while laughing at something Sophia says in his ear. He's talking with my little cousin like it's a normal Sunday. And every once in a while, he winks at me as if to say he knew this would happen all along and I was worrying for nothing. But was I worrying for nothing? Does the fact that my family has accepted him mean that everything from the past is forgotten?

Doubtful.

If he knew what I did two years ago, he'd be out the door and probably hiring a lawyer to sue me for indecent exposure or something.

The longer I watch my family interacting with him, the more anxiety creeps in around me. Having him here, entrenched with my cousins and making their kids giggle, makes him more human than ever before. Far more human than the night we met, and I thought he would be the perfect faceless man for my payback plan. *Boy was I wrong.*

Honestly, though, what was I thinking back then? How did I think I could record something like that and put it out there for Ghost Penis and Rosalie to see? That's not me! I'm not that kind of person. I'm this kind of person. The kind who sucks at casual and falls for a guy after introducing him to her family.

I feel my emotions spiraling out of control, so I excuse myself for the bathroom. Instead of stopping at the hallway toilet, though, I move toward the front door, thinking some air might help calm me down.

I drop down on the front step and wrap my arms around my knees, breathing in the fresh air like a lifeline. I'm just finally beginning to calm down when I hear the door open behind me. I turn around, expecting to see Roan or maybe Vi checking in on me, but I'm shocked to see it's actually Uncle Vaughn standing there in all his tall, intimidating presence.

He looks different without a grandchild in his arms, a rare sight I've noticed since coming into his home. Being a grandfather agrees with him, and I can't help but wonder what my own father would be like as a grandpa.

Vaughn breathes deeply and hooks his thumb back toward the house. "I'm sure this gathering is a great deal louder than what you grew up with in America." He moves down the front stoop, lowering himself onto the step beside me. "And to think we put ourselves through this madness every bloody Sunday."

He gets a weary look on his face that makes me smile.

"Don't act like you don't love every second of it."

"You got me there," he replies, the corner of his mouth tilting up into a prideful expression. "As obnoxious as my lot is, I would still prefer they all live right here under my roof forever. There's a great sense of contentment when you have all the players on your team together."

A pang of regret hits me in the stomach because I can't picture my father considering me as a part of his team. Growing up, I always thought his coldness was because he was British and they express their emotions differently. But seeing Vaughn Harris—a famous former soccer player and now a successful team manager—bouncing babies on his shoulders and waxing lyrical about his children makes me realise just how different the two of them truly are.

"Why the sad face?" Vaughn asks, his brows pinching together as he watches me thoughtfully.

I shake my head dismissively. "Nothing…Tonight just makes me realise I don't have the same sort of relationship with my dad." I run a hand through my hair and add, "I didn't leave on the best of terms with him. Things from my past seem to be affecting my present in more ways than one right now."

Vaughn inhales sharply, the subject of my father clearly something that affects him negatively as well. "Do you want to talk about it?"

I shrug. "I'm afraid it's a little too much information for an uncle to have to endure."

I almost laugh out loud when I think about blabbing, "*Hey, Uncle Vaughn, I walked in on my stepsister and boyfriend fucking on my bed, which sent me into an emotional tailspin where I recorded an accidental sex video of a supposed stranger who I'm actually dating. And now my offenders are getting married and my father thinks it's totally fine for him to walk her down the aisle!*"

"Have you met my son Tanner?" Vaughn deadpans. "Too much information is no longer a concept in our family thanks to him."

We laugh at his comment as our gazes follow a crazy squirrel darting up and down a tree.

"I just wish my dad was more like you. Maybe I'd have someone to lean on instead of making stupid mistakes that I can't take back."

Vaughn visibly tenses out of the corner of my eye. When I glance over, I see that he's lost all humour on his face.

"You know, Allie…I'm not a perfect father either. I'm not sure such a thing even exists. But you should know there was a long period of time when the kids were young that I wasn't exactly present. In fact, I was really a ghost of a man." He pauses and I see his body hunch forward as his mood darkens. "It was after Vilma passed, and it's not a time in my life that I'm proud of. That was also when your father and I got in a huge row." He visibly deflates as he hangs his head. "He wanted me to hire a nanny and get back into football to support my family. Shake off the grief. I was in such a dark place at the time that he said one wrong word and I hit him for it, square in the jaw."

"I had no idea," I state, my eyes wide. "I knew you guys had a falling-out, but I never knew what it was about."

Vaughn nods sadly. "In hindsight, he was probably right. I wasn't fit to care for five young children. But I didn't trust his opinion on the matter because your father didn't know love the way I did with Vilma. He loves a different way. More pragmatically."

"That is so true," I say softly, feeling almost cheated that I didn't grow up seeing my father love a woman the way Vaughn loved Vilma.

"But, as I said, my way wasn't any better than his. I didn't do right by my children for many years. Thankfully, they helped each other out when I wasn't capable of doing so. And the beauty and the curse of family is that they're bound to you by blood, which means I'm doing everything I can to make up for lost time."

I stare at him in wonder, having difficulty imagining him being anyone other than the loving, devoted father I see today. "Your kids don't seem to be any worse for the wear."

A look of pride flits over his face at my compliment. "My kids had each other to lean on. Vi was a mini mummy and Gareth…He was the man of the house more than I ever was. I owe everything to them, and I remind myself of that every single day."

Vaughn's eyes turn red around the edges, and a knot forms in my throat from seeing such a strong man become so vulnerable in front of me. I knew things were hard after Vilma's passing because that was when we stopped seeing them as much. But the grave look in Vaughn's eyes makes me realise that I likely had no idea what it was truly like for this family after losing their wife and mother. My mother may be a flighty, emotionally unstable parent, but at least she's still alive.

"But you didn't have that sense of family, Alice. You were with your dad in a new country without any siblings or a mother to lean on. I feel bad that we lost touch with you guys because I'm sure your dad could have used some brotherly advice and you could have used some pushy cousins, even from afar." He puts his arm around me and pulls me into him, dropping a kiss on the top of my head. "I'm glad we're getting a second chance with you."

I smile, fighting back the tears that sting the backs of my eyes. "I'm glad, too."

He releases me and pins me with a fatherly look. "I think you need to be kind to yourself and let whatever you did in the past be forgotten. This is a new beginning here, and I can't wait to see how wonderfully you do."

His words hit me straight in the stomach. Is it that easy? Can I leave the past in the past and forget about what I did?

"But I've done some things I'm ashamed of. Things that I know I should confess to, but I selfishly don't want to wreck what I have now. Things have been so good since I came to London. I feel happier than I've felt in a long time."

"Then let those things go," Vaughn states knowingly. "In my experience, the time to confess is when things are bad and can't get any worse. If life is good, my uncle-y advice is to not rock the boat."

He pats me on the shoulder and moves to stand up, pausing above me. "And cut yourself some slack, darling. My kids aren't perfect. They depend a lot on each other for everything, especially when they screw up, which they have all done hundreds of times. If you're not perfect, you're in jolly good company now."

With a wink and a smile, he walks back inside the house, leaving me alone with the memories of my past. Honestly, what I did was so uncharacteristic of me. If I could jump in a time machine and take it back, I would. *Well, maybe not the multiple orgasms. Those memories are pretty awesome.*

But I would take back the video part. I'd make it disappear. And perhaps the fact that I haven't deleted it yet is why I can't let it go. If I just click DELETE, then I would just have the memories and wouldn't have to worry about hurting Roan anymore.

Before I move to head in, I pull my phone out of my pocket and locate the video in my gallery. I punch the trash can icon and pause before pressing YES. The video was once a crutch I used to feel empowered, but I don't need it anymore. I am not the person I left behind in Chicago who felt alone and betrayed and ruined for all future relationships.

I am a stronger woman in London. I have a family, a job, a love life. Things are looking up. It's time to focus on my future, not my past. If this video ended up in the wrong hands—if one sinister person got a hold of it—it could ruin not only Roan's life, but my life and my newfound family here in London. The video cannot exist anymore. It needs to be entirely erased from my life.

I confirm the request to delete it and feel a tremendous weight lift off my shoulders when it's gone. With a smile, I stand up and head back inside to Roan and back inside to my family, who all make my future feel pretty damn bright.

CHAPTER

Allie

I T'S A GORGEOUS SUNNY DAY IN LONDON WHEN ROAN PARKS HIS car at the Victoria Park Boating Lake with a curious expression on his face.

"Are we row boating?"

"We are!" I exclaim, grabbing the picnic basket I put together and hopping out of the vehicle. I hurry over to Roan's side and yank him toward the dock by the boat rentals. "This place is one of my most vivid memories of London before I moved away, and I've been dying to come back."

"You're skipping again," Roan says, smiling in that special way he's been smiling at me lately. It's almost like he has a secret that he's not telling me, but it's the good kind of secret. Not the "I have a sex video of you'" kind of secret.

I'm too scared to ask him what his smile means, so I just keep enjoying his dazzling eyes because whatever causes them to sparkle makes me want to jump his bones.

I shrug. "Get over it. It's my thing."

It's been three weeks since the infamous Harris Shakedown. After that, I pretty much quit trying to hide my happy skipping. Things between Roan and I have been wonderful. Whether it's because I let go of that extra baggage I was carrying or because we've been spending more time together, I have become totally smitten by this man.

Mac teases us mercilessly whenever he's around. He says that we're like two stray cats in heat. No matter how hard we try to stay apart, we end up prowling around for each other.

The guy is not wrong.

And because Roan has completed his last match of the season, his schedule is free. So free that he's been threatening to show up at my place of work to take me out to lunch. I told him he cannot do that until I talk to my boss about us. Since we're still supposedly just casually dating, I see no need to involve Niall in our business.

We check out a boat and load up, decked out in really sexy life jackets. Roan's actually looks fine on him considering he's wearing a white T-shirt and jeans. I didn't really think the bright orange life jacket part through when I put on my navy blue split dress this morning. At least my legs aren't covered, though.

Roan rows us out onto the calm lake while I admire his arm muscles as they flex and contract with each stroke. His caramel skin is growing tanner as the summer heats up, and all it does is make those stunning pale brown eyes of his pop even more.

He catches me slack-jawed and staring and says, "You liking the view?"

I sit back in my seat and lift my chin up like a proud princess. "I'd like it better if you took your shirt off."

He barks out a laugh. "You've been hanging out with the Harris women too much."

"Not that much!" I retort and then my face twists up, revealing the lie on my lips.

I've been out with the girls a few times since the Harris Shakedown. And every time we're together, I feel like their intention is to give me a fast-tracked lesson on how to handle an athlete.

I lick my lips seductively and lean toward Roan, trying to show off the cleavage that I so painstakingly tried to put on display before this horrible life jacket entered my life. "I've been spending plenty of time with you, though."

"Not enough time." He gets a wicked look in his eyes as he glances down at my chest and my exposed legs that are on full display in my centre slit. "Maybe you should take *your* shirt off. It's been a few hours since I've seen your breasts, and I bet they miss me."

I roll my eyes like I'm offended, but the pleased smile that spreads across my face indicates otherwise. I turn away, taking in all the people who are soaking in the sun on the grassy areas surrounding the water. It's so much fun to be living in such a metropolitan city like London yet have this bit of oasis that makes you feel like you're far away from it all.

"I was seven years old when I came here with the Harrises," I state, looking around and realising that not much has changed. "Gareth had just gotten his license, and he and Vi thought it would be fun to bring me here with Camden, Tanner, and Booker for my birthday."

Roan's brows lift. "No adult supervision?"

I shake my head. "No. I suppose they were still kids then, but they travelled in a pack, so they were never scared of anything."

My mind drifts back to how close they were to each other even then. They finished each other's sentences and knew exactly what each other wanted to order at a restaurant. They would be physically assaulting each other one minute and hugging the next without any interference from a grown-up. Now that I'm thinking about it, not much has changed, even though we've become adults.

"They always seemed so mature and grown up to me. Well, except for the twins on the maturity front," I state, pointing to a man-made fountain spray that's shooting out of the centre of the lake. "That is where Tanner tipped his boat."

Roan chuckles. "Why am I not surprised?"

"Because it's Tanner," I reply with a fond smile. "He and Camden were standing in their rowboat while Vi yelled for them to get down from her boat with Booker. Gareth was rowing with me, and I remember him telling me in the deepest, calmest tone that they were going to tip. Sure enough, into the lake they went!"

Roan laughs heartily and I join him because I can still picture the two nut-jobs trying to turn the boat over.

"I'm surprised Gareth didn't go crazy on them," Roan says, steering the boat toward a small channel. "He can be scary as fuck when he wants to be."

I nod and smile. "He really can be. But he also has a calmness about him, even in chaos. He always said that finding trouble was a fact of life for Tanner and Camden, and it was easier to help them clean up their messes than to stop them from making them."

Roan tilts his head, absorbing that comment for a moment. "That's probably very true. My sisters fight like crazy. Vicious, claws out, hair pulling, nasty business. I always used to get in the middle, but it never stopped them. I'd literally be holding them apart from each other and they'd take swings at me until I let go. I should have gone with Gareth's theory and just dealt with the aftermath."

The image of siblings fighting sends a bizarre aura of sadness through me because I'm actually jealous of people who got to experience that. Rosalie and I never fought. Maybe that was the first sign that what we had wasn't a real sisterly relationship.

"I would have liked to have had siblings," I state, leaning over and dragging my fingertips through the calm water. "Being an only child in a new country really sucked."

Roan stops rowing to let us drift for a while, his eyes serious on me. "What about your stepsister? I know she turned out to be a fucking cunt in the end, but was it ever good between you?"

I let out a long, pensive sigh. A couple of weeks ago, I opened up to Roan about the dirty details of my breakup with both Ghost Penis and Rosalie. Surprisingly, he didn't threaten bodily harm on them the way Tanner and Booker did when they found out. He simply pulled me into his arms and kissed the pain away.

"I think I was blind when it came to Rosalie," I state, lifting my hand to shield my eyes from the sun as I look back at Roan. "I was at such an awkward age and so desperate for a sense of family that I just kind of latched onto her, calling her my sister and best friend. But since spending more time with the Harris girls here, I've realised that our relationship was nothing like what I see between Indie and Belle or Vi and the boys. I think Rosalie and I have been competing my entire life, but I didn't even know it until now."

Roan's brow furrows. "And your ex? Were you blind when it came to him?"

"God, yes," I retort with an exasperated laugh. "I think I loved the idea of love more than I actually loved him. I blew our relationship up in my mind to seem better than the reality. I did that with him *and* Rosalie. I couldn't see what was real and what wasn't."

"What about us?" he asks tentatively and I watch as his body tenses for my answer.

I'm taken off guard by the weight of his question. "What do you mean?"

"Do you think we're real?"

It seems like a silly question, but his expression isn't portraying anything humourous.

"I hope we are," I reply, playing with my dress and trying not to look him in the eyes when I continue telling him one of my biggest fears. "I guess I don't really know how to trust myself again."

Roan looks down into the boat, chewing his inner cheek for a moment. "Then I want you to trust me."

"Trust you for what?" I cave and eye him questioningly.

"I'll tell you what's real and what is fake between us." His eyes hit me with an intensity that takes my breath away. He releases the oars and braces his hands on his knees, bringing our faces closer together when he adds, "Because, when I ask you to be my girlfriend and not just someone you're casual with, I don't want there to be any hesitation on your end that we're real."

My jaw drops. "Are you…asking me to be your girlfriend?"

"No," he snaps and a hint of a smile lights up his face in a way that is so adorable it gives me butterflies. "This very romantic boat ride would be the worst place for me to ask you to be my girlfriend. Obviously." He comically rolls his eyes and I bite my lip to try and hide the surge of anxiety swirling in my belly.

The anxiety is annoying because I like Roan. I like him ten times more than Ghost Penis, whom I supposedly loved. And I'm not going to lie and say I didn't notice the moment we surpassed his usual one-month mark for when he breaks it off with women. I noticed and tried to tell myself it didn't matter. That deep down, we were still just casual.

But the way he's looking at me—and the way I feel when he looks at me—doesn't *feel* casual. It feels significant.

Suddenly, desperation floods through me, drowning out all my nerves and insecurities. So much of what Roan and I have is because he pushes closer when I pull away. It's exhausting. For once, I want to be the one who pushes. I want to be in the moment and show him that I do know what's real and what's fake sometimes.

Biting my lip, I grab a hold of the sides of the boat to steady myself before moving to stand up.

"What are you doing?" Roan asks, looking down nervously as we teeter side to side. "Sit down, Lis. You're going to tip us over."

"I'm not going to tip us over," I reply and take a step forward. The boat pitches to the right, so I quickly balance out my weight to stop it. "Holy shit, I almost tipped us over."

He laughs and shakes his head. "Sit down, you mad woman!"

"That's what I'm trying to do!" I huff and very carefully place my hands on his shoulders. Using him for support, I step over his legs and lower myself to straddle his lap.

"There," I state with a proud smile, glancing down at my skirt that's spread up the middle. "I sat down."

His brows lift as he glances down and notices my pink panties peeking out from under my dress. He wraps his arms around my waist and squeezes my life-jacketed body close to him. "This skirt of yours gives us easy access if you want to get a little more romantic."

I smile mischievously already having had the same thought. "I was just coming over for this."

I press my lips to his full, perfect mouth. It feels soft, and warm, and welcoming…and more real than any kiss I've ever had. Our tongues dance and my mind drifts to how much I've changed since deleting that stupid video. Before, I was guarded and defensive of my heart because opening it to him meant that I had to tell my se-cret. But deleting it has freed me in more ways than one. I don't need the memory of Roan and me in that video to feel strong and capable in life. I just need the real deal, who's pressed up against my body right now.

He breaks our kiss, his chest rising and falling in big, heavy pants.

I press my forehead to his. "This feels pretty real, right?"

"Fuck yes it does, mooi." His voice is raw and husky as we breathe in the scent of each other, our bodies uniting in a deliciously perfect moment of appreciation.

Our eyes connect and I swear I see nerves flicker across his face, a rare sight for my confident, pushy athlete.

"What's the matter?" I ask, pulling back and cradling his head in my hands. "Is this too much?"

"It's not too much." He swallows slowly. "It's not enough. I want…*more*. I want us to be official."

The corners of my mouth lift up into a smile. "I thought this romantic boat wasn't the right place?"

"I can't help it," he replies, staring deeply into my eyes. "Things just got really real for me."

CHAPTER 19

Roan

S ACKED OUT ON THE SOFA WITH MAC, WE'RE ON HOUR THREE OF an epic Fortnite marathon. I'm pretty sure my ass is numb at this point.

"Aye, I told you not to shoot that guy!" Mac bellows, tossing his controller on the floor. "I needed him to complete one of my challenges!"

"Sorry, you looked cornered over there!" I respond defensively, setting my controller down and stretching out my hands. "We need to take a break anyway. We've been playing an embarrassing amount of time."

Mac growls and gets up, mumbling expletives under his breath as he walks into the kitchen to fetch us a couple of beers. He returns, handing me an amber bottle before dropping back down on the sofa with a heavy sigh.

"So, tell me, how are things with the wee lass?" he asks, prying the top off his bottle and handing me the opener.

I remove the cap off mine as well and take a cool drink. "They're good."

Mac huffs out a laugh. "More than good I'd say. You barely spend any nights apart."

My shoulders lift. "When it's good, it's good."

He eyes me speculatively. "It must be more than good because you've passed your four-week cut-off point, haven't you?"

I shrug noncommittally and take another drink of my beer.

"So, what does that mean?" Mac asks because he's a nosey bastard.

I roll my eyes and hit him with a flat stare. "If you're asking if we're in a relationship, the answer is yes. We made it official last week."

"You WAG'd yourself properly?" Mac hoots with a shit-eating grin. He slaps me on the leg. "I called it, mate! I so fucking called it. My wee boy finally got himself a WAG."

He throws his arm around me, yanking me in for an overly aggressive hug that I shove away from. "Would you shut up already?"

"No! This is cause for celebration. Let's order a pizza and have the church bells rung." He turns like he's looking for the takeout menus, but I know he's just having a piss.

"This is why I don't talk to you about shit."

He gets a wounded look on his face. "What are you hiding from me? Don't you know I have pure brilliant enthusiasm coursing through my veins on a regular basis? My maw always said it was my finest feature!"

"Your maw is a liar," I reply with a laugh and then pause when a thought hits me. I set my beer down on the coffee table before turning to face him. "Tell me if this idea of mine sounds crazy," I say, gesticulating with my hands so he knows I'm being serious. "I've been thinking about surprising Allie with a trip to Cape Town to meet my mom."

His brows lift in shock. "What do you mean by surprise?"

"Like, not tell her we're going there until we get there."

"It's an eleven-hour flight," he deadpans.

I roll my eyes. "I'm aware."

"You haven't been home in two years."

"I'm aware of that as well. But flights are cheap right now, and I think it would be a bit of a jol to show her my home."

His eyes go wide and his face gets an odd, tender look on it. "For fuck's sake, man, you're not just WAG'd. You're in love."

I jerk back defensively. "I'm not in love."

"Aye, you are. You guys have been together for what? Five weeks? And you already want her to meet your mum?" His eyes grow wider as he continues, "You've never introduced a girl to your mum. Not once. You told me that when we first met."

"I know, but Allie is just…different," I shrug, reaching back and squeezing my neck at the bone-chilling truth to that statement. "And next season is going to be mad, so I'm not sure when I'm going to get home to visit again."

He nods, his teasing mannerism slightly fading. "I can see that Allie's different. You're different around her, too. Nothing like the other women you've dated. You're more yourself and less Roan DeWalt, the soccer player."

I frown at his remark. "I'm a different person around other women?"

He holds his hands up in defence. "Aye, a wee bit. I'm sorry to say this, but with me you're chill and shouting at me about bad moves on Fortnite. When you're trying to impress a burd, you do this Rico Suave shite that makes my skin crawl."

"Fuck you!"

"Don't shoot the messenger," he howls. "I'm just saying, I like Allie. I like you around Allie. She can stay."

"Well, thanks for your approval," I snap, annoyed by the turn this conversation took. "So, you think taking her home is a good idea or bad?"

Mac takes a big swig of his beer and replies, "Allie is going to flip the fuck out."

I swallow the nerves I've been feeling ever since the idea came to me. "You're right. She will flip the fuck out. That's why it'll be a surprise. That's sort of our thing. She's afraid and I'm confident. I like to push her."

"Yeah you do," Mac leers, shooting me a dirty wink.

It's disturbing. I didn't even know winks could be dirty, but evidently they can be when they're attached to a giant Scotsman.

"So, you think it's a good idea then? You think I should do it?" I ask for final confirmation.

Mac deadpans, "No. I think it's a bad idea. I wouldn't do it."

Allie

I'm sitting at my desk outside of Niall's office, going over the seating chart for the Get Fit Britain Gala when a text comes through from Roan.

> **Roan: Do you think you can get a few days off next week? We'll be back in plenty of time for the gala. I promise.**
> **Me: Maybe…Why?**
> **Roan: I want to take you away.**
> **Me: Take me away where?**
> **Roan: It's a surprise, but it would involve a longish flight.**
> **Me: Is this real or fake?**
> **Roan: It's always real with me, mooi. ;)**

Since Roan and I became an item last week, I've been trying to find the nerve to tell Niall about us. I think coming clean and putting our cards out on the table will make everything easier and less secretive. I have enough past secrets in my life. I don't need to add this one to the mix.

I will admit that becoming more serious with Roan wasn't my original plan. I'm not sure it was his original plan either. But things between us have progressed in such a natural, easy way, it seemed impossible not to take the next step. And the step after the next step is telling my boss.

I stand up from my desk and walk back to Niall's office. Nerves swirl in my belly as I knock on the glass window and see his head pop up from his computer.

He waves me in. "Allie, I'm glad you're here. I've selected the two winners for the Win A Date Campaign, and I want you to run background checks on them." He grabs two papers off the printer behind him and hands them over to me.

"No problem," I reply, gripping the pages tightly in my hand as I linger in front of his desk.

He looks up at me with a furrow to his brow. "Was there something else you needed?"

I nod and swallow. "Yes."

He pauses to examine me for a moment, clearly intrigued by what has me so tense and awkward. "Have a seat."

I sit and take a deep breath before saying, "I wanted to talk to you about a relationship that's developed between myself and a player for Bethnal Green." I look up nervously and see Niall failing to hide a knowing smirk.

"Continue," he states crisply.

I shift to the edge of my seat. "When I came to London, I had a previous, um, history with Roan DeWalt. He was a friend of the Harris family and, well, we knew each other from a couple of years ago…And I guess you could say we've reacquainted now."

"I see," Niall states, propping his elbows on his desk and rubbing his hands together as he ponders this information.

"I looked in the employee handbook and couldn't find anything about fraternising with clients, so I figured I would just tell you if it developed into something more."

"And it has apparently developed into something more?" Niall's face becomes more serious, and it makes it difficult for me to make eye contact with him.

I pull my lips into my mouth and nod.

He splays his hands out on the desk and lets out a laugh. "Allie, do you really think you're telling me new information?"

My eyes lift to his. "What do you mean?"

"I've known about you and DeWalt for weeks now."

"Weeks?" I ask, my jaw dropped.

"Of course," he says and flicks his hand out like it's a silly concept. "I'm in public relations. It's my job to know. That and Vaughn Harris called me and told me everything."

"He what?" I exclaim, my muscles tensing.

Niall lets out a chuckle. "He said you were spending time with DeWalt and that he is okay with it but wanted to ensure it wouldn't negatively affect your position with the firm."

My throat tightens as emotion overcomes me. My uncle called and said all of this? To my boss? I don't think my own father would have been that protective of me.

"I told him it is fine by me as long as you two don't make any media scandals."

"Ooo—kay," I stammer, blinking back my shock. "So then, it's all good?"

Niall nods and then props his elbows on his desk. "It's more than good. I've just received a call from Adidas and they are interested in using Roan for next season's football campaign."

"What?" I cry, nearly dropping the papers that are in my hand. "Are you serious?"

"Very serious," Niall replies with a cocky brow lift. "It's some sort of Dream Big Campaign. They want to highlight his fast-tracked career from his League One team in Cape Town, to Bethnal Green in the Championship League, to next season as a Premier League starter. It's going to be huge, and there aren't many athletes with his type of career trajectory, so I think the competition is slim."

"That is wonderful news," I state, my jaw still dropped in awe. "I know an endorsement like this is everything Roan has wanted."

Niall smiles proudly. "I'm aware, and I'm doing everything I can to help make this deal happen for your boyfriend. That's why it's extremely important you two are picture-perfect out there on the streets. No public arguments, no cheating scandals. Not even photos with people of the opposite sex. You two need to be the model couple. I'm sure you're aware that it's not only Roan banking on this deal but his family back in Cape Town as well."

A pang of guilt hits me in the stomach and I close my eyes and murmur a silent "thank you" that I finally deleted the video. If that got out now and I ruined all the hard work he's done for his family, I would never forgive myself.

I swallow the knot in my throat and reply, "I'm definitely aware."

"Good," he says, pounding his fist lightly on the desk with some finality. "I'm glad we had this talk. None of this should be hard considering you work in PR, so I won't lecture you anymore on the subject. Hopefully now that things are out in the open, you can stop being so afraid of me."

"I'm not afraid of you," I volley back, surprised by his change in direction. "I was worried about telling you, but only because you didn't seem too pleased about my connection to the Harris family when I first started here. I thought this might push you over the edge."

He purses his lips and sits back in his chair. "That's because when I started working for the team, I was exhausted by all the politics of doing things a certain way. It truly is the Harris way or the highway with Bethnal Green F.C. But I've since learned that they're not so bad and it's better to work with them than against them."

I nod my agreement knowing all too well how the Harris clan works. "That is definitely true."

"So, you and DeWalt being together is fine," he adds, clapping his hand on the desk. "Is that all you needed to talk to me about?"

I pull my lip into my mouth, nervous to ask my next request because it truly is yet another Harris request. "I was wondering if I can have a few days off next week?"

Niall quirks a brow. "Have you completed the seating chart for the gala?"

"I was just finishing it."

"And have you had the final fittings for Roan and Mac's clothing for that night?"

"Yes," I reply. "I took them to the boutique last week, and Freya is doing the final alterations now."

"Good," Niall states, turning his attention back toward his computer screen. "Then submit the days you need to take off and I'll get them approved."

"Thank you, Niall," I exclaim, a big smile on my face.

He shakes his head and sighs. "You Harrises are running the world. I'm just living in it."

I laugh and turn to haul ass out of his office, relief, excitement, and anticipation shooting through my veins. I can't believe my uncle actually called and said what he said to my boss. It feels a bit like a boundary was crossed, but I've quickly learned that that's the norm for my family and I think it helped my case in the end.

I'm just pulling out my phone to text Roan the news when an unfamiliar number illuminates the screen.

I swipe the screen and answer, "Hi, this is Allie."

"Allie, it's me…Please don't hang up."

My body goes stiff at the sound of a familiar voice on the other end of the line.

"Rosalie?" I ask on a shaky breath even though I know it's her.

"Yes. Look, just hear me out and then you can go back to never speaking to me again."

I try to wet my suddenly dry lips as a nervous sweat breaks out all over my skin. I haven't heard her voice in ages. Any contact we had before I left Chicago was via scathing text messages, so her contact today is unnerving.

"Hear you out about what?" I ask, schooling my voice to sound firm and not shaken.

"Daddy wants you at the wedding."

My jaw tightens at her words, and I grind out through clenched teeth, "He's not your dad, Rosalie. Our parents aren't married anymore."

"He's the only one I have, Allie," she retorts with a haughty tone. "And you never minded me calling him daddy when we were kids."

"I don't remember you being a traitorous whore when we were kids, but I've learned that my judgement may have been off back then." My voice is louder than I meant it to be, so I quickly look over my shoulder to make sure Niall didn't overhear.

I inhale a deep breath, then slowly exhale. Why am I letting her get to me like this? I don't need her. I don't even need my father. I just need to focus on my new life in London and leave them both behind me.

"Look, I told you in my letter that we were in love and it had been coming on for a while."

I shake my head at that joke of a letter. "Love can start a myriad of ways, Rose. Naked on my bed while I'm still in a relationship with him shouldn't have been one of them. In all honesty, I've thought a lot about this. If you two would have just come to me and told me you had feelings for each other, I would have been hurt, but it wouldn't have been irreparable damage. What you two did and the way you did it is unforgiveable."

"Get over it, Allie! It's been two years! I would have thought you'd moved on by now."

"I have moved on," I seethe back into the line. "Believe me, Rosalie. I've moved way the hell on and I'm ten times happier now. But in all that movement, I've realised what horrible people I let influence my life in Chicago, so I'm not about to come back there and make those mistakes again. Why do you even want me there? It's clear you don't give a shit about me."

"I *don't* want you there, but Daddy says he won't walk me down the aisle if you're not."

"What?" I screech, my face twisting up in confusion. That sounds nothing like my father.

Rosalie scoffs. "It seems he received some phone call from his brother and he's being all weird about the wedding now. He says he won't come unless you're there and are okay with it."

"Wait…Was it my uncle Vaughn who called?" I ask, thinking I didn't hear her right.

"That's him," she snaps. "I don't even know the guy, but he's doing a great job of ruining my entire life from afar."

My mind reels over the fact that Vaughn has apparently made a lot of phone calls on my behalf. Calling my boss was one thing, but I didn't think my father and Vaughn spoke anymore. Now Vaughn is calling him and speaking up for me?

"I, um, don't know what to say," I state simply because it's the truth.

Rosalie squeaks out an annoyed noise. "Say you'll come to the wedding and watch Daddy walk me down the aisle."

I shake my head, my body slumping down in my chair. "After everything that happened, why on earth would I do that for you, Rosalie?"

She pauses and exhales a loaded breath. "Because I have something on you that I know you don't want to get out."

"And what exactly is that?" I mumble, rubbing my temple and not in the mood to hear her empty threats.

Then she says three little words I did not expect.

"A certain *video*."

My entire body freezes. Surely she's not talking about *that* video. She must be referring to something else. It can't be the same.

"What video?" I ask, my hand clenching the phone so hard I swear I hear it crack.

Her voice drops to a low, threatening tone as she replies, "A video that I'm quite certain you don't want released to the public, unless you're planning a future in pornography of course."

She laughs menacingly into the line, and it takes everything in my power not to break down and cry.

"I deleted it," I rush out.

"You're an idiot," she retorts. "Did you forget that I have access to your Cloud?"

No. No, no, no. This can't be happening.

"I knew all your passwords when we lived together, Allie. I've had this video saved for two years now. I saw it right after it happened. I almost threatened you with it when you wouldn't take your name off the apartment lease. Lucky for me, you came around so I could save it for this very special occasion. What were you planning to do with it anyway? Show it to Parker to make him see what he was missing? Make him jealous so he'd go crawling back to you?"

"No!" I exclaim defensively. "I didn't want Parker back."

"Oh, please," she retorts. "You had a plan, Allie. You don't do anything without a plan."

"I just…wanted it for myself," I whisper, my voice soft and unbelievable, even to my own ears.

"Lies!" she exclaims. "Did you even mean to tape the entire fuckfest? It looked like you tried to press stop and missed the button. Not that I'm complaining. That guy in there is hot…Who is he anyway? I want to meet him."

"Stop, Rose," I croak, my eyes welling with tears. "Stop all of this. This isn't some random person in a video. He's my boyfriend."

"Boyfriend?" Rosalie laughs. "Wow, it only took you two years to move on from Parker. How'd you land this one?"

I bite the inside of my cheek, doing everything I can to stop the shaking of my fingers. "He plays soccer for Uncle Vaughn's team. I do PR for him, which means I *know* he can't have that video get out. It will ruin his career. Please, Rose. I'll do anything."

"Good," she snaps back harshly. "Then come to my wedding with a stupid smile on your face so I can have the picture-perfect day I always dreamed of, or I will ruin you."

My head spins with a mixture of complete, utter sadness and hot, boiling rage. How did I allow this person so deeply into my life? How

195

did I ever believe she cared about me? First she took my boyfriend, then my apartment, and lastly, my father! Now she's threatening my relationship with Roan! This isn't family. This isn't love. This person is a monster. And I'm a fucking fool for not even thinking about our shared Cloud we had back then. I basically gave her everything she needs to continue ruining my life from another continent!

I thought coming to London would give me the fresh start I needed. I took Vaughn's advice and left the past behind me. Roan and I are happy and developing real feelings for each other. Now my past is coming back to haunt me, all because of the stupidest thing I've ever done in my entire life.

My voice is weak when I utter, "Did you ever care about me?"

There's a long pause on the other end of the line before she replies, "You had everything."

"What do you mean?"

"A loving father, a perfect boyfriend, a career. Even school was easy for you. You literally had everything growing up."

"I didn't, though," I snap, shaking my head. "My dad practically started to ignore me the moment we moved to Chicago."

"So what!" she exclaims, her voice high-pitched and maniacal. "At least he was there. At least he didn't leave you for another family that he loved more, like mine did."

I bite my lip, stopping myself from saying something I'll regret. "So, is that why you decided to sleep with my boyfriend? Because I wasn't grateful enough for my own damn life?"

"I did it because I wanted to have a taste of perfect. I did it because I didn't want to be second best to you anymore, which was all our childhood was about."

My lips thin. "I don't remember it like that."

"Of course you don't," she scoffs. "You were too busy being butthurt that Daddy was giving me more attention."

"I didn't care that he helped you!" I retort, my anger spiking. "I felt sorry for you."

"And there it is," Rosalie huffs knowingly. "That is what I've spent most of my teens and twenties trying to overcome. I don't want your pity. I just want to be better than you for one fucking day. I deserve one day where I'm the perfect daughter with the perfect fiancé and the perfect father walking me down the perfect aisle. And I won't let you ruin that day for me."

I clear my throat, schooling myself to sound stronger than I feel. "So if I come to the wedding, you'll delete the video?"

"Of course!" she peels in a high-pitched, fake voice that I want to rip right out of my phone.

I exhale heavily, knowing that I have no choice, regardless of how painful the wedding will be. It's not only my reputation on the line. It's Roan's.

"Fine," I mumble and cover my eyes in horror. "I'll come to your wedding."

"Great!" she replies. "Text me your address, and I'll pop an invitation in the mail. Nice catching up!"

We hang up and I press my head to my desk, hating the fact that my fucking payback plan is now paying me back.

CHAPTER

Roan

"Y OU CAN'T SEE THIS," I STATE SERIOUSLY BEFORE TUCKING the printed airline ticket into the pocket of my athletic jacket. Allie smiles and sneakily begins walking her fingers across my abs and underneath the material of my coat. "I mean it, Lis. Don't look at it, or you'll ruin the fun."

She growls in frustration. "You're seriously not going to tell me where we're going? Even now? We're on our way to the airport!"

"Nope," I reply with a grin, sitting in the backseat of the car I hired to take us to Heathrow Airport. "And I brought these." I pull out my noise-cancelling headphones. "You're not going to hear it announced by the pilot either."

"Why are you being so secretive?" she asks with narrowed eyes. "I could have kept your Adidas sponsorship interest a secret, but I didn't. I told you. Because that's what good girlfriends do."

I laugh at her weak logic. "Niall called me in for a meeting the next day and told me. It wasn't really a secret at that point." She juts out her lip in a pout and I dip my head down to kiss it. "Besides, I think you telling me about Adidas was more exciting for you than it was for me."

Her jaw drops in offence. "You scooped me up into your arms and started dancing with me on the street corner!"

I shrug and shoot her a mischievous wink. "I know. But that's only because I knew you were excited to tell me. I'm a giver like that."

"You are so full of shit, Roan DeWalt!" She dives in for the airline ticket once more, but I grab a hold of her hands and stop her, trying really hard not to think about fucking her in the back of this car. She's cute when she's feisty.

I laugh and give in. "All right, I'm excited about Adidas. But nothing is official yet, so I'm trying to keep myself in check."

She stops fighting me and exhales heavily. "Fine. But, why can't you tell me where we're going?"

I pin her with a look and think to myself, *Because if you knew I was taking you to South Africa to meet my mom, you'd flip the fuck out on me.* Instead, I drop a soft kiss on her lips. "Just let me be fucking romantic, mooi."

"Well, okay. But only because you said fucking." She giggles and nestles herself under my arm.

I press my nose to her hair, inhaling her sweet scent that I never seem to tire of. The past six weeks with Allie have been unlike anything I've ever experienced with any other woman. Mac is right. I am different around her than I have been with others. I'm more… me. From day one, I've pushed for more with her because I like who I am when I'm around her. She feels like home. And it's addictive to be with someone you can be your true self with.

Allie Harris is my addiction.

I knew that day we went out on the rowboat that we were past our one-month mark. I also knew if I was going to end it, it was already too late for it to be drama-free. But every day I spent with her, I fell for her more and more. Then, when she opened up to me out there on the water about being an only child, it made me want to be with her forever. So she'd never feel lonely again.

It's a crazy feeling to want the responsibility of another person so fully like I do with Allie. Mac says that's real love, but I don't trust that it truly is since I've never felt it for another woman. Yet here I am, calling her mine and taking her to meet my mother. This sure seems like love.

"Real or fake?" Allie asks, looking up at me, her eyes blinking slowly. "You want to become a member of the Mile High Club and you're using me to get there."

"Really fucking real." I lean down and kiss her on the nose while squeezing her hip.

She smiles and moves in closer. "I knew it. We're probably flying to some place really lame, like Chicago."

"Ouch," I reply. "Do you really hate Chicago that much?"

She shakes her head. "No, I actually love Chicago. I just don't love the people I have to see there in a few weeks."

I let out a long breath. "You really think it's wise to go back for Rosalie's wedding?"

Her stepsister's wedding has been a sore subject since the minute Allie told me what she is going to do. I haven't blatantly told her I don't want her to go because I'm trying to be supportive. I'm not jealous of her ex, but I don't trust her stepsister. Any sibling who could do what Rosalie did to Allie can't be right in the head. But I know Allie seeks closure, despite how strong she acts, so I'm playing the understanding boyfriend act.

"I have to," she says simply. "But it'll be good. It'll be a goodbye of sorts. For real this time."

"What do you mean by that?" I ask, my brows pinching together in confusion.

She pulls out from under my arm and turns to face me in the backseat. "When I left, it was in a rush and I left things with my dad in a bad place. I'm hoping the trip can repair some of the distance we have."

I stare her down for a minute. "And you're sure I can't go with you? We do really good at weddings, if you recall."

My suggestion is charged with sexual innuendo, but she doesn't take the bait as she pulls her lip into her mouth to chew on it nervously. She nods woodenly and replies, "Thank you for the offer, but I'm sure."

She's cagey about her trip to Chicago and even cagier when I suggest going with her. It's making me suspicious.

"If I didn't know any better, I'd say you don't want me to meet your family."

Her eyes widen and she forces out a laugh. "Well, you'd be right then because you'd look at me differently if you met my crazy family, and I quite like the way you've been looking at me lately." She tries to joke it off, but I can tell she's not amused.

"Mooi," I state firmly and gently grasp her chin, locking my serious eyes on hers. "I'd never look at you differently. Can't you see I'm fucking mad about you?"

Her eyes instantly soften with surprise. "I'm pretty mad about you, too." Her gaze moves back and forth from my eyes to my lips as she wars with something deep inside of her heart that makes mine hurt. She pulls away from my embrace and murmurs, "But this is my family mess, and it's important for me to clean it up myself."

I nod my head at her determination and remind myself that it was one of the first things I liked about her. "All right then. I'm here whenever you need me."

She licks her lips and smiles. "I know. You're kind of a good human like that."

We arrive at Heathrow a few minutes later, and I manage to get her all the way through the airport without her seeing where we're going. However, the size of the jet is a dead giveaway that we're going far.

"Real or fake? We're going somewhere warm," she says, pulling back her noise-cancelling headphones to hear my answer.

"Fake. It's not too warm, but it's not too cold."

She nods, obviously confused by my response. "Real or fake? We're going somewhere that has water."

"Real."

Her brows knit together as she considers some options in her head. "Real or fake? We're going to have lots of sex when we get there."

I hesitate with my answer, and her face falls before I reply, "Probably real."

This seems to confuse her. She sits back, adjusting her seatbelt and quietly contemplating my answer as we take off for a trip that could essentially make or break us.

Allie

Our plane doesn't land for hours. Hours and hours. I lost track of time, but I'm pretty sure we flew as far as I did from Chicago to London. When we finally land, I look out the window with wide eyes.

"Where are we?" I ask and several passengers turn to look at me curiously because I forgot I'm still wearing Roan's headphones.

Roan laughs and pulls them off of my ears. "Welcome to Cape Town, Lis."

My jaw drops. The next thing I know, we're de-boarding the plane and wheeling our small carry-ons through Cape Town International Airport. We're in Roan's hometown? In South Africa? Holy shit!

When we step outside into the cool air, Roan begins waving at a tall, thin woman with fair skin and short blonde hair. She looks old enough to be his mother.

"Mom!" he shouts to get the woman's attention, and I think I die a thousand deaths.

The woman's eyes find us in the crowd, and she looks like she could explode from happiness. She grabs two teenage-looking girls beside her and they all race toward us.

I remain frozen in place as the three of them embrace Roan like they haven't seen him in years. Come to think of it, I do remember Roan saying he hasn't been home since his transfer to Bethnal Green. Now I'm here to witness their reunion.

My mouth turns to cotton and my palms begin to sweat as I realise that I'm meeting my boyfriend's mother...and I had no idea. I anxiously finger-comb my hair because I've been on a plane for hours and I probably look like I just rolled out of bed.

Roan turns his attention to me. "Allie, I'd like you to meet my mother, Diana, and my two sisters, Mia and Ava."

"Um, it's really good...I wish I'd...Lovely to..." I'm stammering like an idiot and Diana laughs knowingly.

She wraps her elegantly long fingers around my hands and says in a posh British accent, "You had no idea you were meeting me today, did you?"

"Of course I knew!" I giggle unconvincingly and then get a horribly guilty look on my face. "No, sorry. I don't know why I'm lying. I'm just in shock, I guess."

Diana shakes her head, rolling her clear blue eyes up toward the clear blue sky. "This is so typical of my son. He doesn't do anything small." She wraps her arms around my shoulders and pulls me in for a hug. "It's nice to meet you, Allie. I've heard a lot about you."

"You have?" I ask.

She laughs like she thinks I'm joking and turns to walk with me under her arm. "Come along, you guys. I only have you for two days, so we're going to make the most of it."

I look over my shoulder at Roan, who looks so pleased with himself that I kind of want to punch him.

Mia and Ava talk a mile a minute, giving me a fast and furious tour of Cape Town in the car on the way to Roan's grandmother's house. It's a bustling city situated in a valley of mountains, the most notable being Table Mountain National Park. Every hilltop we go over offers sweeping views of gorgeous scenery of water and beaches. The wine farms are nearby as well.

Roan smiles from the front seat at me in the back, sandwiched between his two sisters. He looks at me like this is the most normal thing in the world as they jump from subject to subject like little frogs hopping from lily pad to lily pad. I do my best to listen politely, but I am silently freaking out that he's done all this without telling me. Meeting the family is a big deal. A a very big deal. I still can't believe I'm actually here. In Cape Town. With Roan's family. I'm not even sure this isn't some delirious jet lag illusion.

But I'm here, looking at the faces of my boyfriend's family, who all look very different from each other. I recall Roan telling me the girls had a different father than him and it's quite obvious. Their pale colouring is just like their mother's, apart from their sandy brown hair. Roan, on the other hand, has darker features. It is his extended family we are on our way to visit right now.

We arrive in a neighbourhood called Bo-Kaap, which features brightly coloured, two-story houses that remind me of Easter eggs. They are situated on hilly, cobblestone streets that look like they belong on a postcard. We park in front of a small, lemon-yellow coloured home, and I can already hear laughter coming from inside as we get out of the car.

"How many people are in there?" I ask Roan, feeling nervous heat clawing up my neck as he walks around the car and takes my hand.

He smiles proudly. "Probably a dozen or more."

Roan's mother strides up to the white, gated front door while I pause, feeling dizzy. I pull Roan away from the house. "We need to talk," I state quietly, my eyes pleading with his for a moment.

He furrows his brow and looks over his shoulder at his family. "Go ahead, guys. We'll be right behind you."

Roan's mom holds the door open for the girls and offers me a sympathetic half-smile.

As soon as the door closes, I let go of Roan's hand and run my hands through my hair, barely holding it together. "Holy shit, Roan. What are we doing here?"

"What do you mean?" he asks, reaching out to pull me into his arms.

I jerk away from him, shaking my hands out like I'm preparing to run a 5k race , or maybe more like I just finished one with the way my heart is racing in my chest. "We're in Cape Town! I just met your mother and sisters. Now we're walking into your grandmother's house?"

"Yes, they do a Sunday Braai every week. It's like a backyard barbeque with family and neighbours. It's very causal and really not a big deal." He steps forward to clasp my face in his hands for a kiss, but I pull back again.

"This is a very big deal!" I exclaim, ignoring the heavy sigh he releases over my emotional reaction. "I'm filthy, I look like crap, and you thought it'd be a good idea for me to meet your family without warning me first? This is the definition of a big deal."

He tilts his head, eyeing me warily for a moment as he assesses my reaction to this crazy idea of his. "Do you want to leave?" he asks in a guarded tone.

"No!" I retort, propping my hands on my hips. "How the heck would that look?"

"What do you want then, Lis?" he snaps, losing his patience with me.

I step closer to him and shake my fists between us in frustration. "I want you to tell me why you chose to spring this on me."

He exhales heavily, his eyes narrowing. "Because I wasn't sure you'd come if I asked you in advance."

His response stings. "Why would you think that?"

He licks his lips and rubs them together for a moment. "Because that's sort of our rhythm, Lis. I always want more and you always want less."

My jaw drops, my eyes taking in the hurt in his body language that he's apparently been hiding from me for quite some time. "Why do you say that?"

"You didn't want to date me when we first met. You didn't want to tell your family about dating me. And now you don't want me to go to Chicago with you, which actually fucking kills me because I know how hard that trip is going to be for you. I'd say it's pretty clear that you want less."

His words are like a guilt-soaked knife straight through my heart. I don't want him with me in Chicago because I'm terrified of what Rosalie would do if she saw him. Not because I want less from him.

I reach out for his jacket and pull him in close. All this time we've been together, he has seemed so confident and at ease with where we're at. This is the first time he's shown me that he's not one hundred percent secure with us.

I hate it.

When our bodies are flush together, I look up and say, "I don't want less."

He looks away, his jaw muscles ticking with frustration.

I turn his face to mine. "I don't want less. I just…My family is complicated. Not wanting you to go with me to Chicago has more to do with them than you. That's all."

He closes his eyes and takes a long, deep breath I feel through his chest. As he lets it out slowly, his eyes open and his guarded gaze softens as he looks down at me. "My family is complicated, too. Really complicated. It doesn't change the fact that I want you to meet them."

His words rush through me like a wave of emotion that threatens to swallow me whole. Shaking my head, I reply, "You could have just said that. I think we've reached a point where things are different, and I wish you would have trusted me enough to just ask."

He rubs his lips together and nods in agreement. "I'm sorry. You're right. I should have asked you first. You make me do crazy things, Allie Harris. You always have." He lets out a little growl and kisses me on the forehead. "But seriously, if you want to leave, we can go find a bar and get a drink, just the two of us. My family will understand."

His words are sweet and sincere, but I can tell that this trip means a lot to him. He wouldn't have gone to such lengths to surprise me if it didn't.

"Didn't you hear me say I don't want less?"

He smiles a small, shy smile as he wraps his arms around me. "Got it, no need to shout." He lowers his head and kisses me gently on the lips. "Now come and meet my gran. She's the best."

I laugh and allow Roan to pull me inside of his gran's house. Within seconds, I'm immersed in a melting pot of a brand new culture. I meet so many people that I forget everyone's names as soon as I hear them. I'm practically force-fed foods called tomato bredie, bobotie, sosaties, chakalaka, and koeksisters. The sweet-tasting umqombothi beer flows freely, only adding to the warm welcome from everybody. I hear all about the fun that Cape Town has to offer, and Roan's mother makes plans to show us some sights tomorrow. She's affectionate with her son and it's adorable to watch her proud smile when everyone comments on his incredible soccer season.

Roan's gran, whose skin is a shade darker than Roan's, takes me over to a wall of photos to show me a picture of her son, Thando. Thando was Roan's father. She explains that she and her husband, who is now deceased, were one of the rare multiracial couples in South Africa during apartheid. Roan's grandfather was Italian, and because their relationship was illegal, they had to live apart the majority of their lives, living only for weekend visits behind closed doors. When Thando was born with lighter skin than hers, she was forced to tell people outside of her family that he was albino. It wasn't until after apartheid ended in 1994 that Roan's grandparents were able to be legally married. By then, Thando was off studying to be a doctor in England and meeting Roan's mother, Diana.

Gran shows me more photos of the missionary doctor whom Thando met in the early 90s. The doctor was so taken by this local boy's self-taught knowledge in medicine, he made it his mission to fund Thando's education outside of South Africa.

We look through her husband's journals next, which were written about liberation campaigns for South Africa. They discussed the work he did to free Nelson Mandela and fight against apartheid.

I shamefully admit that there was a good majority of this nation's history that I wasn't aware of. When I begin tearing up during some of the heartbreaking tales his grandmother shares, she simply holds my hand and continues. It feels important to be touched by her in this moment. To see her skin against mine as she recounts the history of her family. And when I look over at Roan and see his reaction to his grandmother embracing me, I know exactly why I am here.

I am in love with him.

And I am in love with his family. Hearing all of their history and witnessing Roan's fraternal family accept Roan's white mother and sisters is a beautiful testament to how inclusive they truly are, in their very bones. I am lucky to be in their presence.

When we leave, I feel Roan's eyes on me as his grandmother pulls me close for a long hug on the front steps of her home. She steps back and holds my face in her hands, her light brown eyes glistening with unshed tears in the street lights as she whispers in her accent, "I'm glad the world has changed because it made it possible for me to see true love in my grandson's eyes."

I open my mouth, but no words come out. What kind of response do I give to a woman who knows so much of the world and just revealed a truth I wasn't even aware of yet?

I take a deep breath and feel a tear run down my cheek when I whisper back, "I hope you see true love in mine as well."

She smiles a knowing smile and taps her nose in the most ador-able way a grandmother can. She kisses my forehead and says some-thing to Roan in Afrikaans as she gives him a hug next. He nods, his eyes sincere as he takes my hand and leads me away from the tiny, lemon-yellow house that's so full of history and love I find myself hoping it's not the last time I visit.

When we get back in the car, my heart feels like it's grown two sizes because this is more. This is definitely so much more.

Roan

It's ten o'clock at night by the time we arrive at my mother's small apartment above the dance studio where she works. Allie's eyes barely stayed open the entire drive here, so I know she's beat. It was a long day of travelling and a full evening of family time that she was not at all prepared for.

We shuffle up the three stories to my mom's flat.

"Mom, are you sure this is okay? We can get a hotel room."

"Absolutely not!" she exclaims as she unlocks the deadbolt. "I only have you for two days, and I won't lose a minute of it. The pull-out sofa is all ready for you."

We walk inside with our suitcases, and I smile because it still smells like home. Like a strange blend of garlic and lavender. Mia and Ava head down the hall to their rooms, probably dying for some cell phone time, and my mother rushes around to get us towels and extra blankets.

Allie takes her turn in the bathroom first, showering the long day off of her body and changing into her night clothes. When she walks out in a short, sexy nightie, she looks sheepishly at me. "I need one of your T-shirts."

My chest shakes with silent laughter, but I keep my mouth wisely shut as I dig in my suitcase and hand one over to her.

She takes it from my hand. "This is why it's nice to warn your girlfriend about important trips where sexy nightwear might not be appropriate."

I shake my head. "No way. The image of you walking out of the bathroom will keep me warm for months, mooi."

She chucks my T-shirt at me. "Go get changed."

With a happy sigh, I toss my shirt back to her and head to the bathroom. When I return a few minutes later, my mother is giving Allie a big hug.

"It's good to have you here, Allie."

"It's good to be here," Allie replies, pulling back and tucking her wet hair behind her ears with a shy smile.

My mom strokes her hair affectionately. "You impressed me today. I can see why Roan chose you to be the first girl he brought home."

With those parting words, my mom turns on her heel and kisses me goodnight before heading toward her bedroom.

Allie turns her suddenly wide awake eyes at me. "First girl?"

I exhale heavily and walk around to the far side of the sofa bed. "Don't get all weird," I say, pulling back the covers and crawling in.

"Weird?" she exclaims, her voice giddy-sounding as she slides in next to me. "Why would I get weird?"

She turns on her side to face me, propping her head on her hand. The dim lamp illuminates her amused expression enough to have me rolling my eyes.

"We should get some sleep." I flick the light off, hoping darkness will help Allie pass out sooner so she doesn't hit me with a million questions about why I never brought a woman home to meet my mother.

Unfortunately, I can still make out Allie's cheery face in the faint light streaming in from the window. She has a gleeful smile when she says, "I seriously can't believe I'm the first girl you brought home to meet your mother."

I turn on my side to drape my arm over her. "It's not a big deal."

She giggles at my dry tone and tucks herself under my chin, nestling into me like I'm her own personal cocoon. "Just because you say things aren't a big deal doesn't mean they're not. In fact, everything you say isn't a big deal actually is a really big deal."

I press my nose to her damp hair and inhale deeply before replying, "Fine, it's a big deal. I haven't brought women home because I've never liked anyone enough to share my family history with. But you did brilliantly today. Watching you listen to my gran and ask all those insightful questions…She more than liked you. She connected with you. It was incredible." My heartbeat increases as I feel the weight of that realisation like a thousand bricks on my chest.

"Well, I really liked her," Allie states softly, her voice losing that edge of humour it had before. "She's lived an amazing life."

"She has," I reply with a fond smile as I stare off into space. "So has my mom. They have both sacrificed a lot in their lives. When my mom moved to Cape Town with my dad to help him open up a medical clinic, it was a big deal and her family wasn't very supportive. Then, when my father passed, she was left with a ton of bills she couldn't pay. She did everything she could to keep our heads above water. She could have run back home to her family in England or taken a handout from my gran, but she was too proud for that. She told me that my father used to say overcoming obstacles determined the weak from the strong, and she had to be strong for me since he wasn't here anymore."

Allie trails her fingertips along my back in slow, languid circles as she asks, "Do your sisters see their dad?"

I nod and press my nose to her hair again. "When he's sober, he sees the girls. When he's not, he can't."

"Did you get along with him growing up?"

It's an innocent question that I'm grateful to have a good answer to because not all dark-skinned kids would be accepted by a white man. South Africa has come a long way, but it's far from perfect.

"We got along. He's actually the one who taught me soccer, so I kind of owe my career to him. I think his fondness for me is what made my mom fall in love with him. Sadly, he just loved alcohol more."

Allie remains quiet for several minutes. She's so still I wonder if she fell asleep.

"What did your grandma say to you tonight when we were leaving?"

My body tenses from her question because it's not something I'm ready to tell her yet. "Nothing, mooi," I murmur, dropping a kiss to her hair. "Just granny things."

Allie tightens her arms around my waist, pulling me in so our bodies are completely flush against one another. "Roan…Real or fake? You brought me here to meet your family because you're in love with me."

I pull my head back to look down at Allie's face. She lifts her chin and stares up at me with complete and total vulnerability. No fear. No doubt. No hesitation. Just complete and brave honesty.

Taking a deep breath, I bring my hand up to caress her cheek as I softly reply, "Real."

Her gaze shines in the dim lighting and I swear I see tears welling in her eyes. She brings her hand up to my face, mirroring my touch as she whispers against my lips, "Real or fake? I'm in love with you, too."

My heart thumps hard and fast in my chest because this is a moment I've never experienced with anyone before, and I want to feel it all. I want to remember her innocent face and her exposed expression. I want to remember the sight of my gran embracing her and telling her about our heritage. I want to remember the way her skin feels and looks against my skin. Like a swirl of something special and beautiful, magical and real. I want to remember it all.

I eliminate the space between us and press my lips to hers in a deep, intoxicating kiss. She responds with vigour because she is mine now, in this moment, in this time, in this life. She will never belong to another man as long as I walk this earth.

She laughs against my mouth and pulls away, tenderly rubbing her thumb over my lips as she says, "An answer will make this kiss that much better."

I half smile and it feels like my heart might burst any second. "It better be real, Lis, because I don't know how anything could be fake between us at this point."

CHAPTER

Allie

STARING AT MY REFLECTION IN THE MIRROR, I CAN'T HELP BUT swivel my hips in the bronze, metallic evening gown that Leslie designed for me. As the light catches the material with every flicker of movement, I marvel over Leslie's talents. The dress is the same one I tried on at her boutique several weeks ago, but now Freya has tailored it to me so well, it feels like a second skin. It has the thinnest of spaghetti straps with a sweetheart neckline and cinches tightly at the waist, highlighting my hourglass figure. My golden locks are curled into beachy waves, and my eyes are dark and dramatic with my red-orange matte lip stain.

I look good. I need to look good, though, because tonight is the Get Fit Britain Gala and Roan's date is a leggy brunette from Madrid who looks like a supermodel. She's exactly the type that athletes have on their arms at red carpet events.

When Niall had me run a background check on her, I had a mini panic attack when I came across her Instagram page. She seems to never wear anything other than a bikini. And since she's only twenty-one years old, her body looks airbrushed all the time. I would have much rather picked a different winner for Roan, but I couldn't exactly tell my boss I was in a relationship with Roan one minute and then tell him I wanted to pick a less attractive date for him the next. How unprofessional would that have been?

So I put on a happy face as I greeted Roan's date who was accompanied by her mother at the hotel yesterday. By now, Roan is on a romantic tour of London with her before they will arrive at the red carpet promptly at seven o'clock for the gala.

I keep reminding myself that jealousy can be foreplay. That's what Roan taught me in his kitchen a while back. Hopefully that means after he says goodbye to his date tonight, I'll have plenty of opportunity to show him just how green-eyed I feel over this evening.

In all honesty, though, I trust Roan. Even after the heartbreak that finding Ghost Penis and Rosalie in bed together caused me, I don't worry that Roan will do the same. Our trip to Cape Town changed things between us.

The final day of our trip was spent entirely with his mother and sisters. We saw sights. We drank wine and sampled local foods. I watched Roan salsa with his mother in the kitchen. Mia and Ava French braided my hair at the beach. It was like I was one of the family. Different from my own family dynamic in Chicago, and even different from my extended family in London. It was completely special and something that will stick with me forever.

When Roan's mother squeezed me goodbye at the airport, she brushed a piece of hair out of my face and said that she was going to sleep better knowing that Roan had someone like me taking care of him in London. It was amazing.

It felt like I was home when I was only a visitor.

Sleeping on Roan's shoulder on the plane ride home, I felt content for the first time in a long time. Everything I feel with Roan—the love I am embracing for him—is a truer, more honest, and more genuine love than I've ever experienced. The only thing standing between me and my future with this sexy and surprising South African of mine is my trip to Chicago.

I'll get the gala over with tonight and then next weekend is

Rosalie and Ghost Penis' wedding. I plan to be in and out of the wedding as fast as I was when I came to London for Aunt Fiona's. I'll stay long enough for Rosalie to get married. Then she will hopefully forget that I exist.

I'm just putting my phone into my clutch to leave when my father's name illuminates my cell screen with a call. My brows furrow because I haven't heard from him since moving to London, other than a short email asking if I got settled in okay.

I swipe to answer. "Hello?"

"Hello, Alice," Charles Harris says crisply into the line, sounding like he's conducting a business call instead of speaking to his daughter whose voice he hasn't heard in weeks.

"Hi, Dad," I reply warily. "Everything okay?"

"Everything is fine. I just wanted to wish you luck on your big night tonight."

My head jerks back. "You know about the gala?"

"Yes. I have Facebook."

"I didn't know you actually use it."

He exhales into the line. "I checked it out after I got a call from Vaughn a few weeks ago. He seems to think I'm not taking enough interest in you. Is that how you see it?"

I wince at his bluntness. My father has never been one to beat around the bush, but this conversation is not something I was prepared to have right before I walked out the door. This is more like a topic for family therapy.

"Dad, look. It's fine. I'm fine. I'm doing really well in London actually."

"Yes, that's what I hear from Vaughn. It would have been nice to hear it from you."

I hold back a laugh. "You're joking, right?"

"Why would I joke about such a thing?"

"Because you never ask about my life," I snap, my frustration from this ridiculous call bubbling over.

"That's because you always tell me," he retorts simply. "You're the one who always initiates communication."

"And you think that's okay?"

"I don't bloody know. I just know that's how it's always been between us. Ever since we moved to America, that's been our system."

"Some system," I scoff.

"What's that supposed to mean?"

I shake my head and think to myself, *Why bother?* Why bother telling him everything when he's just going to dismiss it and tuck it away in a drawer like he always does. But then I think about Roan's family and my cousins, and eating dinner with Camden and Indie at their kitchen counter, and watching Vaughn buzz around with a grandchild on his shoulders. All those images are far superior to the grey, sterile life I lived in Chicago and I feel cheated.

"Dad, I'm happier in London than I have been for years because I have a sense of family here. A sense of belonging. I have people who reach out to me, who want to see me. Vi calls and checks in on me every week. I go to Uncle Vaughn's house almost every Sunday for family dinner with everyone. My cousins threatened to pummel my new boyfriend if he doesn't treat me well."

"Boyfriend?"

"I'm not done," I state firmly, cutting him off. "Even Uncle Vaughn has given me more time and attention in the short time I've been here than you have the past couple of years."

"Divorcing Hilary was difficult, Alice. You know that. I was with her longer than I was with your mother."

"Catching Rosalie in bed with Parker was difficult, too. Why do your problems completely block out mine? I'm your daughter. You should care about my well-being," I seethe through clenched teeth.

"I do."

"Then why the hell are you forcing me to come back for Rosalie's wedding to watch you walk her down the aisle?"

"Rosalie said she spoke to you about it and you were fine."

"Rosalie is a liar and a sociopath. How can you possibly think I'd want to attend the wedding of my ex and my ex-stepsister who only ended up together after I caught them in bed together? Are you really that dense, Dad?"

He clears his throat gruffly. I can almost see him pacing back and forth in his office, regretting making this call in the first place because it's forcing him to experience emotions he hasn't tapped into in years.

But I've let him off the hook for far too long.

He begins stammering into the line—something I've never heard him do. "I didn't know. Rosalie made it seem…She's so hard to talk to…She has always needed more from me than you," he says, finally finding his words. "She's so different from you, Alice. You were easy. I never had to worry about you. I worry about Rose, even though her mother and I divorced."

I swallow the knot in my throat. "I know, Dad. And I don't hate you for it. I just…I miss you."

Silence spreads and I swear I hear a faint sniffle that he's trying to hide. "I miss you, too, Alice. And I'm proud of you for doing so well in London. Maybe I can come for a visit once my schedule clears up later this summer?"

The smile on my face is genuine. "I'd really like that."

"Good." He pauses and then softly adds, "We're going to be okay, right, darling?"

I nod even though he can't see it. "We're going to be okay."

Roan

Catalina points her phone in my face one more time, waving at me so that I wave back. I do. For the forty-seventh time tonight. Her

Instagram Story is so full of photos and videos of us during our hour-long tour of London that the line at the top of her phone is tiny dots instead of dashes.

She's a sweet girl, but she's more focused on her phone than on me, which suits me just fine because my eyes keep drifting over to my stunning, golden goddess of a girlfriend.

When Catalina and I arrived at the gala, Allie was in full business mode with Niall as they organised interviews for me and Mac by the velvet ropes that separate the red carpet from the media. It seems all of London's press showed up for this event because all of the photographers are piled on top of each other as they try to get photos of the A-list athletes with their dates.

The Win A Date Campaign helped raise more than one hundred thousand pounds for the cause, and it's kind of an incredible feeling to be walking the red carpet and have the press recognise who I am. I don't chase fame. Far from it. But I do chase success. And if these people know my name, I'm doing something right in my career.

Vaughn Harris, the Harris Brothers, and Vi are ahead of us, decked out in suits with their ladies clad in beautiful gowns. It's no surprise they all showed up to support this cause. I think they'd do just about anything for Allie.

I watch Tanner walk over to Allie, who's standing out of the spotlight next to Niall. He grabs her around the shoulders and pulls her over to their group, announcing to the press that she is their cousin and she belongs in the family photos. The press go crazy, snapping pictures like wildfire. The entire scene makes me smile. I know how much Allie enjoys being a part of a real family and the Harrises have treated her like a sister from the second she came back to London.

Mac's loud voice breaks my focus as he hoots loudly at something his date said. The person who won the company of Mac tonight is a guy named Michael from Boston who's been hanging on

Mac all night as they pose and smile for photos. It's a comical sight watching Mac ruffle the guy's hair in a brotherly way only to have the boy freak-out and rush over to a nearby mirror to fix it.

Catalina and I slowly make our way through the steps and repeat, stopping for all the interviews with various newspapers and magazines. Most ask Catalina about her trip to London and if I'm showing her a good time. Many ask about Bethnal Green's promotion to the Premiership and how I think next season will go.

I'm just finishing an interview when I feel a delicate hand slide up my back. I turn to find Allie standing right beside me. She smells fucking divine and is even more stunning up close. Her skin is glowing like she's been dipped in gold, and her blue eyes are bright against her heavily mascaraed eyes. I glance down at her red lips and I have to stop myself from kissing her senseless.

Her eyes drift down my body appreciatively before snapping up to Catalina with a polite smile. "How was your tour of London, Catalina?"

"Super good!" Catalina chimes and holds her phone up to take a selfie of the three of us.

Allie frowns briefly but then schools her features to look professional. "Are you ready to be shown to your table?"

Catalina nods and begins recording a video of the paparazzi, who are calling after us for more questions. Allie turns to lead the way, but I wrap my hand around her waist and pull her into me.

I press my lips to her ear and whisper, "As sexy as you look in that dress, all I can think about is how much fun it's going to be to take it off of you later."

Allie anxiously looks around the crowd before plastering on a smile and tucking a stray strand of hair behind her ear. Her actions don't stop the adorable blush that stains her cheeks.

I lean in again and add, "Are you wet for me, mooi?"

She laughs nervously and pulls away, noticing that Niall is watching us curiously. Clearing her throat, she loudly replies, "Yes, I think I can accommodate that request."

My eyes dance with amusement. "That's so generous of you." My voice is low when I add, "I hope you're good with being fucked against a wall tonight because I don't think we'll make it past the entryway."

She's prepared for my dirty comment and playfully brings a finger to her chin like she has to think. "Yes, I do believe we can get you a table by the wall."

I shake my head with a wide smile, dying to fucking carry her away from this place and show her how much I've truly fallen for her. Instead, I lean in one last time and my lips brush her ear as I murmur, "The truth is, you're the most beautiful woman here tonight and I'm a lucky bastard because I know that's the least interesting thing about you."

All humour vanishes as she pulls back and stares at me with wide, glistening eyes. I stare back without any hint of a smile so she knows I'm one hundred percent serious. Allie has always been beautiful. It's probably something she's been told her whole life by countless men. But the closer we've become, the more I've realised that it's not her beauty I fell in love with. It was everything else.

We continue gazing at each other for a long, meaningful moment while the rest of the world disappears around us, leaving only me, her, and our hearts that now beat for each other.

Our tender moment is thwarted when Niall walks over and says, "Let's head inside, shall we?"

I can't stop staring at Allie as Catalina and I follow her and Niall into the May Fair Hotel. The woman is fucking skipping in an evening gown. It's slight and not noticeable to everyone, but it's happening and I think I just fell more in love with her.

We arrive at the ballroom where our table is located. Sitting with us is Mac and his date, Michael, Catalina and myself, Niall and Allie, and Vaughn and Vi Harris are right beside me. The rest of the Harrises and their wives are seated at the next table over.

Dinner is served and conversation flows easily. Allie and I exchange several glances from across the table, but I try to pay attention to my date, even though most of her focus is on her phone.

When dessert is served, Vaughn turns his attention to me and says, "So Niall told me about the Adidas endorsement."

I inhale a nervous breath. "Nothing's official yet. I'm meeting with them in a couple of weeks."

"You'd be a great face for them," he says, grabbing his coffee and bringing it to his chest. "You've done a bloody good job of moving here and not getting caught up in the party scene like so many rookies do. London isn't an easy city to stay focused in, especially with all the extra attention from media and fans. But you've really impressed me, both on and off the pitch."

"Thank you, sir," I reply, exhaling through my nose in surprise.

"Enough with the sir nonsense," he says, waving me off. "You're practically family now. Call me Vaughn."

I swallow down his statement because it means more to me than he realises. I turn my eyes to watch Allie, who's laughing so hard at something Mac just said that she has tears in her eyes. She looks happy and at ease. Light and completely carefree. I did that. I gave her that sense of contentment.

She glances at me and offers the tiniest shift in her expression that tells me she knows I did that. She knows she's this happy because we're together. My heart thunders in my chest because I realise in this exact moment that I want to watch Allie Harris laugh for the rest of my life.

"I like the idea of being considered family," I state in a low voice and turn to face Vaughn, whose expression turns from lighthearted to serious as he picks up my change in tone.

"Good," he replies with a nod.

I inhale deeply, preparing to ask a question I never expected to ask tonight. "Does this mean if I were to ask Allie a certain question, you would give me your blessing?"

Vaughn blinks back at me in shock. "If you're asking what I think you're asking, you're speaking to the wrong Harris brother."

"I know," I reply, my jaw tight with determination. "But something tells me that Allie would want your blessing just as much as her father's."

Vaughn sits back, an incredulous look of pride written all over his face. "I'd be honoured to have you as a part of the family."

I huff out a nervous laugh because I can't fucking believe what I just did. I just…*Fucking hell.* Shaking my head, I swallow the knot in my throat and stammer, "Don't, erm, tell Allie about this conversation, please."

Vaughn barks out a laugh and sets his coffee down. "Your secret is safe with me, DeWalt."

He pats me on the back as the guest speaker takes the stage for his presentation. I exhale, relieved for a break from that surprisingly tense moment. I have no fucking clue what possessed me to ask Vaughn for his niece's hand in marriage, but ag, I think that's what I just did. The other shocking thought is that I don't regret it. It just felt right. Allie feels right.

I do my best to focus on the long presentation, but I notice that Niall is paying very close attention to his phone. A rude amount of attention, if I'm being honest. His brow furrows as he taps on the screen and pulls it closer to his face. After a few minutes, he taps Allie on the shoulder, who had been completely focused on the speaker up until now.

He leans in and whispers in her ear. Then Allie takes a sharp breath and covers her mouth with a shaky hand as she stares at his phone. Niall's face looks furious at her, pissed at whatever they are looking at on the screen.

I begin to notice other people's phones illuminating their faces all around us and wonder what the hell kind of breaking news has just occurred. Was there a bomb? A terrorist attack? A shooting? Who the fuck died?

Suddenly, Allie's eyes lift, connecting with mine. The look on her face is so terrifying, it takes everything I have not to jump across the table and ask her what's wrong.

I frown back at her and she shakes her head, tears slipping down her cheeks, one after another. I've never seen Allie cry. I've seen her tear up. I've seen her eyes water. This? Crying? Never.

Just as I plan to go to her, she looks at me and parts her lips to whisper, "I'm so sorry, Roan."

At the same time, Catalina gasps beside me. I turn to find her eyes locked on her phone, her jaw dropped. She looks up at me and blinks, her gaze sliding up and down my body before she finally leans in and says, "How much would I have had to donate for this kind of date?"

She holds her phone out to me, and at first it just looks like an array of moving shadows in a dark room. I squint and grab her hand, pulling the screen closer to me to make out what's on the video.

It's then that I see something I recognise.

Garter belt.

Wet dress.

Wet suit.

Wet…Allie.

I yank the phone out of Catalina's hand and jam my finger on the screen, fast-forwarding to see what comes next because I'm too impatient to watch the familiar scene that I've replayed in my mind a thousand times. But I have to say, my memory wasn't this vivid.

Allie's face suddenly fills the screen, making no mistake she is the woman wearing the garter belt. She fumbles with the phone for a second and then the video continues. My own face eventually comes into view. It's dark and shadowy, but it's obviously me. And let's face it, I was just outside talking to the press for a fucking hour. People know my face now. That means that this shit is out there for all of them to identify me.

I click the BACK button and see that the video is posted on some seedy-looking website written in a foreign language. The one headline I do catch sight of reads, "Striker Roan DeWalt Scores a Goal with a Harris."

The thumbnail video that plays on a loop is horrifying. In my memory, this night was only flashes of passion and lust. Laughter and enjoyment. It was sexy and pure. This video is anything but that. It shows everything. The oral, the different positions we fucked in, me spanking her ass, Allie riding my cock, the two of us looking like goddamned porn stars.

This video takes all those feelings I developed for Allie—feelings that I started having our first night together—and turns them into a seedy, disgusting, public, fucking sex tape.

The crowd begins to applaud because the guest speaker finished his presentation. I can't hear anything other than the ringing in my ears. Thank fuck I couldn't hear the sound on the video because I probably would have flipped the fucking table.

I slam Catalina's phone down and stand up from my chair. Allie stands up with me, watching me like I'm a lion ready to pounce.

"Roan, please—" she says through a choked sob.

"Don't," I growl, my teeth clenched together so hard, they could crack.

"What's going on?" Vaughn asks, his voice low and authoritative.

I ignore his question and shoot Allie a warning look that says, "Don't fucking follow me," before I turn to walk out of the ballroom.

Fuck this date.

Fuck this gala.

Fuck Allie fucking Harris.

And fuck her whole fucking family.

I storm out the front doors of the hotel without even thinking, and I'm instantly assaulted by paparazzi. Flashes go off and voices shout horrible questions at me about the twenty-eight-minute-long sex video that was just revealed by a porn site in India called Garish Entertainment.

"DeWalt! Do you always record your sexual encounters?" a voice calls out.

In a split second, I'm tearing toward the velvet ropes and grabbing the fucking photographer by his shirt.

The crowd gasps at my assault. And before I can grab the ass fuck's camera and throw it on the ground, two large hands grip me by the shoulders and pull me off the squirmy asshole who continues snapping photos despite his near-death experience. That's what would have happened to him if I had another second with him. A fucking painful death.

"Calm down, lad…You don't need this," Mac's Scottish accent growls in my ear.

He drags me down the red carpet and waves for one of the cab drivers who's parked in the line by the curb. The first one pulls up, and Mac shoves me inside, tucking himself in behind me and stating our home address at the driver.

As we pull away, I look out the window and see all four of the Harris Brothers jogging down the red carpet after us. They look fucking murderous, but it's a different kind of murder than I remember from when we played soccer at Vaughn's house. This look is for real.

They bang on the trunk as we take off, and I look back to see them waving down the next cab.

Mac looks at me wide-eyed and terrified. "Fuck me. What did you do?"

I lean forward and run my hands over my head, crouching my head between my knees. "What the fuck is happening?"

"You tell me!" Mac bellows. "All I know is that your date started saying shite about you being in a sex video online, and now we're being chased by the Harris Brothers by the looks of it." He looks behind us and shakes his head. "I think I can take Booker, but they have us outnumbered."

I sit back in the seat and purse my lips together, rage coursing through my veins. Without pause, I thrust my fist into the backseat of the cab.

"Knock it off, or I'll drop you off in the middle of the street!" the cabbie snaps at me.

"Aye, sorry, lad. We're having a bit of a moment. I'll tip you well, dinna fash." Mac turns to me, his voice deep and serious. "Fucking cool it and tell me what's going on."

"Allie made a fucking sex video of us and it's been published to some porn site."

"Fuck you!" Mac barks in disbelief. "How do you know it was her who did it?"

"There's a point when she looks like she tried to press something on the screen, but it kept recording."

Mac runs his hand over his jaw, shaking his head. "When did she do it?"

"Our first night together, fucking two years ago."

Mac huffs, "What is that? Some kind of kinky fetish she has?"

"Mac, I swear to fuck," I growl, clenching my fist and holding it up to his face. "I want to hit something so fucking bad right now, so keep it up and it'll be your damn face."

He frowns, sitting back in his seat and shaking his head. "But why did she do it? It doesn't seem like her."

"I don't fucking know."

"And you're sure she did it?"

I nod, my jaw ticking like a heartbeat. "She was trying to apologise before I saw it on Catalina's phone."

"Christ on a cracker, this is fucked."

I shake my head and look out the window, racking my brain for reasons why she would do this to me.

Is this why she didn't want to see me when she came back to London? Was she trying to make a quick buck by selling the video? Why is it coming out now? How is she fucking okay with having herself out there like that? None of it makes any sense.

The rest of the ride back to our house is in eerie silence, and a second cab pulls up right behind us when we arrive at our duplex. I step out of the cab first and wait on the sidewalk, ready for whatever the fuck the Harris Brothers have to say to me.

Gareth is the first one out of their cab. He strides straight toward me, his hands balled into fists at his sides. I know what's coming. I can tell the second I lay eyes on him. But rather than duck or protect myself, I stand my ground and watch him pull his arm back and clock me square across the jaw.

"Gareth!" Tanner yells, running up behind him as I stumble backwards and drop down on one knee.

My head is spinning, my vision blurred, and all I hear is the muffled sound of Mac shouting in front of me like a watchdog ready to rip the faces off a band of burglars.

When my ears stop ringing, I hear Mac say, "You don't even know the whole story!"

"What do you mean?" Gareth's voice booms.

"It was your—"

I grab Mac by the shoulder and shake my head in warning. "Don't say a word."

His eyes go wide as he silently compels me to tell them what happened. To tell them that the video had nothing to do with me. That it was all Allie's fault. But I won't give these guys the satisfaction. And if I'm being honest, I wouldn't mind if all four of them kicked the living shit out of me. The physical pain on the outside would be a hell of a lot easier to manage than the emotional torment I'm feeling on the inside.

"We fucking trusted you," Gareth growls, still being held back by Tanner while Booker and Camden stand nearby, rocking back and forth on their feet like they're ready to attack. "How the fuck could you do this to her?"

Mac opens his mouth to speak again, but I grab his shoulder and squeeze him hard into silence. He bites his fist, looking like he's going to explode from frustration, but I don't give a fuck. This isn't his fight. And no matter how hurt, and angry, and confused I am about what Allie did, I won't be the one to call her out to the only family that knows how to love her properly.

"You never trusted me," I state through clenched teeth. "You tolerated me at best."

"For good fucking reason!" Gareth snaps and then backs off enough for Tanner to let go of him.

Tanner turns and steps up to me so we're only a foot apart. He looks more serious than I've ever seen before as he says, "I trusted you. You're my teammate, Roan. My fellow striker. My bloody partner. Why would you do this?"

I shake my head. "If you think I could do this, then we were never fucking partners."

Tanner's brow furrows in confusion, but he juts his chin out and adds, "And next season? You're willing to throw it all away for this?"

"If that's what you need to believe, believe it," I state flatly, turning my icy gaze at all of them. "I'm done caring about what you fucking Harris Brothers think. I played your games. I jumped through your hoops. I tried to get you all to accept me. Christ, I've been kissing Harris ass since the second I stepped foot in London. But I'm done with all that now. If I never see a Harris again for the rest of my life, it will be too soon." I point my finger to their cab. "Now, I would appreciate it if you'd all get the fuck away from my property."

Tanner stares back at me like I'm Brutus who's just betrayed Caesar. Maybe I am. Maybe I was an idiot for getting involved with my teammates' cousin. Maybe it was ridiculous for me to think she was worth the risk.

Booker shakes his head, pulling Tanner away from me. "Come on, man. Allie deserves better."

"She'll find better," Camden adds, narrowing his eyes and turning to walk away.

Gareth points his finger at me and adds, "You stay the fuck away from her."

The four of them slide back into their cab and take off down the road, out of my sight. They love her blindly, I'll give them that. I only wish I was capable of doing the same.

CHAPTER 21

Allie

"Just tell me where he went," I beg one last time, standing in the doorway of Roan's house.

Mac narrows his green eyes at me, making me feel like an ant he wants to stomp all over. "How could you do it, Allie? You of all people?"

"It's complicated," I groan, raking my hands through my hair and pulling until it hurts.

What a fucking mess. Had I known what my father was going to do after hanging up the phone with me earlier this evening, I would have stopped him. I would have told him to walk Rosalie down the aisle. If he didn't want to do it, I would have found a mad scientist to make a clone of my father for Rosalie to prevent this mess from occurring.

But Rose didn't even give me a chance to change his mind. After Niall showed me the video on some horrible website, I pulled out my phone and saw the ominous text she sent me two hours earlier, confirming what she did.

Rose: Daddy backed out of the wedding. You are a selfish bitch.

By the time the media got a hold of the link and Niall was notified via an urgent text from the agency, the video was already up to twenty thousand views. *Twenty thousand people* saw everything Roan and I did in that hotel room.

Fucking mortifying.

Next thing I knew, my cousins went tearing out of the ballroom after Roan while I was stuck with Niall and Vaughn, who were both working tirelessly to find someone to get the video taken down. It was uploaded on a foreign website that was difficult to trace.

It took Vi contacting a friend of hers she called Frank and Beans, who knew a hacker that could get into the site to remove the file. Within five minutes of the call, the video was gone, but the damage had been done.

I officially have a sex tape leaked of myself with an athlete and nothing would ever change that.

I didn't have time to explain what happened to Vaughn or Niall before I asked Vi to give me the keys to her car. I needed to see Roan. I needed to make sure he was okay, that we were okay. I needed to explain that the video was a horrible mistake and that I was so utterly wrong and sorry.

So here I am now, getting mean looks from the friendliest Scotsman on the face of the earth.

"Mac, I would love to tell you why I did it, but I need to speak to Roan first. You really won't tell me where he went?"

He shakes his head. "He's one of the good ones, Allie. You really fucked-up."

"I know!" I shriek, my emotions bubbling over as I turn and walk away, shaking my head and cursing my own stupid actions for the ten thousandth time. Tears stream down my cheeks as I drop onto their front steps and cry. I'm not crying for myself and my public humiliation. I'm crying over my betrayal against Roan that I will never be able to forgive myself for.

"I'm such an idiot, Mac. I was so lost when I made that video. So confused about who I was and what real love actually looked like. That heartbreak turned me into some horrible version of myself who I never even knew existed. But then I met Roan, and I fell in love with the person I became when I was with him. And I fell in love with him. I didn't even know I was capable of feeling love like that after everything that happened.

"And I know I should have deleted the video two years ago. But every time I tried, I couldn't bring myself to do it because I knew there was something special between us, even after our first night together. I couldn't let that go until I realised I didn't need the video. I just needed him."

My breath catches in my throat as the sobs rack through my chest like a child trying to recover from a tantrum. I definitely feel like a child. This entire nightmare is the most immature, idiotic, stupid thing I have ever done, and I'll never be able to take it back.

"Fucking hell," I hear Mac growl as he steps outside of the house and moves down the steps to sit beside me. He pats me on the back awkwardly. "I can't handle women crying. It's a thing for me."

I sniff and wipe away my tears. "I love him so much, Mac. I'll never forgive myself for ruining everything."

Mac gets a pained look in his eyes as he pulls his hand back and braces his arms on his knees. "Ruining everything is a grand statement to make, lass."

"Well, it feels like everything is ruined." I swallow the painful ache in my throat and turn to look him in the eyes. "I may not ever get Roan's forgiveness, but I hope I can earn yours someday, Mac. You're a great friend to Roan, and I'm sorry I've let you down."

His eyes dance over my mess of a face for a moment before he releases a heavy sigh. He shifts to dig into his pocket and grabs a set of keys. He pulls one silver key off the ring and hands it over to me.

"What's this?" I ask, my voice hollow.

He purses his lips and replies, "It's a key to Tower Park. I'll bet you anything he's there. It's where most of us go when we need to clear our heads."

My eyes fly wide as I clutch the key in my hand.

He head nods toward Vi's car. "Park at the northeast player's entrance, then go in and hang a left. It'll lead you out onto the pitch."

I hug Mac with all the strength in my body. He feels like a giant boulder, but I'm still squeezing, even if it hurts. I pull back and offer him a shaky smile. "Thanks, Mac."

He reaches out and wipes a tear from my eye. "Get the hell out of here before I start blubbering, too."

Before I know it, I'm sliding into Vi's car and taking off down the road like a bat out of hell. Minutes later, I pull up to Tower Park, and my heart races when I see Roan's car in the parking lot.

On shaky legs, I step out of the car and straighten my gown that I'll likely want to burn after the mess that this night turned out to be. The look on Roan's face when he saw the video will haunt me forever, and I deserve to be haunted by this. It was probably the worst thing I could have done to him.

I unlock the player's entrance and let myself inside of Tower Park. I take a quick left like Mac instructed and see lights shining at the end of the hallway. When I reach the wide opening, I see the Tower Park field. It looks different at night, the electric green grass almost cyan because of the faint blue security lights.

My eyes land on Roan, who's hunched over on the sideline bench about halfway down the field. His suit coat is draped over the bench and his white dress shirt is unbuttoned at the top with his bow tie hanging loose around his neck. He looks so beautiful. Beautiful and broken. I did that to him. I caused him this pain.

My heels sink into the soft grass, and my hands shake as I stop to pull them off. My metallic dress drags noisily as I walk barefoot toward him. Roan hears me coming and instantly stands up from his seat like he's going to run.

"I'm not ready to see you," he snaps, pacing back and forth like a lion in a cage.

"I need to talk to you," I reply, my voice shaking with anxiety. "I need to explain."

"Explain what?" he growls, turning to face me as I stop a good ten feet away from him. His face is dark in this light and the right side of his jaw looks red and swollen. Has he been crying? "Explain that you filmed us fucking without telling me?"

I pull my lips into my mouth, wishing a thousand more times that I could take that night back. "It was an accident."

"An accident?" he barks, his hands flying up to grip the back of his head as he stares up at the sky. "An accident that you propped your phone up to face the bed? Or an accident that you pressed record?"

I inhale a shaky breath. "I didn't mean to let it run that long."

"How long did you mean to let it run?" he exclaims, his eyes wide and accusing on mine. He marches closer, looming his anger over me and spreading his heady scent in the process. His face looks positively evil when he asks, "Long enough for me to stroke my cock in front of you? Long enough for me to eat your pussy? Long enough for me to slap your ass? Or were you just waiting for me to make you squirt because you knew it'd be good to sell?"

"Stop!" I yell, jerking away from him, feeling slapped across the face by his vulgar words. My chin trembles as I fight back tears. "You know none of that sounds like me."

"I thought I knew you, but the woman I fell in love with wouldn't have pressed that fucking record button in the first place!" he yells and backs away from me, looking at me like I'm a piece of shit he found on the sidewalk. "That was you who pushed record, right? Or was I fucking some secret twin sister you've been hiding from me as well?"

"It was me," I confirm, tears running down my face. "I just…It wasn't supposed to show your face. It wasn't supposed to even show mine. I tried to stop it after I took off my clothes for you, but I guess I missed the button. I don't know. I was caught up in the moment. But I was never going to show us having sex. That wasn't a part of my plan."

"Do you fucking hear yourself right now?" he roars, his hands clutching his head in complete and utter disbelief as he turns away from me. "You clicked a button on your phone to record the two of us fucking in your hotel room…You fucking used me, Lis! You used me like I was nothing. How did your conscience not stop you from doing that?"

"I don't know!" I scream and cover my face in horror. Hearing everything described back to me—hearing what I did and how I did it—makes me sound disgusting. Despicable. Unforgiveable. I *was* using him at the time and telling myself it was okay because he was a stranger. But none of that defence makes any sense to me now.

My voice is hoarse from crying when I say, "I was a mess when I met you. It had only been two weeks since my entire world had been turned upside down. I thought if I could record myself doing a striptease for a faceless stranger, it would make my ex jealous and show my stepsister that she didn't break me. It was a stupid plan, okay?"

"You're goddamned fucking right it was stupid!" he growls and swerves toward me, hovering close to me again. His eyes fill with anguish as he adds, "I could get kicked off the team. My mom and my sisters depend on me. They depend on my support. And I can kiss that endorsement deal goodbye. You have completely fucked-up my life, Allie!"

"I'm sorry!" I sob, reaching out for him, only to have him jerk away from me like I'm a diseased animal. My voice is a garbled mess as my body shakes violently with regret. "Truly, I'm so sorry! But you have to know I was never going to show them. After I got to know you that night, I knew I couldn't go through with showing them. You were too special."

Roan barks out a disbelieving laugh. "Well, lucky fucking me, you waited to release it until after I fell in love with you."

"I didn't release it." I sniff and wipe away my tears, my chest heaving with emotion. "Rosalie had access to my Cloud, and she threatened to leak the video unless I came to her wedding and supported my father walking her down the aisle."

Roan freezes in place, dropping his hands to his sides as he stares back at me in complete silence, communicating only with the pain radiating from his entire body. Finally, he says, "That's why you didn't want me to go with you to their wedding? Because you were afraid Rosalie was going to call you out?"

I rake my hands through my hair, hating how this keeps getting worse and worse and knowing that my words won't make any of it go away.

"Was anything you said to me true, Allie?" he asks, his voice composed with a tone of finality to it. I see tears shining in his eyes and it kills me. It kills me that he's letting this one mistake discredit everything we experienced together.

"Yes," I croak, moving toward him. My hands reach out, longing to touch him and pull him to me. To comfort him and show him that I'm still me, not the monster that he currently sees me as. "I love you, Roan. I love who I have become with you. I love my life here in London with you. This place doesn't feel like home without you."

"Home," he laughs and shakes his head. "I can't believe I took you home. I can't believe I introduced you to my gran. I can't believe I was so fucking stupid."

Pain. Searing, torturing, relentless pain slices through me at his words. My knees threaten to give out, and as he moves past me, I hear myself call out to him, "Is that it then?"

He stops midstride, only turning his head to reply, "Yeah, that's it…because you definitely weren't worth the chase."

I drop down on my knees, sobbing as he walks away and leaves me alone on the pitch. Each step he takes further from me feels like a vice squeezing my heart. I want to run after him. I want to chase him the way he chased me and beg him to forgive me, but I know it's too late. It's all much too late. Closing my eyes, I let the pain of losing the man I love overcome me.

CHAPTER 22

Roan

Normally when I walk into Tower Park, I feel like a man on top of the world. I feel like someone who won the fucking lottery and gets paid to play his favourite game.

Today, I feel like the tattered nets that are tossed into the trash.

It's been five days since the video released. Five days since my world was turned upside down. And five days since I walked away from the only woman I've ever loved.

The press have been relentlessly trying to get me to do an interview. Other pornography sites have been calling with offers of huge sums of money to let them publish the video legally. It's been a disaster.

And my mother…My mother is at a loss for words, which is a rare thing when it comes to her. She didn't see the video, thank fuck. Nor did my sisters or gran. But it's been reported on the news, even down in South Africa, so the shame that I've brought to all of them kills me. It *kills* me.

Our team lawyer, Santino, has been working around the clock, issuing takedowns for every pirated copy of the video that pops up on the internet. Legal action has begun to sue the owner of the IP address that uploaded the video without consent, which happens to be Allie's very lovely cunt of a stepsister.

Today, I'm at Tower Park to meet with Vaughn, Niall, and Santino to sign a statement for the world because the longer I stay silent, the worse it all looks. And I'm ninety percent sure today is the day I'm getting fired from Bethnal Green F.C.

I wish I could care. I wish I could muster the strength to stand up and fucking fight for my place on the team. But my heart is too empty to fight. My soul has shrivelled up to nothing and my drive has disappeared into thin air. Right now, I just want to go the fuck home.

Vaughn's secretary waves me through toward his office. As I walk in, Vaughn states in an ominous tone, "Close the door behind you, son."

I do as I'm told and take the open seat in front of Vaughn's desk beside Santino, who smiles sympathetically and pats me on the shoulder. It feels patronising even though I know he doesn't mean it that way. I don't like needing help. I don't like being someone who causes waves and creates drama. I've spent the majority of my life completely drama free and now I've managed to reach my lifetime max of drama in less than a week.

Avoiding eye contact with Vaughn, I glance over at Niall, who's perched on the credenza in front of the large glass window that overlooks the pitch. He's dressed in another one of his perfect grey suits with a banana-yellow tie that sets me on edge for some reason.

Finally, I force myself to look at my manager—a man who has been like a father to me since I came to London—and my stomach rolls when I realise he can't even make eye contact with me.

Vaughn clears his throat and stares down at the papers on his desk as he says, "Thanks for coming in today, DeWalt. I'm sure the last few days have been difficult for you."

I nod silently, my jaw ticking with fear, but I steel myself to remain composed.

"We've drawn up a statement to the media," Niall says, pushing himself off the back desk and walking toward me with a piece of paper in his hand. "But we need you to sign it before we can have it issued."

I look at the paper in his hand and inhale deeply. "Does that statement say I'm no longer a player for Bethnal Green F.C.?"

Vaughn's eyes snap up from his desk. "What?"

I swallow the knot in my throat, trying to be strong but feeling like I could break into a million pieces over the thought of leaving the team. I even hate the idea of leaving Tanner, who hates the ground I walk upon right now, but it's the fucking ground we walk on together.

"I assume you've brought me in here to let me go," I clarify, needing to hear the words out loud before I see them in black and white.

Niall barks out a hyenic laugh that grates on my nerves. "We haven't brought you in for that. This is a strategy meeting."

"Strategy?" I ask, looking back and forth between Vaughn and Niall.

"They need someone to fall on the sword is more like it," Santino says, sharing a displeased look with Vaughn.

"What do you mean by that?" I ask.

Niall grabs a chair from the side of the room and props it right in front of me. He unbuttons his suit jacket before lowering himself into the chair. "Look, I know Allie is Vaughn's niece, but the truth of the matter is she is not a player for the team and Vaughn's loyalty must go to you in this matter."

"All right," I reply slowly, still not following.

Niall hands me the paper and continues, "This statement says that Alice Harris knowingly recorded a nonconsensual sexual video of you and that legal charges have been filed."

"What?" I exclaim, sitting forward and swerving my eyes to Santino. "Have legal charges been filed against Allie?"

Santino shakes his head, eyeing Niall sternly. "No. We've only filed charges against Rosalie Dawson since she is the individual who illegally uploaded and distributed the video."

"But the public doesn't give a shit about Rosalie Dawson—a nobody from Chicago," Niall states, leaning forward and bracing his elbows on his knees and getting annoyingly close to me. "They need someone they recognise to take the blame. This statement says that Alice Harris has been terminated from all employment pertaining to Bethnal Green F.C., as well as the PR firm representing the team. It says that *she* knowingly published the video without written consent from you and will accept all legal action here forth."

"Allie was fired?" I ask, standing up and dropping the sheet of paper on my chair like it's poison. "Has that already happened?"

Niall narrows his eyes, obviously annoyed by my reaction. "Yes, Roan. Of course she was fired. We can't have a PR nightmare working at a PR firm." He grabs the paper and places it on Vaughn's desk, jamming his pointer finger on it. "This statement is your ticket out. This statement turns Roan DeWalt into the martyr everyone wants to feel sorry for."

"I don't want to be a fucking martyr," I snap and grip the back of my neck, my mind swirling with an array of emotions I can't fully comprehend right now. "And I'm not letting Allie take the blame for this. Hell no."

Niall scoffs and looks pointedly at Vaughn to take over.

Vaughn splays his hands out on the desk, looking pained as he states, "Allie very willingly signed the statement, admitting that you had nothing to do with the video and were completely innocent. I know you want to protect her, but she has a lot less to lose here. You have your entire career to think about. And Adidas."

"Adidas is still on the table?" I ask, jerking my head toward Niall.

Niall gets a wormy look on his face, like he's pleased with his mad skills. It makes me want to punch him. "Yes. They can't blame you for the illegal actions of others." He straightens his tie. "We throw this scandal all on Allie and label her the black sheep cousin of the Harris family. You put it all on her and we'll get you back on track with Adidas for your endorsement deal."

I blink at him, shocked and somewhat amazed that I came in here today expecting to lose my job and my endorsement deal. Instead I'm being told that I have a chance to save them both. But at what cost? Does Allie deserve my loyalty? Why am I so resistant to letting her take the blame? It is entirely her fault. She kept this monumental secret from me the whole time I was falling in love with her. Doesn't she have this coming?

Niall grabs a pen, shoving it in my hand and straightening the paper on Vaughn's desk. "Sign here and get your dreams back, DeWalt."

My eyes swerve to Vaughn, who looks positively ill. "Sir, you're actually okay with this?"

Vaughn exhales heavily, and he looks like he's aged ten years in the past ten minutes. "I'm not happy about it, but Allie was adamant about this and I'm supporting her. And despite our family connection, this is my club and you are my responsibility."

I shake my head, still not convinced. "So I sign this and I get my life back?"

"Yes," Niall states, his eyes widening with urgency. "What are you waiting for?"

Allie

"Unemployment does not suit me," I state aloud as I kneel down in front of Camden and Indie's fishbowl and prop my chin on the edge of the table. "Hello, Snowflake. How's life inside a bowl?"

The betta barely even moves. His tiny, fluttering gills are the only indication that the thing is even alive. I tap on the glass and beg for him to show me some sort of attention, anything to make me feel less lonely.

"It looks pretty nice to me." I glance at the tiny sprig of ceramic coral nestled amongst the red rocks lining the bottom. "I bet it's quiet in there. Peaceful. You don't have any sociopathic family members in there, trying to ruin your life."

"Sociopathic seems a bit harsh," Camden says, and my head snaps to the front door that I didn't even hear open. "I'd call us charmingly dysfunctional."

I stand up and my eyes fly wide as I see it's not only Camden. Indie strolls in behind him with Tanner and Belle. Through the door next is Booker and Poppy, each with a twin on one hip. Behind them is Gareth carrying Milo in a car seat carrier with Sloan and Sophia beside him. Vi, Hayden, and Rocky bring up the rear.

"I, um, wasn't referring to you guys," I state, my eyes blinking uncomfortably because they're all chattering away at each other like it's completely normal for them to hang out at Camden and Indie's house on a Thursday night.

I watch in amazement as everyone hunkers down in the living room. Booker and Poppy each grapple with a one-year-old while Sloan prepares a bottle for Milo. Little Rocky has broken loose from her mother's arms and is currently working hard at pulling all of Camden's James Patterson novels off the book shelf.

Camden wrinkles his nose at the horrific scene. "It's fine…It's totally fine. They're all just sorted based on my favourite puns, and it only took me an entire weekend to get them exactly how I like them. But look, she seems to be using them for a dance floor, so there's the silver lining to my agony."

Vi's brows lift as she doesn't even attempt to hide her amusement. "Let's call it preparation for your own little one, shall we?"

Camden deadpans, "Oh, joy. Maybe our newborn will be an overachiever and wreak havoc on the Dewey Decimal System."

The two of them begin arguing and I start to feel a bit like an outsider who wasn't invited. I move past Vi and Camden to make my way toward the stairs.

"Where are you going?" Vi asks, holding a hand in front of Camden so he'll stop complaining about the books. "This family meeting is for you, so it would be good if you stayed."

"For me?" I ask, my brows furrowing.

"Yes, we need to talk. Where are you trying to go?" she asks.

I point to the steps. "I was just heading upstairs to finish packing. My flight leaves tomorrow morning."

"You're still going to your stepsister's wedding?" Vi asks innocently enough.

I shake my head. None of them know that it was Rosalie who released the video. Vaughn knows because I had meetings with him and his lawyer a few times this week, but he swore he wouldn't say a word to anyone until I was ready. So far, I haven't been ready. So far, I've just been doing everything I can to not fall apart.

My eyes divert to the floor. "My dad has a couple of interviews set up for me."

"Interviews?" Indie chimes in from her spot on the ground where she's playing with the twins. She holds her black glasses away from their prying hands. "Interviews for what?"

I exhale heavily, not expecting to tell them all at once like this. "For a job."

"You're looking for a job in Chicago?" Camden asks, his voice tight with shock. "What, like, for good?"

A knot forms in my throat. "I just think it's better for me not to be around all of you guys. You don't need my reputation dragging you down."

"Oh, sod off with that nonsense!" Tanner bellows, draping his arm around Belle. "If we gave a toss about our reputations, we wouldn't have let Gareth pop Roan in the bloody jaw."

"Wait…What?" I ask, my brows furrowing in confusion.

Booker pipes up next. "Gareth socked Roan right in the jaw on Saturday night, outside of Roan's house. It was a proper swing, too. DeWalt went down on the ground and everything."

"Why did you punch Roan?" I ask, my mouth hanging open.

Gareth looks at me like I have two heads. "Because of the video he made of course."

"He didn't make the video!" I exclaim, my voice reaching a high pitch that probably only dogs could hear. "I did!"

Everyone's jaws drop as they watch me.

I want to punch myself because, not only did I invade Roan's privacy, but he got his ass kicked because of me. I scrub my hands over my face, horrified that they got it all backwards. "Didn't you guys see the video? It's obvious it was me."

"No!" all the boys snap in unison, their faces twisting up in disgust.

I let out a dramatic groan. "I made the video after my horrible breakup, when Roan was nice enough to take me to Aunt Fiona's wedding. I thought it would be a good payback for my ex…Make him jealous or something stupid. I never planned on moving back to London, so I didn't think it would ever get back to Roan. Clearly I was wrong because my stepsister got a hold of it and posted it to spite me."

"What video?" Sophia asks, her eyes bright and innocently quizzical.

"Nothing!" Sloan exclaims, standing up with Milo in her arms. "Let's go see what Uncle Camden and Aunt Indie have for snacks in the kitchen." Rocky cheers and bolts ahead of her toward the kitchen with the twins hot on her heels.

Sloan gives me a sympathetic smile and walks away just as Camden interjects. "If DeWalt didn't know anything about the video, why didn't he say so?"

My mind swims with confusion. "He didn't tell you guys that I recorded it without his consent?"

"No," Tanner barks, standing up and stroking his beard. "He just stood there while we gave him a proper dressing-down."

"Why would he let you guys blame him?" Poppy asks, frowning at Booker.

There's a moment of silence until Vi states, "Dad said that Roan didn't sign the statement either." She turns her worried eyes to me and adds, "I spoke to Dad a little bit ago. He's been really tight-lipped about the whole thing, but he said Roan refused to sign some statement that would make this all go away."

"Oh my God," I say, my entire body trembling from this new realisation. "That statement says it was all my doing. That I recorded the video without his consent and released it without his authorisation. He has to sign that statement. It puts all the blame on me and will save his career. If he doesn't agree to it, he could lose everything. What is he doing? Why is he not telling everyone it was me?"

The room goes quiet again before Gareth's deep voice states, "Because he loves you."

My head swerves to my cousin, his dark eyes staring at me with a resigned look about them, like he's been wrong about Roan all along.

"He did love me. Past tense," I correct because I still can't shake the disturbing way Roan looked at me at Tower Park.

Gareth exhales heavily and stands up to walk over to me. He puts his hands on my shoulders. "Allie-Cat, no man gives up what he's giving up unless he's head over heels in love."

My eyes fill with tears. Tears that I haven't felt since I dragged myself off the Tower Park pitch and cried myself to sleep in Vi's car. I've been numb the past week. Numb when I signed the statement. Numb when I packed my bags and prepared myself to move. Numb to the idea of moving away from my cousins whom I've grown to love more than I ever imagined. The idea that Roan might still love me is a hope I won't allow myself to have.

Gareth's face softens as he takes in my tears. He pulls me to his chest and rubs the back of my head. "It's going to be okay, Allie-Cat," he says, his chest rumbling against my cheek.

I shake my head, pulling out of his arms, knowing I don't deserve the comfort. "You all have been so good to me since I moved here. Including me in your family, making me feel like a friend. And Vi, you were so kind to set me up with Roan, and I…I just…I ruined everything. I brought this horrible scandal to your family, and I'm seriously sick about this—" My voice cuts off as I begin to sob.

Vi walks over to me and puts an arm around my shoulders, stroking my back in a motherly way that makes the tears in my eyes fall even faster. "You don't need to explain anything to us, Allie. We're your family, too. We've got your back no matter how stupid you are."

I huff out a garbled laugh and wipe away the tears. "This is certainly the stupidest thing I have ever done. It makes the stuff Tanner has done look like child's play."

"That's the bloody truth," Vi says with a small laugh.

Tanner nods knowingly. "I do have to hand it to you, Allie. It is a grade-A fuck-up and I'm mildly jealous about losing the Biggest Harris Screw-up throne."

Vi laughs and turns to face me, hitting me with her bright blue eyes as she says, "Regardless, it doesn't change how much we love you and how much you are still a part of this family and always will be."

I pull Vi in for a hug, needing the affection and comfort more than I realised. "Thank you," I croak and pull back, sniffing loudly. "But, honestly, finding a job in London with the reputation I have now is going to be hard. I think I owe it to my dad to do the interviews in Chicago. Perhaps he and I can have a fresh start now that the Rosalie drama is behind us."

Vi looks around at everyone, clearly not liking the idea but holding her tongue. "If going back to Chicago is what you need, we'll support you. But we're always here when you need us."

I nod and exhale deeply, believing that more now than I ever did before. But there's still one very important thing I have to take care of before I leave.

CHAPTER 23

Roan

A LOUD BANGING ON MY DOOR HAS ME DROPPING MY XBOX controller and heading down the steps toward the front door. When I open it, I'm whacked in my chest by a tiny little fist.

"You idiot!" Allie exclaims, standing in the rain on my doorstep and pushing me so hard I stumble back into the foyer. She slaps a piece of paper against my chest, her blonde hair wet around her face as she stares up at me. "If you don't sign this right now, I will park myself on your doorstep in this miserable rain."

"What are you doing?" I ask, grabbing her by the wrist and pulling her through the entryway.

My hand releases hers instantly, feeling an intense burn from the brief contact my skin had with hers. My eyes look her up and down. It's been days since I've seen her, but it feels like years. Her T-shirt and jeans are damp, and her chest heaves as she fights to catch her breath. A shiver runs up my spine because it hurts to have her this close to me. I can smell her floral scent and see the stress in her eyes. She looks tired and not like herself. If this were last week, I would have pulled her into my arms to soothe whatever pain she has away. I would have rubbed the furrowed line on her forehead until she smiled.

But everything is different now.

"I'm trying to save you, you idiot!" she bellows, crinkling the soggy paper in her hand, her shoulders rising up to her ears. "Why won't you sign this, Roan? They said it can save your endorsement deal. You've been working toward that for so long."

"Don't you think I know that?" I snap, my tone acidic as my hands ball into fists to fight the muscle memory they have to pull her in close and feel the weight of her in my arms.

Allie's anger dissipates, her fierce blue eyes softening into a silent plea. "Then sign it. Sign it and you can leave this all behind you. You can leave me behind and get on with your life."

"Oh, is that all I have to do to forget about what you did? I sign that and it magically erases that video from my mind forever?"

She sags against the open doorframe, her eyes swimming with tears as she looks anywhere other than my face. "It's a start."

"Do you think I give a fuck about my endorsement deal anymore?" I bark, shoving a hand through my hair and gripping the back of my neck. "Right now, I'm just trying to figure out how to fucking function with the crater-sized hole you left in my heart."

Her chin trembles and she sniffs hard, shaking her head sharply as she fights back her tears. "I can't fix your heart and I can't change what I did. But this…This I can do."

I scoff, shaking my head at how she still doesn't get it. She doesn't get that what's broken in me cannot be fixed. My voice is hollow when I ask, "Tell me this, Allie. Why the fuck did you do it?" I lean down to look her square in the eyes. "Because I've spent the past week going over all of our time together. Every day, every hour, every fucking minute, and kiss, and caress, and I can't figure out how I didn't see this coming. How could I be so goddamned blind to this dark side of you?"

"I did have a dark side," she replies, exhaling heavily and swiping at the black mascara running down her cheeks. "But it was only because I was in pain, Roan. I was in more pain than I think I even realised. When I found Parker and Rosalie in my bed together, my entire world

249

was turned upside down. Until that moment, I thought I had a good life. I knew my dad wasn't real affectionate, but I was okay with that. I thought Rose was my real sister, but that was a lie. I thought Parker loved me, but it turned out he loved her more. I truly thought I had a family and a good life, but one betrayal turned everything I knew into a lie."

"I know the feeling," I retort, narrowing my eyes at her.

She deflates under my gaze, biting her lip nervously before she adds, "I didn't even cry when I found them in bed together. I just left. I cut ties, but I wanted to get back at them instead of grieving my losses. I wanted to get back at the world for putting all those false relationships in my life and telling me I was safe when I so clearly wasn't."

She pauses, pulling in huge breaths of air as she works through feelings that I don't know if she's ever truly worked through before.

"The striptease video idea was fucking stupid," she adds, continuing with her explanation. "It was something I thought would only hurt them, but it turned out to be something very different in the end."

"I'd say," I snap, my jaw ticking with frustration. "It turned out to be a sex video of us for the whole fucking world to see."

"That's not what I meant," she replies as she steels herself to step forward, closer to me. So close I can smell her scent again, which causes an involuntary reaction in my body.

"That video, Roan…I couldn't bring myself to delete it for the longest time because it helped me. As horrible and stupid as it was for it to even exist, I watched it after I left you and it made me feel desirable at a time when I should have been insecure and doubting everything about myself because Parker chose Rosalie over me. Just having it on my phone, in my possession, and knowing I was capable of doing what I did in it made me stronger. Hell, it's what made it possible for me to fall in love with you!"

My head jerks back, unable to comprehend her logic. "It was a video of us fucking, Allie. Nothing more."

"It *was* more and you know it!" she snaps, whipping my vulgar words to the ground. "The way you looked at me that night…The way you spoke to me and how my body reacted to you…We had just met and you had already made me feel more alive than I had been in my entire life. You saw me better than anyone else had ever seen me! And when I went home, that video gave me a piece of myself back that I lost years ago."

She touches my hand, sliding her delicate fingers against my palm before holding it. "Then we reconnected and you confirmed that what we had was special. I couldn't help but fall in love with you and once that happened, I didn't need the video anymore. I had the real thing looking at me and everything felt right in the world."

I pull my hand out of her grasp, unable to accept her affection because it hurts too much. All of this hurts too much. We were so good, I wanted to spend the rest of my life with her. But can we come back from something like this?

"Why didn't you just tell me? You had so many chances," I finally state.

She nods knowingly and steps back to lean against the doorframe again. "I wanted to tell you a million different times, but I was too afraid to break our happy bubble. I've never been as happy as I was when I was with you. Never. So I told myself that deleting the video would erase the memory. That we were already making so many new memories together, we didn't need the old ones."

I close my eyes, a burning ache forming on the backs of my lids. "I just don't see how I can ever forget what you did."

"I know," she replies, the corners of her mouth turning down as her voice shakes. "And I can never fix that for you. But I can try to fix your career if you'll sign this damn statement."

I cross my arms over my chest. "Letting someone else take the fall isn't how I do things."

"Well, making sex videos isn't how I do things either, so I think it's time for trying new things." She forces a smile that hurts my fucking soul as she hands the paper over to me. "Sign the statement, Roan," she says with a final tone to her voice, pursing her lips and trying to fight back tears. "And I hope you can find it in your heart to forgive me someday. But please know that I will never forgive myself."

She pauses like she wants to hug me goodbye but knows she shouldn't. The entire act feels final and distant for some odd reason, like she's not just going back to Notting Hill but far, far away. With one last withering look, she steps out into the rain and I watch her leave.

When I can no longer see her, I look down at the piece of paper in my hand that has an offer on it. An offer that I really shouldn't refuse. The problem is, the offer I thought I was going to spend the rest of my life with isn't on the table anymore.

Sweat pours down my back as the automatic soccer ball track kicks out the last five balls at me in five-second intervals. I zig and zag, eating up the Tower Park training room and stopping the balls with my foot before launching them into the unguarded net. The sound of the ball hitting the net every damn time is music to my ears and a welcome distraction from my roaring, painful thoughts.

I've been at it for two hours, trying to sweat away the look on Allie's face when she left yesterday. Trying to sweat away the tender touch of her hand on mine. Trying to sweat away the memory of a body that I knew so intimately that I could bring it to life with a single breath of air.

My body aches from exertion as I walk over to my duffel bag and drop down on the ground to fish out a water bottle. I drink half the contents and hear a door open in the distance. I look over to see Vaughn Harris walking toward me. He has that all-business look on him again. The same one he had when I met with him about the statement.

"DeWalt, did you forget it's the off-season?" he asks, coming to stand above me with his arms crossed.

"This is the only place that quiets my brain," I reply by way of explanation.

His brows lift. "Is it working?"

I huff out a laugh. "Not really."

He half smiles and lowers himself to the ground beside me. "That's women for you."

I turn to look at him, surprised by his candidness. "Does it ever get easier?"

He shakes his head slowly. "Not if you find one who's worth it."

I frown at him curiously. "How do you know when someone is worth it?"

He releases a heavy sigh. "For me, it was when I realised that I cared more about her than football." He offers me a resigned smile. "I quit football after my wife got sick, you know. I was the top player at Man U at the time and life was good. Really good. But then Vilma became ill and nothing else mattered. I actually got into a massive row with my brother about quitting. That's Alice's father, Charles. He couldn't believe I was breaking a million-pound contract to watch my wife die. I couldn't believe he didn't see that it wasn't even an option for me to stay. At the time, I knew that there was no career or amount of money in the world that was more important than my family."

"Did you ever have any regrets?" I ask, hanging on his every word.

"I had regrets for years, but only because I lost myself when I lost her. I didn't appreciate the legacy of my wife who lived in the eyes of my children. It was a dark time for my whole family."

I straighten my legs out and absorb his comment for a minute. "You seem to be great with all of them now. Sunday dinners and all that."

"That's because if there's enough love, all is forgivable." He shrugs like it's a simple comment, but it doesn't feel simple. "Sometimes you just don't really know how much you love someone until they're gone. And I'm referring to Alice here, son, not my wife."

I frown at his last remark. "What do you mean by that?"

He exhales through his nose knowingly. "You know she went back to Chicago today, right?"

My brows furrow in confusion. "She went back for Rosalie's wedding? Why would she do that?"

He shakes his head. "Not just for the wedding. She packed up all of her stuff and moved back for good from the sounds of it. Her father lined up a job interview for her with a friend of his. She thinks it'll be better for her to leave London after everything that happened. I guess I'm glad her father is at least trying."

I jump to my feet, my heart racing at the words coming out of his mouth. "What are you talking about? She can't just move back to Chicago without thinking about it first," I bellow, my shoulders high and tense. "What the fuck is she thinking?"

Vaughn stares up at me incredulously. "Why can't she move back? She lost her job and the man she loves. There's nothing really keeping her here."

"Her home is here!" I exclaim defensively. "With you guys," I hurriedly add to the end, gesticulating with my hands like a mad man as I pace back and forth on the artificial grass.

Vaughn's brows lift curiously. "Her home is not with you of course."

I stop in my tracks and stare down at the man who's supposed to be my manager, my coach. Someone to push me in my career, not advise me on my love life. I shove my hands through my hair, my whole world feeling like it's spinning. "I don't know."

Vaughn laughs and shakes his head like a knowing father. "Well you better figure it out, son, because she's flying an ocean away from you right now."

CHAPTER 24

Allie

"DARLING, ARE YOU SURE YOU WANT TO DO THIS?" MY FATHER asks as I turn around in a red, satin, floor-length ball gown that magically fits me like a glove.

"I'm positive," I state, taking one last look at myself in the bathroom mirror.

My hair is curled in loose waves down my back, and my dramatic smoky eyes and sky-high, fuck-me-heels bring back a memory that I never want to forget. When I arrived in Chicago less than twenty-four hours ago, I never thought this would happen.

The day started off awesome because I went out for brunch with my dad and we talked. *Really* talked for the first time in what felt like years. He asked me about my job back in London and I caught him up on all the Harrises and their growing little families. After beating around the bush, he finally brought up the video. No, my father did not watch the video. *Thank. God.* But Rosalie did send him the link the night it went live, before I even had a chance to call and explain it to him. Apparently she had hoped that his shame toward me would convince him to go to her wedding after all, but all it did was add the final nail in the coffin in regard to his relationship with her.

By the time we finished our food, we were in the middle of a

Rosalie bitchfest, recalling all the ways she manipulated us into giving her what she wanted. It was highly therapeutic.

Finally, he asked about the guy in the video, and it was then that I broke down crying. My father stared at me awkwardly from across the table as I recounted all the ways I screwed up the best thing that ever happened to me. I wasn't even sure he was listening until he added that I was never that upset when Parker and I split up.

He's right. I was with Parker for five years and only with Roan for a couple of months, yet the heartbreak I feel over the loss of Roan will be something I will live with forever. Like an ulcer in my stomach that will never truly heal.

I eventually pulled myself together because I had to leave my father to head to my coffee shop meeting on Michigan Avenue. I was being interviewed by friends of my father's, so I couldn't have them seeing me as a complete wreck.

The couple who interviewed me were a husband and a wife who own a whisky distillery, and they were looking for outside-of-the-box publicity ideas. They actually brought up the sex tape ordeal first thing. I was humiliated and felt myself stammering out my excuses, but the woman named Marjorie hushed me. She said my experience going through all of that scandal would be an asset to their business, not a liability.

They were a fun couple and I could tell immediately that they have a very interesting company culture. It's most likely a bit of a party scene, but it would be nice to work for an industry that isn't concerned about keeping a squeaky clean track record all of the time. Life isn't always clean. Sometimes it's messy. And good PR is what helps turn the mess into beautiful chaos.

After the interview, I was on a high, feeling like my career in PR wasn't completely over, so I nearly missed it when I walked by.

The dress.

I wasn't even looking for a dress, but I swear it found me for a reason. It was a vibrant red hue and had a plunging neckline and tiny straps. The skirt was full and would most likely twirl like a dream on the dance floor. That is, if I still had a boyfriend who knew how to dance.

Before I knew what I was doing, I walked into the store, tried it on, and bought the dress. It was as I was walking back to my dad's apartment that my payback plan to get Rosalie back for leaking the video evolved.

I was going to crash Rosalie and Parker's wedding, and I was going to look damn good doing it.

Well, I'm not technically crashing the wedding because I was invited. But I'm certain Rosalie won't be expecting me to show my face around a crowd of people after she put that video out there for the world to see.

Ultimate payback. And definitely a better plan than my last one.

My dad props himself in the open bathroom doorway, a worried look on his face.

"I'm not going to stay long, Dad," I state soothingly as I put the lid on my red lipstick and drop it into my makeup bag. "And I'm not going to cause a scene. I'm just going to walk into their wedding reception wearing my scarlet-*A* dress and show Rosalie that she can't break me no matter how much she tries."

Dad sighs heavily. "*The Scarlet Letter* was about an adulterer, Alice. If anyone should be wearing a scarlet *A*, it's Rosalie."

I bark out a laugh at his small attempt at humour. "Nice burn, Dad!"

He crosses his arms over his chest, trying to hide his smile before stating seriously, "I wish I could make it all disappear for you, darling. I know the video isn't online anymore, but I hate the idea that she did that to you. I feel responsible. If I had just stuck to the original plan, none of this would have happened."

"Don't," I reply, turning to face him. "You were actually listening to me for once and I really appreciate that."

He smiles sadly. "I wish I would have listened a long time ago.

My brother really had a go at me. He's certainly taken you under his wing, hasn't he?"

I pause, watching his reaction carefully for any signs of jealousy or resentment. Thankfully, I don't see it. I only see gratitude. "The entire Harris family has been amazing. Truly. I'm going to miss not living close to them anymore."

He nods thoughtfully. "I'm sure they never would have done what Rosalie did to you. That girl isn't right in the head."

I laugh because, at this point, I have to laugh. I'm done crying. I'm done feeling sorry for myself. I fluff out my dress and let it fuel my strength. "In some ways, I'm glad she released the video. As bizarre as that sounds, now she has nothing more to hold over me. And having it out there in the world has shown me just how strong I can be."

My father smiles sweetly and walks into the bathroom, awkwardly putting his hand on my shoulder. "You must take after your cousins with this spirit because I bloody well don't have this kind of fight in me."

I laugh and pull him in for a hug. He's tense as he pats me on the back, but I don't mind because he's at least trying.

"I'll be home soon." I do one final twirl before walking out the door and heading to my ex-boyfriend and dear stepsister's wedding.

The ballroom is a sea of white and taupe. Very tasteful. Very clean. Very unlike Rosalie. Wreaths of baby's breath and candles illuminate the round tables. I stand in the doorway, recognising many faces but not feeling a desire to reconnect with any of them. It's funny how a couple of months in London has changed my perspective on the life I left here. Everything is pale in comparison to what I experienced overseas. And even though I'm moving back, I'm determined to make a new start for myself, detached from all of these past acquaintances.

The DJ announces into the microphone that Parker and Rosalie are going to share their first dance, so I decide now is the big moment. I take a deep breath and glide through the door, doing my best to keep my head held high. I feel eyes following me, and I can't tell if it's because of my dress, or because everyone here knows that Parker was my boyfriend before he and Rosalie became an item. Never mind the fact that I was recently featured in a sex video with a sexy athlete in London. Nobody cares about that!

I make my way to the edge of the dance floor, grabbing a flute of champagne off a server's tray as I walk. I sip the fizzy bubbles and move close enough for the colourful DJ lights to illuminate my skin. My eyes can't help but admire Rosalie's princess-style wedding gown as it sways back and forth like a broom across the dance floor. Clearly she didn't make Parker take dance lessons before this affair, and I feel a small sense of victory over that. After meeting Roan, I now know what it's like to truly move to music. But regardless of their limited mobility dancing, she's beautiful. Her makeup is fresh and half of her blonde hair is pinned back. She makes a gorgeous villain all things considered.

"Allie?" a voice says and I turn my gaze to see my ex-stepmother, Hilary, blinking her wide blue eyes at me. "Oh my God," she says, her gaze lowering to my dress and taking me in like she's just seen a ghost. "I didn't know you were coming."

I smile and shrug my bare shoulders. "I was hoping to surprise Rosalie."

Hilary nods and her eyes look around the room. "Is…your father here?"

She looks hopeful. Hilary always was a bit clueless. Clueless in life and extraordinarily clueless when it came to her daughter.

I shake my head regretfully. "No, he had to work."

She nods, disappointed by that answer. "When Rosalie said

Charles was going to walk her down the aisle, I'll admit I was shocked that he agreed to it after everything that happened between you and Rosalie and Parker."

"You and me both," I reply coldly, pressing my lips together so I don't say more.

Hilary winces. "I'm sorry, Allie. I could always tell Rosalie had feelings for Parker, but I never thought they'd—"

I force out a laugh because I will vomit all over my pretty dress if she finishes her sentence. "Honestly, Rosalie did me a favour."

"Oh?" Hilary asks, stepping closer to me. "Have you moved on? Are you with the boy from that video?" She softens her voice. "Don't worry, I never watched it. You're like a daughter to me."

I huff a disbelieving breath out of my nose because I've never felt like a daughter to Hilary. She certainly didn't pay me any extra attention the way my father did with Rosalie.

"I have moved on, but that video ruined the relationship I had with him. It was heartbreaking that it got leaked."

She gets a conspiratorial look on her face. "So, it wasn't him who released it? I assumed it was."

"No," I exclaim and feel everyone in the ballroom watching us. "Roan was my boyfriend, and he would have never put that out in the public eye. Not in a million years."

She holds her hands back defensively. "I'm sorry, I didn't know. But how did it get out there then?"

I smile and tilt my head, staring back at good ol' clueless Hilary, who really doesn't know the first thing about her own child. "You really should ask your daughter that question." My voice is louder than I intended as the end of the song begins to fade.

When the music stops completely, I slowly turn my head toward the dance floor to see Rosalie and Parker both staring openmouthed at me like a tacky Big Mouth Billy Bass that sings on the wall. I smile and wave, throwing my free arm around Hilary just to get under Rosalie's skin.

They look at each other with confused expressions, not understanding what my presence here means. The DJ breaks all of our focus as he announces to the crowd that everyone should grab a stranger and drag them out onto the dance floor.

The sound of Frank Sinatra fills the quiet room as Rosalie strides purposefully toward me with Parker following in her white, bridal wake. He looks nervous, like a whipped puppy, and I can't help but wonder what I ever saw in him.

Rosalie's eyes are slits as she looks at my dress. "Allie," she states my name like a curse. "You came."

My brows lift as I smile brightly at her. "I wouldn't have dreamed of missing your big day!" I set my flute of champagne down and waltz over to her, wrapping my arms around her strapless shoulders like Judas kissing the cheek of Jesus. When I pull back, Rose's brows are pinched together. "Congratulations, sis." I turn my painted-on smile to Parker. "Congratulations, Ghost Penis—I mean Parker."

He frowns, clearly not understanding my reference, and then shakes his head, mumbling a pathetic thanks. He lowers his gaze and stares unabashedly at my breasts. Granted, I'm wearing a plunging neckline, so you can't help but notice the cut. But he's not just glancing. He's staring at my cleavage like it has just come home from war.

Rosalie notices Parker's focus and elbows him in the ribs before turning back to me. "What's your plan here, Allie?"

I give her my best doe-eyed look. "Plan?"

She purses her lips. "Yes. You're obviously here for something. So, what's your deal? Are you serving me with legal papers? I've already heard from your lawyer."

Hilary steps up beside us. "Rose, a lawyer? What is going on?"

"Nothing, Mother," she snaps. "Parker is handling it." She turns her icy blue eyes on me. "Are you here to out me to all my wedding guests? To tell them all that I accessed a sex video off your Cloud and published it to a pornography site without your consent?"

Hilary gasps in shock as I stare at Rosalie, blinking slowly with a small, satisfied smile.

"Or are you here to get Parker back?" Rose continues. "You think you can show up in a slutty red dress and he'll forget he loves me more than you?"

Her last comment has me rolling my eyes toward the ceiling. "Rose, I am not your competition."

She glowers at me, crossing her bony arms across her chest. "You ruined my day for me. I had to have my mother walk me down the aisle. Do you know how humiliating that was?"

"Rose!" Hilary exclaims, her eyes wide with hurt feelings. "I thought it was a really special moment for us today."

"Mom!" she growls, turning her eyes on Hilary in warning.

I shake my head at the sight. "I had nothing to do with my father backing out on you. If you *are* looking for someone to blame for ruining your picture-perfect day, you can blame yourself for not understanding the concept of boundaries."

She barks out a laugh. "Oh, and you're the moral compass on life after filming a sex video with a random stranger?"

"He's not a stranger," I volley back, my own anger spiking hard and fast at any reference of Roan coming from her mouth. "He's a real person with responsibilities and he didn't deserve what you did to him."

She laughs, turning away from me and back to Parker, who looks horribly uncomfortable with the entire conversation. Rose hits me with a withering stare over her shoulder. "So, is that why you're here? To tell me I ruined some guy's life?"

My body recoils from her vindictive tone. She has no remorse. No reaction or feelings. No memory of any time in our lives that she didn't hate me. She's filled with nothing.

I exhale heavily and step right up to her, my heels giving me an extra inch of height that makes me feel like an Amazon warrior princess. "I'm here to show you that you didn't break me."

She narrows her eyes, not believing anything I'm saying.

"I'm here to show you that I will find my place in this world, and the laundry list of malicious, horrible things you've done to me won't ruin my life."

She laughs maniacally. "Well, I'm sure I didn't ruin your man's life either. He probably has a line out the door by now of all the over-eager women ready and willing to be his rebound. You'll be easily forgotten, Allie. No shocker there. After all, Parker forgot about you before you even split up."

I open my mouth to reply, but the reality of her words suddenly penetrates the thick skin I've been wearing since the moment Roan walked away from me at Tower Park.

Rosalie is right. Roan will move on. He'll find someone else. He'll love another woman, and she will get to dance with him and laugh with him. She'll sleep in his bed and enjoy the way he tries to rub away her worry lines. She'll probably go to his games and wear his jersey. She'll go to Cape Town and meet his gran, and sightsee with his mom and sisters, and make love to him on a creaky sofa bed. She will have Roan's children.

My hands move to my stomach because the idea of another woman being with him, loving him, and starting a family with him guts me to my very core. My insides begin to churn, and I suddenly feel sick and desperate to get out of here.

I take one more look at Rosalie before I turn to leave. She looks smaller somehow, like a cracked porcelain doll that could break at any moment. How did I let her have this power over me? Why?

My body begins to shake as the true nature of my feelings become crystal clear. I'm not even here for her or Parker. In the grand scheme of my emotional state, they are microscopic fleas of annoyance. Nothing more.

I have been a fool once again. I thought this payback plan tonight would help me move on and feel strong.

But I was wrong.

Because it wasn't the video or this stupid red dress that made me strong.

It was Roan.

His touch, his presence, his faith in me was all the revenge I ever needed. I need him.

My watery eyes lift as I make my way toward the exit and glance past an attractive man in a suit standing at the threshold. The familiar figure registers in my mind and I feel my heart stop.

It's in that moment that the entire world freezes.

Roan.

Roan DeWalt.

Is here.

At my stepsister's wedding.

My chest heaves as I realise I stopped breathing. As soon as my mind has regained the oxygen it needs to function, I do a double take to make sure it really is the man I love standing here of all places.

Roan pauses in the doorway—tall, dark, and handsome like always. His skin glows like fresh caramel and there's a hopefulness in his eyes that I thought was long-lost. He's wearing a dark grey suit that reminds me of the one he wore the first night we met.

When my eyes stop checking out the thickness of his muscles, they lift back to his pale brown eyes. That are currently locked on me.

I hold my breath. Roan's brows lift as he slowly looks me up and down like I'm a mural he must appreciate. His lips part in silent awe, and his heated expression tells me he likes what he sees.

When his eyes have drank their fill, he looks at me and places a hand on his chest like I've just taken his breath away, too. I hope I did. I hope that him being here means what I want it to mean because I will get down on my knees and beg if I have to.

He moves toward me with purpose and I briefly notice all eyes are on him. How can they not be? He's the kind of man who women fall in love with without even trying. I think I might have even fallen in love with him the first night we met.

I resist the urge to skip over to him, every muscle in my body charged and ready to feel his closeness. When he reaches me, the three words that come out of his mouth are not what I expect.

"Dance with me."

He holds one hand out to me while placing the other on the small of his back in a bow like he's some sort of prince asking a princess to be his queen. With no reply, I reach my trembling hand out to his and let him lead me onto the dance floor.

He wraps me in his arms—his firm, capable, perfect arms—and I realise that we're not just dancing. We're Viennese waltzing.

The few couples slow dancing around us stare open-mouthed at our movements that look as though we've been dancing together our entire lives. They stop their side to side swaying, backing away to appreciate the splendour of Roan twirling me in my magnificent red dress all over the dance floor.

I fall into step with him and it feels effortless and easy. Any time I stumble, he shifts it into a turn, making my flaws look like a flourish. He lifts me above his head at one point, and it's then that I realise the dance floor is completely empty and the entire ballroom is watching us. Everyone is lining the edges, enjoying the spectacle that he's creating. That I am creating because of him.

He slows the waltz and looks deeply into my eyes. "Hi, mooi."

I huff out an exasperated breath, my heart pounding in my chest in disbelief. "How are you here?"

He smirks, his eyes twinkling as he replies, "There is this really modern flying vehicle called an airplane."

I roll my eyes and give his shoulder a shake. "I know how you're here, but how are you here, here?"

"Your dad told me where to find you. I had to buy a suit for the occasion."

My eyes threaten to shed tears. "How are you not hating me with every fibre of your being?"

He swallows slowly, his eyes growing more serious as they

dance all over my face. "Hating you would be easy, but I've never taken the easy road in my life."

I smile at his response because, after everything I've learned about this man, I know it's true. "So, what does this mean?"

"What do you want it to mean?" he asks, his question putting all the pressure back on me.

I shake my head and press my forehead to his shoulder before pulling back to gaze at him. "I want it to mean that our love is strong enough for us to get past everything that's happened. This whole thing…You and me…The sex video that's out there of us. It's never going to go away. I mean, yes, they've taken it down. But people don't forget, and it might pop up again."

"All very true," he states simply.

"And I know if I stay in Chicago and away from London—away from you and away from the Harrises—the less people will see of me, so the less likely they will bring up that stupid, awful video. They could forget about that nut-job Harris cousin."

"So, you want to be forgotten?"

"No," I answer, my shoulders tensing. "Not anymore. I thought coming home and showing Rosalie and Parker they didn't break me would help me be strong enough to get past everything. But, good-god, I'm more miserable now than when I arrived."

"That's because this place isn't your home, Lis," Roan's voice is soft but his eyes are fierce as they gaze into mine. "Chicago isn't your home. These people aren't your family." He looks around at the crowd of faces that I knew once upon a time, but now they feel like judgmental strangers to me. "Your home is around the ones who won't cast you aside when you screw up because they know you're better than that."

Tears well in my eyes because I don't know if he's talking about himself, or if he's talking about my cousins. "Where is my home, Roan?" I ask, my voice cracking with fear because there's only one answer I want to hear.

He gazes at me with so much tenderness that I have to hold my breath while he answers, "Your home is with the man who knows that what his woman did was fucked-up, but he also knows that a lifetime of fuck-ups with her would be a life well-lived together."

Tears fill my eyes from his words. Words that I want to believe, but I still have fears. "What about your career? Your endorsement deal?"

He shakes his head, his eyes softening around the edges as he replies, "I used to only care about soccer. Making it big and getting an endorsement deal were my only dreams. But somewhere along the way, my dreams changed. Something changed them…Someone changed them…You."

Hot tears pour down my face as I stare up at Roan's pale brown eyes twinkling in the ballroom lighting. He's looking down at me with so much warmth, and love, and forgiveness, I feel completely unworthy.

"I'm so sorry, Roan. Truly. You changed me, too, and I love you so much. I regret every second of what I did that night."

Roan's brows lift in mocking challenge. "I hope not every second of it."

I cringe and shake away the nervous laughter bubbling up in my throat. "I mean it. When I first met you, I thought there was enough distance between us that, that horrible video would never touch you. That you were just a stranger who would never be affected. But after we slept together, I knew I'd never show a soul that video because you were something I wanted to keep to myself."

Roan rubs his lips together. "I know the video is out there, Lis. I know it sucks, and I know it's something we'll probably never be able to fully shake. But we can survive it together because you belong with me. You are mine and I am yours. I want to be your home and your family. Hell, I want to marry you."

My eyes fly wide and my entire body begins shaking. My voice is trembling when I croak, "Don't say that if you don't mean it."

He shakes his head, his face as serious as a heart attack. "When Vaughn told me you were moving back here, I swear to God, my heart stopped. I didn't even pack a bag before driving to the airport and taking the first flight out. I haven't slept in twenty-four hours, your dad had to loan me a toothbrush, and I spent way more fucking money on this suit than I should have because I'm here to tell you that I want you, mooi. Forever. And if you're here to get some payback on your stepsister, I'll drop down on one knee right now and ask you to marry me. Stealing her spotlight would be the ultimate payback."

He moves to drop down on one knee and my jaw drops as I yank him back up onto his feet. My mind is spinning with emotions as I shake my head and bat away my tears. "Not here."

He looks at me in confusion, glancing over at Rosalie and Parker, who are watching us like we're on fire. I grab his face and press my lips to his, tasting this moment he's just given me. This moment…This magical, unbelievable, unforgettable moment. He responds, sliding his tongue into my mouth and holding my face in place just as he did for our first kiss.

Finally, I pull away, my voice breathless when I say, "Real or fake? You just tried to propose to me at my stepsister and ex-boyfriend's wedding."

His breath is warm on my lips with his quiet laughter. "Fucking real."

My smile is wide as I shake my head. "I don't want the question you're apparently ready to ask me to be tainted with revenge. These people have invaded enough of my life. They don't get this moment, too." I rub my hands over his face, imprinting his loving expression into my memory. "I want this to be pure and perfect and just what we always should have been."

"Pure and perfect," he replies with a sexy laugh. "So, asking you to make a sex tape sequel when I propose is out of the question?"

"Yes!" I exclaim with a laugh and pull him to my lips again. I kiss him chastely and add, "I don't care when or how, but please just hold onto your question until we get home."

"Home?" He says it like a question. "And where is that exactly?"

I exhale heavily. "Wherever you are."

EPILOGUE

Roan
Several Months Later

"ALLIE HARRIS," I STATE, LOOKING UP AT MY GORGEOUS girlfriend from down on one knee. Her bright blue eyes go wide and her hands cup her cheeks in anticipation. "Would you do me the honour of…getting me a double Americano?"

Allie's body instantly deflates and she lunges for me, shoving me off my knee and onto the floor of the coffee shop near her new place of work in East London. "You are such an asshole!" she exclaims, her voice getting that growly tone that I love so much.

I chuckle because this never gets old. "You really think I'm going to propose in a coffee shop?"

She juts out her lower lip in a pout. "Don't you think we've given the media enough excitement? It's been months of this now!"

I stand up and throw my arm around her, ignoring everyone as they stare open-mouthed at the spectacle I just made. My voice is a whisper when I reply, "I'm not sure. What's the statute of limitations on the press forgetting we have a sex video together?"

She sighs with defeat. "Probably never."

I laugh and move to stand behind her to wrap my arms around her waist and press a kiss on her temple. "Come on, mooi. We're giving them a bigger better story with this. You may as well laugh. Everyone else is."

We both look out from our little bubble of teasing bliss to see several onlookers pointing their phones at us. One of these videos will likely be sold to several of the entertainment channels that have been reporting on Allie and me for the past five months.

Thankfully, they aren't reporting about our sex video anymore. Well, not very much anyway. These days, Allie and I are being regularly featured in the papers because the entire city of London knows that I am torturing my girlfriend with what the media are calling "Proposal Fake Outs." It was Mac's idea actually, which is no surprise there. He casually suggested one night that I give the media something else to talk about and I guess I kind of ran with it.

When Allie and I returned to London after her stepsister's wedding, we both decided that getting engaged right away was a bad idea. Don't get me wrong. I meant what I said that night. I want to marry her. I'm going to marry her. But we knew we needed to take some time to see what our new normal was going to be post-sex tape scandal.

Turns out, things are pretty great.

The worst aftermath was that my gran wouldn't talk to me for several weeks. But she eventually came around, even making a trip up to London with my mom and sisters a couple of months ago. The visit was nice and only forty percent awkward during brunch when both my sisters asked Allie where she buys her lingerie.

Things with Allie's family have improved as well. The Harris Brothers have done a complete one-eighty with me, especially after finding out that I was protecting Allie while getting my face punched in and refusing to sign Niall's statement. Not only am I required to attend all Harris Sunday dinners, but I was even invited to help out with a Harris Shakedown that occurred after Tanner and Belle had their daughter, Josephine. When Belle's father showed up to meet little Joey at the hospital, the Harris Brothers decided he needed to be shown who Belle's real family is now. Evidently I am one of them now, too.

Allie ended up accepting a position at Sloan and Leslie's clothing boutique as their marketing and public relations consultant. The two of them felt that if Allie could navigate her way through a sex tape scandal, she can do pretty much anything they need for their flourishing shop.

And since working at the boutique so much, Allie has become extremely close to Freya. Ironically, Freya and Mac are new best friends now, so hanging out with our closest friends is pretty damn fun these days. Allie and I keep watching for any signs of romance between them, but the unlikely pair seem perfectly content watching Netflix on the sofa together. The way they argue like an old married couple is actually pretty fucking cute.

As for my career, playing for Bethnal Green F.C. in the Premier League is going brilliantly. Our season started off a little rocky, but we all found our stride once we shook off our nerves from playing in the big leagues. Things even turned out okay for me on the endorsement front. I lost my sponsorship opportunity with Adidas but ended up shooting three commercials for the whisky distillery that Allie interviewed with back in Chicago. It turns out there are businesses out there that don't look at scandal as a bad thing. In fact, I was worth a lot more money to them post-sex tape than pre-sex tape, so there are many silver linings to everything that happened.

And while I hate that our video is out there, it has actually made Allie and me closer than I ever thought possible. We're the only two in the world who understand what it's like to live with it out there. We can't click delete on the people who have seen it or may have copies of it, but it's all a part of our unconventional love story.

Once we took the, "if you can't beat them, join them," approach, our lives filled with a lot more joy. Hence, Proposal Fake Outs. It's way more fun having the media inquire about those instead of the sex video. And even though Allie acts like she hates them, she's been skipping more than ever the last few months. I know that means she's happy.

Hell, I'm happy, too. Yes, what she did hurt me. Fuck, it hurt me a lot. But being without Allie devastated me more, and Vaughn's words to me at Tower Park really struck a chord. *"If there is enough love, all is forgivable."* No matter how much pain her betrayal caused me, I never stopped loving Allie. That's why I'll live with this video out there and protect her for as long as I live. She's it for me, and nothing else matters more than her.

"You're done after this, right? We can leave once you get the girls their coffee?" I ask impatiently because I have a tight schedule to keep today.

"Yes, I'm free as soon as I finish this last task," Allie says as she hands the slip of paper with Sloan, Leslie, and Freya's coffee orders over to the barista. "Still not going to tell me where we're going?"

"No," I reply with a smirk. "I told you, it's a surprise."

Allie pins me with a skeptical look. "Does it involve a plane ride?"

I laugh at the notion. "Not this time, mooi."

She nods with appreciation. "Well, at least I know you won't be doing another fake proposal. Good-God, I really thought that was going to be the one last week when you dropped down on one knee before your game at Tower Park."

"You and thousands of fans in the stands," I reply with a chuckle. "Christ, that one will be impossible to beat."

She plasters on a fake smile. "Thankfully, we have YouTube links to remember it for the rest of our lives. Lucky us."

I shrug. "At least that one has more views than our sex video."

She rolls her eyes. "I'm starting to wonder if the sex video was less painful than this."

My jaw drops as I mock piercing a dagger through my heart. "I thought you like my fake out proposals?"

She laughs and shakes her head. "I find them amusing, but only if it's going to be real one of these days."

Oh, my beautiful, Lis. You have no idea.

We deliver the coffee to Kindred Spirits Boutique and then jump in my car to take the long way toward a location that I've been to with Allie before. She's holding my hand over the console, completely clueless about the fact that I'm killing time so everyone can get into place.

When I park in front of the familiar hotel, she finally realises where I've taken her.

"I remember this place!"

I mock gasp. "You do?"

She looks at me in confusion. "This is where my aunt Fiona was married. This is where we met."

"Huh, I'd almost forgotten," I state, sliding out of the car and doing a horrible job of hiding my smile as I pass my keys off to the valet.

I walk around and grab her hand as she narrows her eyes at me. "What are we doing here?"

I roll my eyes. "Mooi, I told you it's a surprise."

We walk through the door and into the posh lobby. The marble floors shine in the daylight streaming through the large windows. I point to the floor and then toward the elevator. "This is where I first noticed you are a grown woman who still likes to skip."

She laughs and gives me a light shove. "Only when I'm really happy."

My brows lift with amusement. "You've been happy a lot lately."

Her smile turns soft and warm, sending a jolt of emotion straight to my heart. "I have indeed."

We hang a left toward the doors of the ballroom where her aunt had her reception. We walk through the deserted space and muse over the annoying things her aunt said to us that night as I pull her toward the double-door exit that leads to the fountains out back.

"If you're planning to get me drenched in those fountains again, you're damn lucky it's warm outside today," Allie says, squeezing my hand in warning. "And I hope this means you booked us a room."

274

I chuckle and bring her hand up to my lips to press a chaste kiss on her knuckle. "I know you like getting wet, mooi."

She bites her lip and I hit her with a wink before pushing through the doors that lead to the concrete courtyard where the fountains go off at the top of every hour. It's a good fifteen minutes until they'll go off again, so people are walking around the area without a care in the world. I pause us at the top of the steps and gaze out at the space where I first fell in love with her.

"You know I fell in love with you out here, right?" I ask seriously and exhale the heady feeling that's tightening in my chest. I wrap my arms around her waist and pull her against me to feel the warmth of her body on mine.

She splays her hands out around my arms and looks up at me with wide, wondering eyes. "I still say you fell in lust."

I shrug my shoulders. "It was something I'd never felt before, I know that much."

She nods thoughtfully and looks out at the space. "I don't know how you managed to make me smile that night, but you did. I was a mess, yet you somehow made everything fade away."

I kiss her forehead and inhale her scent. "I'll always be here for you, mooi."

"I know that," she replies with a sad look in her eyes. "And I'll never lie to you again."

"I know you won't," I reassure her and lean down to take her lips with mine.

This is a thing between us right now. Allie still struggles to let go of her guilt over the video. But she doesn't realise that I would forgive her a thousand times over because of how happy she makes me. *She also doesn't know that I'm lying like crazy to her right now.*

Suddenly, Frank Sinatra's "Strangers in the Night" echoes through the empty courtyard. We pull apart and look down the steps to where the sound is blaring from the speakers in the bushes surrounding the smooth concrete. The passersby pause and look around nervously, their eyes landing on a couple in the back corner. The couple step out of the bushes and into full sight, dressed in colourful ballroom dancing outfits. The man takes the woman in his arms and they begin waltzing around the large, flat surface.

"Are we interrupting something?" Allie asks, her eyes confused by the sight of people dodging to get out of the way of the dancers.

I shrug my shoulders, and we both turn our attention back to the couple who move with seasoned training. They are obviously professionals, and they don't seem bothered by the crowd of people lining the edges of the courtyard to watch their performance.

I frown when I feel Allie tense in my arms. "Wait…Aren't those the dance instructors who trained us at that dance studio Vi took us all to?" she asks, looking up at me for confirmation.

I lift my hand to block the sunlight from my eyes for a closer look. "It might be. I'm not sure."

She presses her lips into a fine line, but our attention is back on the courtyard when the music shifts from smooth and dreamy Sinatra to feel-good, punchy pop. The song "Perfect Strangers" by Jonas Blue fills the space as several other couples hustle out onto the concrete, wrapping each other in their arms. The remaining crowd backs off further when the chorus starts and the dancers begin waltzing beside each other in perfect unison, like they've rehearsed this number a thousand times.

We watch for a minute, enjoying the show, and I'm doing my best to hide my pleased smile because Allie still thinks she's witnessing something that has nothing to do with us. Then she catches sight of movement to the left and looks over to see yet another group coming in. This groups falls in step with the other, making at least twenty people dancing to a song that talks about complete strangers having a night together that could change them. As I allow myself to listen to the familiar lyrics, my emotions threaten to give the secret away.

The reasons Allie came into my life may have been because

of her ill-conceived payback plan, but that payback set us up for the perfect comeback. So for that, I'll never regret our first night together.

Suddenly, the music shifts again to Ed Sheeran's "Photograph," and Allie's grip on my arm tightens to a near painful squeeze when she sees a new set of dancers emerging.

Mac and Freya tango out to the front of the dancers and stop smack dab in the middle of everyone. Mac has a rose clenched between his teeth as he dips Freya dramatically and almost drops her on the ground. She whacks his shoulder and then grabs the rose out of his mouth and tosses it behind her. Allie looks at me, silently asking, "What the fuck?"

I smile proudly and point to the next group strolling out to join our friends.

Allie turns her attention to them, and I hear her gasp as my mom, my sisters, and my gran make their way to the front of the dancers as Mac and Freya and the other couples behind them spread out into two rows. As soon as they are in place, everyone begins dancing in unison.

"Roan, what is this?" Allie asks, her voice garbled and thick with unshed tears.

I wrap my arm around her shoulders and kiss the top of her head. "Keep watching."

She shakes her head in disbelief, covering her mouth as everyone performs simple moves that even my gran can pull off. I have an inner battle with myself about who I want to watch more…The dancers or Allie.

Allie wins. I think she might win forever.

Suddenly, her eyes go to the right and she lets out a small cry as her own family marches in together.

Her father, Charles, and her mother, Karen—whom Charles helped me get in touch with—lead the pack of Vaughn and the rest of his Harris bunch into the courtyard. First there's Gareth with Milo in his arms and Sloan walking hand-in-hand with Sophia. Then there's Booker and Poppy with their twins practically dragging them out toward the other dancers. Next there's Vi and Hayden, who has Rocky perched up on his shoulders, waving to the crowd.

Behind Rocky is the proud new father, Tanner—in all his bearded, man-bunned glory—holding his three-week-old baby girl. Belle is walking beside him, anxiously checking on Joey, who appears to be asleep and missing out on all the jol.

Bringing in the rear is a hugely pregnant Indie walking with Camden, who is holding onto her like she might tip over at any minute. Honestly, I wasn't sure they were going to make it. Indie is due any day now, but she practically forced me to hurry up this flash mob proposal idea because she didn't want to miss out on it for something silly like childbirth.

The Harrises really are the fucking best. And they all look so happy, it may as well be their sister getting engaged, not just their cousin.

I look down and Allie is a crying mess, shaking uncontrollably as she covers the shock on her face. The noises coming out of her sound somewhat alarming, but I won't say anything because I'm fighting back some really unmanly sobs myself. *Fucking hell, there's something in my eye.*

The Harris crew joins in with the choreography that they've been rehearsing for weeks now in that little dance studio. It was a mess to organise, but ag, it's a perfect mess right now. Sort of like Allie and me.

Sophia attempts to spin the twin boys because that was her choreographed dance, but the boys are more interested in running around like little terrors and stealing the show with their devil-like cuteness. Vi is crying full tears as Hayden marches to his own beat with Rocky bouncing on his shoulders. It's perfection.

Even Charles is dancing. Although, he's dancing quite poorly. But he looks proud and happy all the same. I'm glad he's a part of this. And I'm glad he gave me his blessing to ask his daughter to marry me because there's no way for me to live in this world without her.

Finally, the notes of Ed Sheeran fade, so I quickly pull Allie down to the bottom of the steps for the big finale. She's laughing and crying as she notices the cameras popping out from behind the bushes in addition to all the strangers filming the scene on their phones.

Let them film it. This is a memory I give my full consent to record.

I position Allie on the edge of the makeshift dance floor and take my position, front and centre of the crew. Tanner and Gareth both pass off their babies, and Allie's face lights up when the next song starts.

"I'm Too Sexy" blares through the speakers, and the Harris Brothers all whoop with excitement as the dancers leave the area open for them and me. Two brothers flank me on either side with Mac in the back as the six of us bounce to the beat until the vocals start again. Once the verse begins, we bust into a routine that we worked on day and night with my mother via Skype.

Like I said…A fucking mess.

But fuck it, we're owning it now.

Allie howls with laughter as the rest of our family lines a make-shift catwalk for us six to strut down. Tanner lies down at the front to take fake pictures that we all pose for like paparazzi whores.

When the "I'm Too Sexy" chorus repeats, the five of us slowly begin to unbutton our shirts. But before we get too far, the ladies run out to stop us, shoving the other guys to the back of the court-yard and leaving me out here all alone.

Then the music shifts to Etta James' "At Last," and I walk toward Allie with a giant smile and ask, "Remember this song, Lis?" I grab her hand and pull her out to the middle of the courtyard.

Her eyes are glossy as she fights back more tears. "I do."

I whisk her into my arms and twirl us around the dance floor for a measure. "Real or fake? I told you that night at the dance studio that this could be our wedding song."

She inhales a deep breath and releases it in a small sob. "So real."

I take a deep breath and step back to drop down on one knee. "That means this isn't a fake out, Allie Harris."

I reach into my pocket for the ring box and, as if I timed it this way, the fountain spouts suddenly come alive.

Allie squeals and shifts out of the stream that's shooting up into her face. I stay on my knee, ducking my head against the rainfall of cold-ass water coming down on us. This wasn't exactly a part of my plan. I had hoped to pop the question before the waterworks and have a magical moment of her saying yes, *then* all of us dance in the water.

But it's no surprise that this moment isn't perfect. Allie and I aren't perfect. We're just us.

"Are you sure this is real?" Allie cries, her face scrunching up against the onslaught of water spraying all around us. She looks at the enormous crowd that's assembled. "Because this would be a really good fake out if you were trying to burn me good!"

"This is real, mooi," I state loudly over the thundering sound of water hitting concrete.

I lick some moisture off my lips and slide over on my knee to an area that's not getting pounded by water. Allie follows, her eyes drifting down as I open the lid on the box to reveal a sparkly round diamond that I spent way too many hours picking out.

I reach out and grab her wet, trembling hand. "Allie Harris, you say you're not a dancer, but what you don't know is that dancing is just skipping in circles. And from the moment you skipped into my life, I haven't been the same. And I don't want to be the same. I want to be who I am when I'm with you. I would do anything for you, mooi. And I want to do anything for you for the rest of our lives. Will you marry me?"

"Yes!" she cries, her lips turned up into an overjoyed smile as mascara runs down her face. She side steps a new fountain spray, laughing the whole time as she adds, "Yes, Roan. You are my home, my family, my life. Of course I'll marry you!"

She falls down onto my knee and kisses me with everything she has. And I give it right back because there's no better payback in life…

…than a happily ever after.

The End

Did you know that all the Harris Brothers have books?
Binge their complete series in Kindle Unlimited now!

More Books by Amy Daws

The London Lovers:
Becoming Us: Finley's Story Part 1
A Broken Us: Finley's Story Part 2
London Bound: Leslie's Story
Not the One: Reyna's Story

A London Lovers/Harris Brothers Crossover Novel:
Strength: Vi Harris & Hayden's Story

The Harris Brothers Series:
A spin-off series featuring the football-playing Harris Brothers!
Challenge: Camden's Story
Endurance: Tanner's Story
Keeper: Booker's Story
Surrender & Dominate: Gareth's Duet

Payback: A Harris Family Spin-off Standalone

The Wait With Me Series:
Wait With Me: A Tire Shop Rom Com
Next In Line: A Bait Shop Rom Com

Pointe of Breaking: A College Dance Standalone by Amy Daws &
Sarah J. Pepper

Chasing Hope: A Mother's True Story of Loss, Heartbreak,
and the Miracle of Hope

For all retailer purchase links, visit:
www.amydawsauthor.com

Acknowledgements

After thinking I was done with the Harris Brothers for a while, I shouldn't be surprised those cheeky bros dragged my creative muse back to their world for another book! I hope you all enjoyed Allie and Roan's scandalous and unconventional love story.

I must take a moment to thank all the people who helped get this book here today! First of all, my alpha readers, Jen, Beth, Franci, and Jane Ashley Converse. Thank you all so much for tolerating my emotions and the constant push and pull I feel daily with my characters. They all seem to make me want to yank my hair out sometimes, and I know my stories would suffer if I didn't have you three to bounce ideas off of and to encourage me to be better.

Thanks to my PA, Julia for being just the best and always there for me when I need you. Both as an assistant and as an alpha reader!

Thanks to my editor, Stephanie, for making this baby shine like you always do. And to my proofers, Lydia, Teresa, and Lynsey for adding that final coat of varnish. Lydia, you do a hell of a lot more for me than proof and I appreciate you always and every day!

A special word of appreciation to the South African readers I spoke to for advice on this story. Even though this is a fictional romance novel, I wanted to acknowledge some of what your country has been through. I thank you for your candour in helping me honour your history.

Thanks to my hubby for being patient with me when I get in the zone and ignore life responsibilities. And thanks to my daughter, Lolo, who never lets me completely disappear into a story. Nothing makes me happier than hearing you play barbies on the sofa in my office while I work. It's seriously the best part about working from home.

To my angel babies that I know are always looking out for me: Thank you for giving me perspective in my life so I'm able to appreciate the little things that can so easily be overlooked.

More about the Author

Amy Daws is an Amazon Top 25 bestselling author of sexy, contemporary romance novels. She enjoys writing love stories that take place in America, as well as across the pond in London. When Amy is not writing in a tire shop waiting room, she's watching *Gilmore Girls*, Instagramming, or singing karaoke in the living room with her daughter while Daddy smiles awkwardly from a distance.

For more of Amy's work, visit: http://www.amydawsauthor.com

www.facebook.com/amydawsauthor
www.twitter.com/amydawsauthor
instagram.com/amydawsauthor

59066221R00174

Made in the USA
Columbia, SC
01 June 2019